What Others Say

"*You write with an easy, fascinating, living style which moves the reader along rapidly—caught up in the story—and becoming almost part of the action. You kept my interest to the end...I'm sure your purpose is not to proclaim faith but to tell a story from a very human point of view. You do that well...Your purpose was to stop at His death. But your comment that the story doesn't end there was insightful and helpful to understanding.*"

—Rev. Carl W. Segerhammar, D.D., Past President
Pacific Southwest Synod of the Lutheran Church in America

"*You are, I believe, a true descendant of Jewish tradition, reflected in your great gift as a story teller. The tale you tell is compelling and at times makes the heart beat faster and gets the adrenalin really flowing. It is a pleasure to read a description of the trial and ordeal of Jesus from a Jewish perspective. Obviously, I believe that even history is better served from such a version.*"

—Rabbi Moshe J. Rothblum
Adat Ari El, North Hollywood, CA

"*I found it very readable and the story was so well told that I wanted to keep on reading. The story gives a running Biblical account of the life of Christ, and the reader should find great delight in its clarity. I believe you have well fulfilled the purpose for which you have taken time to write it...I would like to encourage you to complete your dream and write the story, as you understand it, of the days that followed His death and perhaps the spreading of this gospel story throughout the world."*

—Dr. A. George Downing, Executive Minister
American Baptist Churches of the Pacific Southwest

"I (have) read your fine Biblical novel. It certainly moves at a fast pace and provides your readers with some excellent insights. I was especially intrigued with your suggesting that there was a <u>political Sanhedrin</u> operating in Jerusalem."

—Rabbi Allen I. Freehling, PhD
University Synagogue, West Los Angeles, CA

"The author, using his prerogative as a novelist, alters the Biblical account at points for dramatic effect, but otherwise uses the Biblical material (selectively) and basically follows the Biblical story. He has an easy, readable style. He tells us that he wrote the book 'to give readers a deeper appreciation for, and better understanding of, Jesus' Jewish roots.' (The author) has given us a reverent, enjoyable work, and he has reminded us once again, as we need to be reminded, that Jesus and his disciples were Jews…"

—William Sanford Lasor, Professor of Old Testament,
Fuller Theological Seminary, Pasadena, California
(reviewed in *The Reformed Journal*, May 1978)

"This book does help us again to experience the passion as a drama involving live people. And it helps us understand Jesus and his inner circle as Jews, with a more sympathetic picture of Judaism than we see in the Gospels."

—Review, *The North American Moravian*, March 1978

"This is a novel you can be proud of for the rest of your life. It shows a grasp of the craft. I've never been a reader of Biblical novels, but was quite engrossed. You handled the subject matter very well, never heavy-

handedly. It is individual, has a fresh point of view and is told in human terms."

—Sylva Romano, Executive Vice President,
Ernest Tidyman International Ltd.

"I would like to congratulate you for this interesting and enlightening manuscript."

—Rt. Rev. Meletios, Bishop of Christianoupolis
Greek Orthodox Archdiocese of North and South America
Fourth Archdiocesan District

"The approach…is an extremely interesting one. This is an old-fashioned novel with moral, psychological and theological overtones."

—Bertha Klausner, Bertha Klausner International
Literary Agency, Inc., New York, New York

"I found it most absorbing and stimulating, a really astonishing work of writing, research and spiritual insight."

—Roy Huggins, President, Public Arts, Inc., Universal City, CA

A JEWISH NOVEL ABOUT JESUS

Books by Rolf Gompertz

Abraham, The Dreamer: An Erotic and Sacred Love Story
(Biblical novel)

A Jewish Novel About Jesus
(Biblical novel)

SPARKS OF SPIRIT (A Handbook for Personal Happiness)
How to Find Love & Meaning in Your Life 24 Hours a Day
(Personal Development Guide)

The Messiah of Midtown Park
(Play/Comedy-Drama)

A CELEBRATION OF LIFE
(Poetry and Prose)

For additional information, please see
About the Author/Books at back of this book

How to Obtain These Books

These books are available as paperbacks from the publisher's online book store at http://www.iUniverse.com or from http://www.amazon.com. The books may be inspected and browsed at either place before ordering. At the web site _select_ the _book store_ and _search_ by _author's name_ (Rolf Gompertz) or the particular _book title_. If a title has not been posted yet, it will be shortly. You may also contact the author for more information and updates. Mailto: rolfgompertz@yahoo.com.

Please address any correspondence with the author to:
P.O. Box 9761, North Hollywood, CA 91609
Telephone/fax: 1(818) 980-3576 E-mail: rolfgompertz@yahoo.com

A Jewish Novel About Jesus

Author of **Abraham, The Dreamer, An Erotic and Sacred Love Story**

Rolf Gompertz

iUniverse, Inc.
New York Lincoln Shanghai

A Jewish Novel About Jesus

iUniverse, Inc.

For information address:
iUniverse, Inc.
2021 Pine Lake Road, Suite 100
Lincoln, NE 68512
www.iuniverse.com

Originally published as: *My Jewish Brother Jesus*
First edition 1977, The Wordoctor (Word Doctor) Publications, Copyright © 1977 by Rolf Gompertz,

Cover image by Menachem
Author image by Debra Halberstadt, HalfCity Productions

ISBN: 0-595-28437-X (pbk)
ISBN: 0-595-65796-6 (cloth)

Printed in the United States of America

This book is dedicated to

ANNA N. COFFEE BAER COOPER

—*who saved us from the Holocaust and preserved our life,
so that we could see visions and dream dreams*

MY PARENTS, OSCAR & SELMA GOMPERTZ

—*who encouraged my dreams*

MY WIFE, CAROL

—*who helped me realize my dreams*

and

OUR CHILDREN, RON, NANCY & PHILIP

—*so that they may see visions, and dream dreams*

Contents

About This Book

I have felt the need to write this book for many years—ever since I was in college. For years I did not feel up to this awesome task. But the need to write this book persisted, and one day I made my commitment to it.

I spent three years on it.

Why did I write it?

I wanted, first and foremost, to deal with Jesus, the Jew. However else he is to be understood, I felt that he also must be understood as a Jew. He was born a Jew, he lived as a Jew, and he died a Jew.

I was curious about the Twelve Apostles. Who were they? What were they like? What drew them to Jesus and his cause?

I was intrigued with Judas. What draws a man to a cause, and what makes him betray that cause—and its leader? Or was it a betrayal? Was it possible that Judas was loyal and devoted to the end, and that he saw himself as the instrument of Jesus' triumph rather than crucifixion?

What about Mary Magdalene, a prostitute who became a devoted follower? What makes people change?

And what about the death of Jesus? Who really wanted it? Could it have been pagan Rome? Judea was an occupied country. Did Pontius Pilate, the Roman governor, fearful of revolution, mastermind the death of Jesus? If so, how and why?

These are the elements of my book.

The book stops with the death of Jesus. The story, of course, does not end there. However, what happened three days later, and after, is the beginning of another book I hope to write some day. I would like to show what caused Judaism and Christianity to diverge and come to a parting of the ways, with sensitivity to the best in both traditions.

I would like to make my purpose clear in writing this present book:

I hope to give Christians a better understanding of, and appreciation for, Jesus and his Jewish roots.

I hope to give Jews a better understanding of, and appreciation for, Jesus in terms of Judaism.

I do not wish to undermine the validity of Christianity or to convert Jews to Christianity.

I wish only to create understanding, so that the two faiths may live side by side, respectful of one another, in dignity and peace.

These, then, are the elements of this book.

Following are some details that might interest the reader:

My decision to write this book goes back to December 9, 1952, near the end of my college studies, when I made the following diary entry:

"I think that I shall some day write a book to be called 'Judas and The Messiah'…Anything that I would try to say about it now could not do justice to what I envision (only vaguely now)…But only an absolute love and compassion and sympathy and understanding for both individuals…will ever do full justice to them, to the human drama, to life and to God."

What drew me to this theme?

I, myself, had been searching—wrestling—with the nature and meaning of life. Finally the answer had come to me: Love. I saw this as the dynamic principle underlying all of life. Human life, the universe, God started to make sense to me. It was a momentous personal discovery.

It expressed itself first in a couple of major, though then unpublished, philosophical poems which I wrote (now to be found in my book, "A Celebration of Life," together with my other poems). I also became curious about Jesus, the most dramatic exponent of Love in Western civilization.

I was stirred to write his story some day. I also felt overawed by the task and certainly not up to it at the time.

The desire to write the story never left me, but I didn't come to grips with it until late 1962. I was nearing my thirty-fifth birthday and, for the first time in my life, I became truly aware of my own mortality. I suddenly saw the limits of my own strength and days. I realized that life could be over in a flash. I saw that the demands and responsibilities of daily living could become so great that no time would be left over any more for the pursuit of dreams and visions. I asked myself, "If this were it, if life were to end right now, what would you regret not having done?"

I came up with only one regret—that I had not written the book about Judas and Jesus.

That is when I made my commitment to it. I started to work on it in 1963—researching, thinking and, eventually, writing. I finished it around Passover, 1966.

It was a thrilling moment and I was genuinely happy with the results.

I also thought that the hardest part was behind me—the writing of the book. But the hardest part was yet to come—finding a publisher.

I found a very fine agent, Sylva Romano, who was with the Mitchell J. Hamilburg agency at the time. "This is a novel that you can be proud of for the rest of your life," she told me after reading the book. That comment kept me going and believing in the book for the next ten years.

During this time the book was represented by several agents and submitted to a total of thirty publishers, who rejected it. I changed its title to the present one along the way (*My Jewish Brother Jesus*) and I shortened the book, on the advice of one agent. Long books by first authors, I was told, are too risky economically. Publishing costs are seldom recovered. I cut the book in half, down to its bare essentials, as it is now.

A number of individuals have read the manuscript and commented favorably on it. I was curious also how the book would be received in the religious community. I sent copies of the manuscript to a number of religious leaders and scholars, inviting their comments. Some, who had time to read the book, were most kind and gracious in their comments and granted me permission to quote them. (Their quotes may be found elsewhere in this book.)

Finally, I saw no sense in continuing to send the manuscript around to publishers. But I could not abandon the book, either. I decided, therefore, to set up my own publishing company, The Word Doctor Publications, and self-publish the book at my own expense (not to be confused with going to a vanity or subsidy publisher, which should be avoided). This is doing it the hard way, of course. I have no illusions. I have hopes, but no unrealistic expectations. My primary concern is that the book finds readers and is given life.

Why am I going this far? For the same reason that I wrote the book. I feel I must. Part of what is involved, I am sure, is a writer's vanity. But I see something else involved, too.

I am one of the fortunate ones who escaped the Nazi Holocaust with my parents. We fled Hitler's Germany after *Kristallnacht* (The Night of Broken Glass) and came to America as refugees in 1939, shortly before the outbreak of World War II in Europe.

As long as I can remember, I have wondered about the meaning of my life. I also have wondered why I survived. I have felt the need to give life meaning in the way I live it and in what I do with it. In its deepest sense, therefore, I see this book as my answer to Hitler. I see it as an affirmation of what he tried to destroy—the dignity and decency of Judaism and, by extension, Christianity. It is an affirmation of faith and belief in the triumph of the spirit over persecution and oppression—whether in the form of pagan Rome or Nazi Germany.

I know that it is not possible to fully satisfy the various points of view when it comes to Jesus. I hope, however, that my book will be judged for what it is, rather than for what it isn't, and that its merits will outweigh its shortcomings.

R.G.

Acknowledgments

I am indebted to all the authors listed in the bibliography for their scholarship and perspectives. I have singled out some for special mention in the Postscript of this book. I am grateful to all these authors who provided me with information, insight and understanding.

The extensive bibliography also lists the Jewish and Christian scriptural sources which I consulted. I have quoted from two of these, and from a Passover Haggadah.

Grateful acknowledgment is given for:
The use of passages from *The Holy Scriptures, According to the Masoretic Text*. Copyright © 1917, 1955 (New Edition, fourth impression, 1965.) Approved version of The Jewish Publication Society. Used by permission of the Jewish Publication Society.

The use of passages from *The New English Bible* © Oxford University Press and Cambridge University Press 1961, 1970. Used by permission.

The use of passages from *The New Haggadah/For the Pesah Seder*, edited by Mordecai M. Kaplan, Eugene Kohn, and Ira Eisenstein, for the Jewish Reconstructionist Foundation, published by Behrman House, New York, 1941; second printing, revised, 1942, sixteenth printing, 1959. Out of print. Used by permission.

I used these particular translations because their contemporary language blended in best with the modern speech and contemporary language that I aimed for deliberately, to cut through the centuries and make the period and the people come alive for us. They did not think of themselves as speaking "biblically." They were contemporaries. That's how they saw themselves. They spoke to each other as you and I speak. That speech may have changed over the years, but, at the time, it was *modern*.

I wish to express my special appreciation to the libraries of the University of Judaism in Los Angeles and the Los Angeles Public Library, where I had access to the many valuable books which I have cited.

To all who read this book while it was still in manuscript form my deep thanks for your thoughtful comments, valuable quotes and generosity of spirit.

Finally, I am grateful to iUniverse and its partners for creating new publishing models for authors, so that our books have a better chance to see the light of day and find their audiences. To those who have worked with me on my book in particular, my heartfelt thanks for your special skills, creative talents, constant caring and friendly, patient guidance.

CHAPTER 1

Crucifixion

Judas had been walking all morning.

It was near noon now and he was nearing his destination. He was in Galilee and he could see the town of Magdala ahead of him.

As he came closer, he saw what appeared to be an unusual amount of activity outside the city gate. Soon he could make out the nature of that activity.

The Jews of Magdala had come out to witness the crucifixion of one of their own: Reuben ben Jacob, the nineteen-year-old son of Rachel and Jacob.

They had come, the Jews of Magdala, to lend moral support to the youth and to his parents. They came as silent witnesses not for, but against, the might of Rome before God.

A contingent of Roman solders was busily at work. Some of the soldiers made sure that the six-foot upright post was firmly in the ground while four others—two on each end—placed the thirty-pound crossbeam on the ground, ready to receive the prisoner who stood a few paces away under guard.

The spectators watched in horror and mute contempt. There, in the alien image of the cross, stood the full indignity of Rome. The slow, inhuman torture of crucifixion was an abhorrence and an abomination in the sight of God and man. It was the Roman way.

On arrival at the scene Judas joined the silent spectators, who hardly regarded him, being more concerned with what was going on.

The soldiers formed a cordon around Reuben.

Rachel and Jacob, the parents of the youth, looked on in anguish, their arms around each other for comfort and support, tears streaming down their faces.

"Don't!" Rachel screamed.

Jacob gripped his wife tightly and tried to turn her away.

"Don't look!" he exclaimed.

But he could not turn her away and Rachel continued to stare, terror-stricken.

The youth's body and face trembled with fear as the soldiers removed his clothes and wound a cloth around his loins. Now he was ready for crucifixion and all but two soldiers on either side of him withdrew.

"Oh God! My son! My son!" Rachel screamed. "Help him, somebody! Please help him!"

The anguished outcry penetrated to the very heart and soul of Judas, like a knife. He wanted to leap forward and tear the prisoner away from the Roman soldiers, but he, as everyone else, stood frozen helplessly to the spot, staring in horror and disbelief.

The executioner assured himself of the adequacy of the preparations and nodded to the two soldiers on either side of the prisoner.

They seized Reuben's hands and threw him backwards to the ground, so that the crossbeam fitted under his neck.

The soldiers stretched his arms out on either side and knelt against the inside of his elbows.

The executioner pulled out two five-inch nails and knelt beside the prisoner. As one of the soldiers held the right forearm flat against the wooden beam, the executioner placed the square-cut iron nail upon the hollow spot near the wrist and, taking the hammer, drove the first spike into the crossbeam.

He repeated the process with the left wrist.

Reuben screamed with pain. Rachel and Jacob heard him, being barely able to see him through the blinding flow of their tears.

The executioner assured himself that the prisoner was securely anchored, then threw his hands up in the air as a signal to the soldiers to raise the crossbeam on which the prisoner was nailed.

The two soldiers grasped each end of the beam and lifted it into the air, while Reuben dangled from it as best as he could. They brought the beam over the upright post and maneuvered the mortised hole into position.

Now that the T-shaped cross was in place, the executioner nailed the board bearing the prisoner's name and nature of his crime upon the beam.

What did he do?" Judas asked a nearby townsman.

"He struck him," the townsman said, nodding towards a man, a mountain of fat, who stood isolated from the other townspeople, watching the proceedings with smug satisfaction.

"Who is he?" Judas asked.

"Necho ben Obadiah, the tax collector," the townsman answered contemptuously.

"He only struck him?" Judas asked.

"That's Roman 'justice' for you!" the townsman replied sarcastically.

Judas was not really surprised. Another "example." He could only speculate on the specific circumstances involved. Rome was bleeding the Jews dry through ever-increasing taxes, and so were the tax collectors, who could charge anything above the Roman rate and keep for themselves whatever they could collect above that rate. Judas speculated that the youth had struck the tax collector in outrage at seeing his parents bled dry.

Two soldiers grasped the calves of the prisoner's legs and placed the right foot over the left. They pushed the legs upward, to prolong death, while the executioner took a single spike and drove it through the feet. They dispensed with the small seat sometimes attached to provide rest for the prisoner. There was no need to offer the youth relief from his agony.

When the executioner was finished, he looked with satisfaction on his work. The prisoner would be dead within a few hours. Until then, he would move up and down upon the cross in search of relief. He would push upward to relieve the pain in his arms and in his legs, so he could breathe. He would sag suspended from his wrists to relieve the throbbing pain in his legs and feet. Death would be an eternity in coming.

In time, the onlookers would drift away one by one, to look after their affairs. Soon only the soldiers and the flies would remain to guard the prisoner.

"Let me take you home," some said, addressing Rachel and Jacob.

"No," wailed Rachel, "we will stay."

They would stay, too—they, the guards and the flies.

"He will not know that you are here," the friend suggested gently. "Don't torture yourselves more by staying. Don't remember him as he is now—try to remember him as he…was."

"We will stay!" Rachel insisted.

Maybe he would feel their presence, she thought. Maybe once or twice he would see them and recognize them and know them. Maybe it would help, if only for a moment.

But there was no real help now. Reuben ben Jacob, writhing in agony, could find relief only in death.

'You are not from around here," the townsman who had spoken with Judas earlier said. "Where are you from?"

"Jerusalem," said Judas. "Incidentally, could you tell me where I could find Barabbas?"

"Barabbas?" the townsman repeated. "Sure. There!"

With that, he nodded in the direction of a hard-looking man, medium in height, rippling with power. Judas had noticed him before, struck by the fact that while others were watching the crucifixion, Barabbas kept studying Necho ben Obadiah.

"Thanks," said Judas to the townsman and walked over to Barabbas.

The mute multitude now began to find its voice, chanting the ancient blessings in the face of death.

> "The Lord is King!
> "The Lord was King!
> "The Lord will be King for ever and ever."

Three times they chanted it.
Then they chanted the second blessing.

> "Blessed be His name, whose glorious kingdom is for ever and ever.
> "Blessed be His name, whose glorious kingdom is for ever and ever.
> "Blessed be His name, whose glorious kingdom is for ever and
>   ever."

They continued chanting, seven times, as prescribed:

> "The Lord He is God.
> "The Lord He is God.
> "The Lord He is God.
> "The Lord He is God.
> "The Lord He is God.
> "The Lord He is God.
> "The Lord He is God.

The guards gripped their spears more tightly.

"Sh'ma yisrael, adonai eloheynu, adonai echad."
"Hear, O Israel, the Lord is our God, the Lord is One."

Some left now. Some left later. Some stayed. But in their heart all knew that before long, Israel would triumph over Rome, with the coming of the Messiah, when God's kingdom would be established upon earth, in the end of days!

Judas had made his way over to Barabbas. "Barabbas?" he asked.
"Yes?"
"Shalom. My name is Judas."
Barabbas nodded. Then they walked off together.

❧   ❧   ❧

Judas watched as Barabbas busied himself around the courtyard of his house. The tools gave evidence that Barabbas was a butcher by profession.
"Why did you come here?" Barabbas asked Judas.
Judas watched as he sharpened a knife. "To come to work for you," he said.
"As a butcher?"
"Yes," said Judas.
There was ambiguity in the answer, which did not escape Barabbas.
"Here!" he said, thrusting one of the knives at Judas. "Show me!"
He indicated the lamb nearby. Judas inspected the knife. It had a notch in it.
"It is unfit," he exclaimed.
"Unfit?"
"Unfit for ritual slaughter, as in accordance with our laws," Judas declared evenly. "It has a notch in it."
"Then make it fit!" Barabbas exclaimed.
Judas went to sharpen it. He tested it with his nail and finger, then showed it to Barabbas, who inspected it and nodded his approval.
Then Judas walked over to the lamb which awaited him quietly, trustfully. He laid a comforting hand on its head and then recited the appropriate blessing:
"Blessed art Thou, O Lord, our God, who has sanctified us by Thy commandments and commanded us concerning slaughtering."

The knife now flashed across the lamb's throat with lightning speed in one prescribed motion. The life blood ran out, the lamb crumpled to the ground, the glassy eyes pleaded and, in a moment, the breath of life left the body.

Judas looked at Barabbas, who nodded his approval.

Judas regarded Barabbas.

"I am not the only butcher in Galilee," said Barabbas. "Why did you come to me, here in Magdala?"

He had passed the first test, Judas thought. Now for the crucial part.

"I want to work for the Movement!" said Judas, deciding to be direct, figuring that one does not play guessing games with Barabbas.

"The Movement?"

"The revolution—against Rome!"

"You know how to slaughter," said Barabbas evenly. "But can you kill?"

"I think so," Judas said.

"You may stay," said Barabbas simply, but before Judas had a chance to respond, Barabbas continued with rapid-fire recitation. "You were born in Kerioth. Your family moved to Jerusalem. Your father is a physician, the son of a merchant. Your father is considered a society doctor. He caters to the rich and powerful. He is the personal physician of Caiaphas, the High Priest, and of Rabbi Gamaliel, head of the Sanhedrin. Your father aligns himself with the Sadducees. He is no friend of the Zealots or the Movement to overthrow Roman rule. Your mother loves her social status. One of her childhood friends, Mary, lives in Nazareth. Mary has five sons and two daughters. They have visited you at the time of the Three Festivals. One of the sons is Jesus, your friend."

Judas was glad that he had been direct with Barabbas. It was obvious that Barabbas had an effective intelligence network at his command. Judas knew that he was face to face with the brilliant Zealot leader of the militant underground movement against the Roman occupation.

Judas nodded as Barabbas finished his recitation of facts.

"About Jesus," Barabbas asked. "Where does he stand?"

"I don't know," Judas said artlessly. "I haven't seen him in three years."

"Anyone here?" A woman's voice stopped further conversation.

'Yeah!" yelled Barabbas. "Out here!"

Judas was surprised to see a beautiful young woman appear in the doorway.

"I need some meat for tomorrow!" she declared bluntly.

"You could at least first say 'Shalom,'" Barabbas snarled.

"I'm in a hurry!" she snapped.

"Well, I'm busy!" Barabbas shot back.

"All right, Shalom!" she conceded.

Now she noticed Judas standing over the slaughtered lamb.

"Oh!" she gasped. "Shalom!"

"Shalom," he answered.

"My helper, Judas Iscariot," Barabbas explained by way of introduction. "My cousin, Mary, of Magdala."

"Shalom," Judas said once more, smiling, looking apologetically at the dead lamb at his feet, the pool of blood, the knife and the bloodstained hands.

"Shalom," Mary said, invitingly.

She was a beautiful Jewess, her blue eyes contrasting strikingly with her long, raven hair which fell softly, undulatingly to her waist. Her lips were full and inviting. Her face was pale, as if great care had been taken to protect it from the sun, which dried and burned the skin. The fineries she wore covered but did not conceal the exciting rhythms of her voluptuous body.

"I'll take a leg of lamb," she said to Barabbas.

"Wait, and you can take it with you!" Barabbas growled.

"Have Judas deliver it tomorrow," she said.

Barabbas grunted.

"Shalom, Judas," she said, regarding him enigmatically. "I'll see you tomor-row."

"Shalom," said Judas, already anxious to see her again.

Mary left and the two men began preparing the lamb.

"She is beautiful, isn't she?" Barabbas said, without looking up.

Judas laughed self-consciously.

"All men find her beautiful," Barabbas snarled.

"You two don't seem to get along," Judas said.

"She's foolish!" Barabbas said angrily. "Don't get involved with her!"

"Are you trying to protect her?" Judas asked.

"No!" Barabbas snapped. "I'm trying to protect you!"

"I can take care of myself," Judas insisted.

"She's trash, filth, garbage!" Barabbas blurted. "Don't dirty your hands!"

"How can you say…," Judas began, appalled.

"Stay away from her, Judas!" Barabbas ordered. "She's a whore!"

Judas was stunned. Before he could figure out how to respond, Barabbas continued matter-of-factly: "You have two jobs tomorrow. First, you will deliver the leg of lamb to Mary. Then, in the evening, you will ambush Necho ben Obadiah, the tax collector, on his way home, and kill him."

Judas nodded, speechless. His mind reeled as it tried to absorb what had happened in so short a time and what lay ahead.

❋   ❋   ❋

The next day Judas approached Mary's house with uncertainty. He was curious about her; he felt drawn to her, yet the attraction frightened him. He was afraid that he would not be able to resist her.

He remembered how he felt the previous day and how desire had welled up within him. He remembered, too, a feeling that was more than desire—a strange, mystical feeling, as if they were meant to meet and know each other, as if they had a common purpose and a common bond.

Judas dismissed both feelings quickly. Barabbas was right. It was best not to get involved with Mary.

The curtains were drawn discreetly when Judas arrived at the house.

"Shalom!" he called, knocking on the door.

A man answered. "Yes?"

At first Judas thought he was a customer of Mary's. But he revised his estimate quickly, deciding, rather, that he was Mary's pimp.

Judas took an instant dislike to Eliezer ben Jochanan.

He was unnaturally handsome, with sensuous features and a face that smiled easily. Judas had the uncomfortable feeling that it was a treacherous smile, one that masked unspeakable cruelty and evil.

"I would like to see Mary," Judas said.

"What for?" Eliezer asked.

"I have something for her."

"I'll take it! said the pimp curtly.

"Who are you?" Judas demanded.

"I said I'd take it."

Judas had no intention of being intimidated—or of leaving without seeing Mary.

"She asked me to deliver it to her," he exclaimed.

Suddenly Eliezer snatched the leg of lamb away from Judas and began backing into the house. The move took Judas by surprise for a brief moment. Then, before Eliezer had a chance to disappear inside, Judas exploded into action.

He twirled the pimp around and wrestled him to the ground, tossing him into the road as the leg of lamb went flying out of Eliezer's hand.

For a moment, Judas lost his grip, causing both men to scramble to their feet. Seizing the advantage, Eliezer lunged at Judas' legs, sending him sprawling to the ground.

Eliezer threw himself on Judas, who caught him with his feet and sent him flying through the air. Eliezer landed hard but before Judas had a chance to reach him, he was on his feet again. As Judas charged, their bodies locked in combat.

Eliezer caught him in a hammerlock which Judas broke as Eliezer stumbled on an unseen rock. With Eliezer off balance, Judas let his weight fall on him, forcing him to the ground. Grappling in the dust, Eliezer kicked himself loose, sprang to his feet, reached inside his sash and whipped out a knife.

Judas caught the reflection of the knife and stopped. As Eliezer advanced, Judas reached inside the folds of his sash and pulled out a dagger.

Eliezer stopped and evaluated the situation. He could fight or run. He was not about to run.

The two men circled each other in deadly silence, carefully watching every move. Once or twice Eliezer slashed and missed.

Suddenly Judas stumbled and Eliezer threw himself at him.

Judas rolled away, kicking hard with his feet as he rolled over. Eliezer uttered a sharp cry as Judas' foot struck his hand, sending the knife flying from him.

Judas now threw himself at his assailant. The next moment the tip of Judas' knife pressed against Eliezer's throat.

"Don't kill me!" Eliezer begged.

"Bastard! Rotten bastard!" Judas hissed.

"I won't bother you any more!" Eliezer promised.

"Parasite!" Judas exclaimed. "I'd do the world a favor if I killed you!"

"Please!" Eliezer pleaded.

"I don't want your rotten life!" Judas exclaimed finally.

With that, he removed the knife from Eliezer's throat and released him.

Eliezer scrambled to his feet and ran off down the road, quickly disappearing from view.

Judas now noticed Mary, who had witnessed the whole thing from the doorway. He picked up the leg of lamb and brought it to her. "Here!" he said.

"Won't you come in?" she asked.

Judas followed her inside.

"Sit down," she said. "I'll get you some water and a towel."

She took the meat from him and returned presently with a bowl of water, washcloth and towel, which she brought over to where Judas was sitting.

"Are you all right?" she asked.

"Yes," he said, as he cleaned himself.

"You should have killed him," Mary said.

"Would that have pleased you?" Judas asked.

"Perhaps," Mary said ambiguously. "He'll make trouble for you now."

"I don't think so."

"You don't know Eliezer ben Jochanan," Mary said. She studied Judas silently for a moment as he continued cleaning himself. Then she asked, "What did Barabbas tell you about me?"

"Nothing," Judas lied.

"Don't be polite," Mary said. "He either wants you to help me or not get involved with me. Which is it?"

Judas chuckled. "He said not to get involved."

"Well?"

"I'll make my own decision," Judas said.

"I give men their money's worth, and more," Mary said bluntly. "They always come back. Will you be back?"

'I expect to be," Judas said, aware of her effort to put him on the spot.

"Good," she said.

"That leg of lamb won't last forever," he said.

Mary laughed, amused at the remark, but also annoyed at the way he had taken the offensive away from here. "I could make life interesting for you," she said.

"You already have," he replied.

Judas rose from where he had been sitting. Mary sensed that he was about to leave and stepped close to him.

"I haven't even started," she said. "If it's the money, you can…"

"It's not the money," he said, interrupting.

"What is it, then?" she asked.

"A strange feeling."

"You never had that feeling before?" she asked suspiciously.

"Not that feeling," Judas said, laughing, realizing what she had reference to. "Another feeling."

"What other kind is there?"

"A feeling of something very special between us," he said quietly.

A trite, old line, Mary thought, one she had heard often. "Oh," she said.

"I have this feeling about only one other person," Judas admitted.

His mother, Mary figured. "Oh?" she asked, pretending curiosity.

"Jesus!" said Judas.

"It was worse even than she had suspected.

"He's a friend of mine," Judas explained. "A very special friend."

"So I gather," Mary said wryly.

"No, not that kind of friend," Judas added quickly, realizing the implications. "I hope you'll meet him some time."

Mary thought she spotted the difficulty. It was a typical one. "Look, Judas," she said, "next time you come, just tell me what you want and I'll give it to you. It's as simple as that. Don't waste time trying to make me or you feel right or good."

It was obvious that he wanted to leave now. She walked him to the door, where he turned to her a final time.

"Mary," he said, "if there's nothing special ahead for us, I'll just look foolish acting this way. But if there is something special, then I want it to start this way."

With that, he disappeared out the door. Mary looked after him, smiling wryly, convinced that he'd be back, on her terms.

*   *   *

"Are you sure he's coming this way?" Judas asked nervously.

"Yes," said Barabbas. "I know his habits. Relax."

It was shortly after dark. The moon, a full moon, was out as the two men lay in ambush along the road taken regularly by Necho ben Obadiah on his way home.

Judas checked his knife again.

"Stop worrying," Barabbas said. "You'll make out all right. The first time is always the hardest. When you get ready to strike, just remember one thing—the face on the cross!"

"All right," Judas said.

"Tonight you become one of us!" Barabbas said, firing up Judas. "'No God but Yahweh! No tax but to the Temple. No friend but a Zealot!'"

Judas nodded, recognizing and acknowledging the familiar Zealot battle cry, a flush of excitement passing through him as he stood on the brink of his crucial initiation into the ranks of the militant underground liberation movement whose method was violence, whose weapon was the knife, and whose enemy was Rome and those who did its bidding throughout the land.

"You'll do all right," Barabbas added reassuringly.

Suddenly the two froze as they heard the sound of approaching footsteps. Judas drew his knife and waited, his breath coming quickly.

Presently a man's form emerged from the darkness.

"That's him!" Barabbas said softly.

"Are you sure?" Judas asked.

"Yes."

Within a moment, Judas, too, was sure.

It had been agreed that Judas would work alone. He was to stay under cover until Necho ben Obadiah had passed him. Then he would leap up behind the tax collector and, before the man had a chance to react, Judas would cut his throat and plunge the knife into the man's heart.

Judas thought Necho ben Obadiah would never get there. The distance, though short, seemed infinite. Then, suddenly, he was there and, in another instant, had passed the place of ambush.

A few quick, silent steps and Judas was behind Necho ben Obadiah. The next moment he put a stranglehold around the neck of the tax collector, with the knife poised for the kill.

Barabbas had watched every move and was pleased with the flawless execution of the task so far. But suddenly, before he even knew that it was happening, he sensed that something was going wrong.

"Strike!" he whispered hoarsely, as Judas seemed to hesitate at the crucial moment.

Judas heard the command but his hand refused to obey. He felt Necho ben Obadiah struggling to free himself and he knew that if he did not act quickly, there would be trouble.

"Kill him!" Barabbas hissed.

Judas might have done so if Necho's head had not become twisted in such a way that his eyes suddenly stared upward and gazed at Judas. Judas had seen those frightened, pleading eyes before. He wondered when. Then he knew. He had seen them the day before, on the cross!

As Judas relaxed his hold slightly, Necho ben Obadiah struggled free, running off in panic as fast as his short legs and fat body could carry him.

"Help!" he screamed. "Help!"

Before he had a chance to run far, Barabbas dashed after him. The next moment, his powerful arms grabbed Necho ben Obadiah. One arm encircled his head, holding him like a vice, as, with the other knife-wielding hand, Barabbas slit the man's throat and stabbed him through the heart. With that, Necho ben Obadiah sank to the ground, dead.

Barabbas straightened up and regarded Judas.

"I'm sorry," Judas said, confused by what had happened.

The two men walked off silently.

❦   ❦   ❦

Arriving home, Barabbas put some left-over meats on the table, together with a loaf of bread and a flask of wine.

"Eat!" he said, as they sat down to supper.

Judas shivered, thinking with what casualness Barabbas could kill a man and then sit down to eat. Judas studied him, again struck by the man, in light of what had just happened. Barabbas was of medium height, but his whole body rippled with power. The legs, the arms, the neck were solid bone, flesh and muscle, even when their owner sat relaxed, as now. The face was hard and square. The eyes were blue, cold, intense. The lips were thin, firm, grim.

"Well?" Barabbas asked, looking up.

"I'm not hungry," Judas said.

"You must eat!" Barabbas said, almost parentally.

"I can't!"

You never know about people, Barabbas thought to himself. He knew of men who killed for the sheer joy of it. They were rare, of course. Most needed strong motivation, especially the first time. He had counted on Judas to come through, but he had misjudged him, obviously. But then, he had seen that before, too.

"You'll make it the next time," Barabbas said, seeking to restore Judas' confidence.

"There won't be a next time," Judas said slowly.

Barabbas stopped eating and regarded Judas searchingly.

"You're just upset now," Barabbas said slowly. "I've seen it happen before. Don't worry. You'll come through, the next time."

"There won't be a next time," Judas repeated.

"What do you mean?" Barabbas asked.

"I can't kill!" Judas declared.

Barabbas recalled the words of Ecclesiastes: "'To everything there is a season and a time to every purpose under the heaven…a time to kill, and a time to heal…a time to love, and a time to hate, a time of war and a time of peace.'"

"I can't kill," Judas said with quiet, firm conviction.

For a moment Barabbas did not speak, his thoughts going back to a time long ago. When, finally, he addressed Judas, it seemed like a different person talking—the vulnerable, sensitive, injured being that still lived at the very heart and core of the man who had become the hard, harsh leader of the Zealots.

"You would have liked my mother and my father," he said softly, "especially my father. He was a gentle man, who believed in the goodness of all men. He always kept his own counsel. He had nothing to do with Judas the Galilean, who, some years ago, claimed to be the Messiah and led the Zealots in an uprising against the Roman occupation of our land. But the Romans did not draw fine distinctions. They picked two thousand Jews and crucified them, including my father. I was only a boy at the time. I saw them crucify my father. That day I became a Zealot!"

Judas was deeply moved. "I can understand," he said softly.

"So?" Barabbas asked.

"I don't know," Judas said. "I just know that I must leave tomorrow."

"Leave? You just got here!"

"I can't stay!"

Barabbas was more puzzled. "Judas?" he asked.

"What?"

"What are you looking for?"

"I...don't know," Judas said honestly.

"One day soon you will have to take sides," Barabbas said seriously. He cut off a piece of meat and stuck the knife into the wooden tabletop.

Judas watched.

"Judas?"

"Yes?"

"Just remember..."

"What?"

"It's better to die by the sword than on the cross!"

Judas considered the words as they continued the rest of the meal in silence.

CHAPTER 2

Messiah

The next morning Judas left the house of Barabbas and proceeded toward the city gate without any particular destination in mind. The cross was still up, but the body of Reuben ben Jacob had been taken down.

As Judas stopped in the shadow of the cross, he saw a man approaching in the distance. As he came closer, Judas made out his features. First he was startled, then delighted.

"Jesus!" he exclaimed, moving forward to greet him. "Shalom!"

"Shalom, Judas," Jesus answered, almost expectantly.

The two looked like brothers, with Jesus, who was around thirty years of age, the older of the two by about seven years. He was dark haired, bearded, an inch or two short of six feet, strong, though not particularly muscular in appearance.

"What are you doing here?" Judas asked.

"I'm on my way to Capernaum," Jesus said. "And you?"

"I came…to join the Zealots," Judas said.

Jesus regarded him thoughtfully. "And…?"

"I couldn't kill!" Judas explained.

Jesus looked pleased. "Why did you want to join them?" he asked.

"To drive out the Romans and…"

"And what?" Jesus asked, scrutinizing Judas.

"…and bring about the Messianic Kingdom."

Jesus smiled, pleased, then regarded Judas thoughtfully once more. "Do you think it is near?" hde asked.

"Yes," said Judas. 'All Israel is waiting."

"What stopped you, Judas?"

"From killing?"

"Yes."

"Maybe cowardice...maybe God."

"The Zealots will not bring about the Messianic Kingdom," Jesus said with unmistakable authority. "There is a better way."

Judas looked hard at Jesus. Strange feelings stirred within him, feelings that took him back to the last time they saw each other, three years ago, in Jerusalem...

🍁   🍁   🍁

Dinner was in progress and going as expected.

It was questionable what Dinah bat Miriam, Judas' mother, enjoyed more—shopping for the latest in fashionable possessions or entertaining the prominent. In a sense, the two went hand in hand, one requiring the other, and both done for effect and status.

Dinah had been slightly miffed that Annas, the former High Priest, and his wife had turned down the dinner invitation. He was a hard one to snag and Dinah had never been successful with him. But then he was the most influential person, politically, in Jerusalem and in the land. Even though he had been deposed by the Romans as High Priest some ten years ago, everyone, even the Romans, knew that he was still the unofficial spokesman for the Sadducean upper class and the priesthood. Everyone knew that he was the guiding power behind his son-in-law, Caiaphas, the present High Priest. Some day, thought Dinah, they would entertain Annas and be entertained by him in turn. That's one reason why she had invited Caiaphas and his wife tonight.

There were other reasons. She had felt socially obligated for some time to have Rabban Gamaliel and his wife to dinner. To begin with, both families were good patients of her husband, the doctor. Dinah believed in purposeful entertaining. Then there was the fact that Rabban Gamaliel was not her idea of a pleasant evening. She felt uncomfortable with him because he wasn't partial to their class or their ideas. That's why she liked to have Caiaphas present. He could handle Rabban Gamaliel, though, in a sense, no one could really handle him. It was a shame.

It was obvious from the seating arrangement that in the estimation of Dinah and her husband, Nathan, Caiaphas and his wife, Sarah, ranked over

Gamaliel and Rebecca, for they occupied the middle couch, which represented the place of honor.

To their left, next in dignity, stood a second couch, on which reclined Gamaliel, Rebecca and Jesus.

The third couch, to the right of Caiaphas, was occupied by Nathan, Dinah and Judas…

In each case, the left side of the couch was considered the most honored spot.

"Uh, I shouldn't," protested Rebecca, as she accepted another helping of meat.

The wife of Gamaliel was a beautiful woman, with a strong sense of justice and of genuine values. She had intense likes and dislikes. She loved her husband. She despised Dinah.

"When you come here, you have to eat," Nathan teased her, "or you don't get invited again."

That, of course, would have been all right with Rebecca, but she said, "If I eat too much, Doctor, I'm afraid I'll get sick."

"That's good for business!" Nathan quipped.

Everyone laughed.

"Nathan!" Dinah chided her husband.

"Well, we have to figure some way of paying for all the food they're eating," he said naughtily.

Everyone laughed once more. It could be argued that they were laughing at him as much as with him. Nathan, the son of Reuel, a small-time merchant in nearby Kerioth, had achieved status in Jerusalem by becoming a skilled society physician. But he continued to think and act like the son of a merchant.

"Oh, you're terrible," Dinah said with amused exasperation. "Just don't pay attention to him."

"Just for that," said Caiaphas, with a twinkle in his eye, "I'll have another helping. Might as well get our money's worth!"

When Caiaphas was relaxed he was good company. he told a good story and he enjoyed being with people. He was only thirty years old but there was no question about the fact that he was capable. He loved power. He knew how it was used and he knew how to use it.

Rabban Gamaliel, on the other hand, was a much older man, about middle age, yet his spirit seemed ageless and indefatigable. He had deep-set eyes which twinkled with perpetual laughter. His brows were heavy, his lips were shaped by kindness. His Semitic nose stood proudly on his broad and handsome face, which radiated with a joy of body and soul.

Only the silver-black hair, thin on top but still full and billowy around the sides, and the slightly protruding stomach, betrayed his years.

Rabban Gamaliel, that is, Gamaliel ben Simon, grandson of the great Hillel, was the first scholarly leader to be honored with the title *Rabban*, "Our Teacher." He was a Pharisee and head of the Great Sanhedrin, the country's highest religious governing body. He was much loved by his people and by his peers.

"Are you here by yourself?" Gamaliel asked Jesus with kind solicitousness.

"Yes," said Jesus.

"You are from Galilee."

The fact was obvious from his manner of speech, so Gamaliel put it more in the form of a statement than a question.

'Yes," said Jesus. "I came down for the Feast of Booths. I'm a few days early."

Caiaphas was bored but decided to enter the conversation out of politeness.

"Where in Galilee?" he asked Jesus.

"Nazareth."

"Oh," said Caiaphas, with noticeable disdain.

"I have been there," said Gamaliel cordially, trying to counteract the High Priest's rude innuendo. "It is a lovely town with a beautiful view."

"Yes," Jesus answered with a grateful smile. "It is lovely—maybe because it is my home."

Gamaliel smiled. He liked the answer.

"You have family there?" Caiaphas asked, trying to be courteous, just in case it mattered, but doubting that it did.

"Yes," said Jesus. "I live there with my parents. I also have four brothers and two sisters."

'They...didn't come?" The note of accusation in the High Priest's voice was unmistakable.

"They...couldn't," said Jesus. "I was sent to represent the family."

This was permissible, though it indicated ill health or modest means.

"What does your father do?" Caiaphas asked.

"He is a carpenter," Jesus said. "He has not been well lately."

"I see," said Caiaphas condescendingly. His original intuition had been confirmed. There was no sense wasting time on Jesus. He had no value to him.

Dinah felt the need to apologize for the awkward presence of their Galilean guest. "My mother and his mother were friends," she explained. She was relieved when Caiaphas smiled back at her tolerantly.

"Well," said Nathan, glad to have a chance to change the subject. "How does it look?"

"How does what look?" Caiaphas asked, knowing all the time what the physician meant.

"The new procurator."

"Pontius Pilate?" Caiaphas asked, stalling. The remark was redundant. Everyone knew who was meant.

Yes," said Nathan.

Caiaphas would have been just as happy to avoid this discussion—not because of Nathan but because of Gamaliel. Nathan just wanted reassurances that all was well. But Gamaliel would probably give him an argument. Caiaphas wished people wouldn't always ask about such touchy matters so casually just to have something to talk about.

"I am optimistic that we can live with him," said the High priest finally.

"Really?" Nathan asked hopefully.

"Yes," said Caiaphas with conviction. "We must accept the fact that he is a Roman and that he'll have his problems understanding us. I'm sure he'll have his faults, like everyone else, but I think he'll make an honest effort to get along—if we'll meet him half-way."

"That was quite a beginning!" Rabban Gamaliel said wryly.

"What do you mean?" Caiaphas asked, knowing well what he meant.

"When he had his soldiers bring the Roman standards into Jerusalem," Gamaliel reminded him.

"Well," Caiaphas rationalized, "that, and the consequences, simply were the results of an unfortunate misunderstanding. The standards were covered, you know. He thought by keeping the images of Caesar covered, it would be all right. He meant no offense."

"He brought them here under the protective cover of night," Gamaliel reminded him with calm, logical precision. "He knew what he was doing. He was expressing his contempt for us—right from the start!"

The High Priest smiled tolerantly at Gamaliel, with that element of exasperation that bright youth reserves for the dense opinions of the older generation.

"That's just what I mean," said Caiaphas. "We're so anxious to see the worst in everything…"

"Everything Roman?" Gamaliel suggested.

"Yes!" Caiaphas agreed slowly. "We're so anxious to see the worst in…everything Roman, that we bring about the worst."

"I would gladly have given Pilate the benefit of the doubt," Gamaliel said, "if he had acted in good faith when he realized that he had offended our religious sensitivities. Even the Emperor insists that his representatives respect the religious feelings of the various provinces—so long as these do not threaten Rome."

"I don't mean to debate here, but Pilate acted in good faith—he recalled the standards," Caiaphas insisted.

Gamaliel laughed.

"Sure," he said with driving truth. "Remember the uproar? He never expected to see that many Jews descend upon Caesarea, where he was staying. Five days of 'conferences.' Remember how he had his soldiers surround the people and how he then informed us that the standards would stay? Well, his soldiers weren't ready for what happened! We all bared our necks and invited Pilate to kill us! He wasn't ready for that, either. He changed his tune. That's why he removed the standards and the images of the Emperor from Jerusalem!"

"Well," said Caiaphas, "that was an unfortunate situation. He was new and…well, everyone's entitled to one mistake—even a Roman."

His effort at humor fell flat, though Nathan, Dinah and Sarah considered the remark funny and laughed.

"I would like to believe that this is all it was," said the head of the Great Sanhedrin with genuine concern. "Even at that, it was quite a mistake. But the man frightens me. I have it on good authority that he is cruel, crafty, mercenary. We must act with great care."

"That's good advice," said the High Priest blandly. "At least here is one thing we can both agree on."

"Yes," smiled Gamaliel. He had to admire the High Priest. He had that uncanny talent of dealing inoffensively with everyone. Still, his inoffensiveness was offensive to Gamaliel.

"The point I'm trying to make, Rabban, is that we must be flexible in dealing with Rome," said Caiaphas, with quiet conviction. "We have no better choice."

"The point I was trying to make was that I hope you will be as fair to our interests as you are trying to be to those of Rome," Gamaliel said pointedly, adding, before Caiaphas could take offense, "but I agree with you wholeheartedly, we must be flexible!"

The High Priest, who had started to resent the head Pharisee's remarks, looked pleased now at his unexpected concession and overlooked whatever slight was intended.

"In fact," added Gamaliel, "I must say that you have demonstrated excellent flexibility yourself."

The remark was so perfectly ambiguous that Caiaphas managed to interpret it as a compliment. The seeming flattery mellowed him.

"Look," he said with obvious sincerity, "I don't mean to be an apologist for Rome. I am not a Roman, I am a Jew, and my first allegiance is to my people, after God! But Rome is a fact, the Roman empire is a fact, and our subjugation by Rome is a fact! We are an occupied country!"

"Yes," sighed Rabban Gamaliel. "Yes."

"Rome," Caiaphas continued, "knows what strings to pull to get her way. She wants only two things—power and money. She knows we are a religious people and that religion is the string that makes us dance. So, if I cooperate, if I manage to maintain peace and tranquility in the land, we are permitted 'freedom' of worship. If I do not cooperate, if there is trouble in the land, Rome will find someone who will cooperate, or else Rome will choke us to death."

The High Priest had spoken honestly, and Gamaliel knew only too well that what he had said was true. It was a terrible dilemma and, for a moment, the two men felt drawn together by their common cause. Beyond this, though, they could not agree.

"I have hopes still that we can deal honorably with Rome," said Gamaliel thoughtfully, "but I am beginning to have misgivings. We are two different worlds. We do not understand each other really, and I doubt whether we will be able to come to terms ultimately. Something will happen, some final outrage, large or small, and the nation's blood will flow. I fear for us."

"That's why it's so important for us to remain wise as serpents and harmless as doves," said the High Priest. "We must move with the mood of the moment and adapt ourselves to the temper of the times. We must stay flexible."

"You have steered a careful course these last years," said Gamaliel, not unkindly.

"And I mean to steer a careful course for a long time to come," said the High Priest with unquestionable determination. Reiterating, he added, "But we must stay flexible!"

"Yes," said Rabban Gamaliel casually, "we must stay flexible, whether we're dealing with Rome or with the Torah!"

"That's not what I said!" the High Priest exclaimed, bridling.

'Yes you did," Rabban Gamaliel argued calmly. "By implication! If it's good for the one, it's good for the other."

"I don't believe in the flexible interpretation of the Law," exclaimed the High Priest. "You believe in that!"

It was true, but it was more than just a difference of opinion between the two leaders. It was the difference between two outlooks that had developed within Judaism. It was the difference between the two groups they represented: the High Priest and the Sadducees on the one hand, and the head of the Great Sanhedrin and the Pharisees on the other.

The priestly class and the aristocracy were Sadducees. They believed in the strict acceptance of the Biblical writings. They were opposed to finding meanings that weren't stated explicitly. They found the Pharisaic custom of reading meanings into words or drawing meanings from words foolish, if not dangerous. They did not go along with such "new" concepts "found" by the Pharisees in the Bible as the immortality of the soul, the resurrection of the dead, life after death, and the reward of the righteous and the punishment of the wicked, ultimately. They restricted their view to this world and to what was stated explicitly in the Bible alone.

The Pharisees, on the other hand, had a good basis for their more flexible approach. They had come into their own as leaders of the people starting with the destruction of the First Temple, followed by the Babylonian captivity and exile some 600 years earlier.

With that calamity, the survival of Judaism was at stake. People without a country, priests without a Temple! New problems demanded new solutions. New conditions demanded new interpretations. New times demanded new views. The scribes became teachers. They established houses of prayer, assembly and interpretation; in short, the synagogue. They learned to interpret the Torah and apply it to Time and Place. This became Pharisaic Judaism.

The Pharisees, who were close to the people, now enjoyed their support and respect.

"Yes," replied Rabban Gamaliel, the Pharisaic head of the Great Sanhedrin. "I do believe in the flexible interpretation of the Law."

'Rabban," the High Priest asked, "once you start, where do you stop?"

"Once you stop, you risk death," Rabban Gamaliel replied evenly.

"You're risking that now!" the High Priest replied gravely. "That's what comes of all your irresponsible flights of fancy!"

Rabban Gamaliel said nothing, waiting for the High Priest to explain himself.

"I'm not worried about the immortality of the soul," said the High Priest. "That's just a foolish idea, as far as I'm concerned. But I'm talking about the Messiah! That's a dangerous idea!"

"Perhaps it has its hazards," Rabban Gamaliel granted, "but it's also a holy hope. it runs throughout our writings, starting as a thin, almost invisible thread…"

"That's exactly what I mean," said Caiaphas. "You start with a thread and you have woven a cloak out of it. That's what comes when you start looking for the 'inner' meaning of words. I see no such evidence in the Torah."

Dinah, Judas' mother, tried unsuccessfully to stifle a yawn. She looked around, embarrassed, but nobody seemed to have noticed except Sarah, Caiaphas' wife.

Dinah apologized silently, but Sarah just smiled, shooting Dinah a look of fellow boredom.

Dinah winked gratefully and rolled her eyes upward in an expression of helplessness. Sarah smiled understandingly. The silent by-play was relief to both.

It was a shame, thought Dinah, that they had to listen to religion and politics all night long. That always happened when she had Rabban Gamaliel over. Of course, there was nothing wrong with religion and politics. It's what men talked about when they weren't talking about business or about…well, telling…stories. She didn't mind it, for instance, when her husband talked religion or politics, or Caiaphas, the High Priest. At least they were sensible about it. But Gamaliel just wasn't realistic! He had such old-fashioned ideas. He was so extreme! That's it! He was a fanatic! Maybe it wasn't a nice thing to say but, let's face it, thought Dinah, it was true. She didn't care how nice he was personally, he was dangerous! It's a good thing, she thought, that there were people like Caiaphas, otherwise they really would have trouble with Rome.

Dinah noticed Sarah fondling a necklace she herself had been admiring all evening. "New?" Dinah mouthed silently, catching Sarah's eye.

Sarah nodded, pleased at the observation.

"Beautiful!" Dinah indicated. Sarah smiled.

Their by-play, however, had not gone unnoticed, from the time of the yawn. It had been caught by Rebecca, Gamaliel's wife, who felt confirmed once more in her opinion that both women were dumb, vapid cows.

"Cows at least breed well!" Rebecca fumed inwardly.

Gamaliel, meantime, would have dropped the matter at this point, knowing that their positions were diametrically opposed and that he was not about to convert the Sadducean High Priest to the Pharisaic point of view. But Caiaphas was anxious to have the final word.

"It all leads to dangerous confusion!" Caiaphas said. "Not only do the various Biblical statements lead to contradictions, but they've led to wild, irresponsible, inflammatory speculations. I'm sure you've read some of them, haven't you—the Psalms of Solomon, the Assumption of Moses, the Testament of the Twelve Tribes, the Book of Jubilees!"

"Yes," said Rabban Gamaliel, partially acknowledging the truth of Caiaphas' concern.

"Don't you see the danger?" Caiaphas pressed. "Take the Psalms of Solomon, for instance. Give us a Messiah, they say! 'Gird him with strength to shatter unrighteous rulers, and to purge Jerusalem from the nations that trample her down to destruction.' That's asking for trouble these days! And such things, as 'With a rod of...of...'"

Caiaphas couldn't remember and looked for help to Gamaliel.

"Yes,' I've heard of it,' Gamaliel said. "'With a rod of...'" He, too, had trouble recalling the exact words.

"'With a rod of iron he shall break in pieces all their substance!'"

Suddenly everyone turned in surprise to Jesus, who had uttered these words and who continued quoting the rest of the passage:

"'He shall destroy the godless nations with the word of his mouth. At his rebuke nations shall flee before him, and he shall reprove sinners for the thoughts of their heart.'"

A momentary hush fell on all present.

"Yes," said Caiaphas slowly, "yes, that's it. You see what I mean? Everyone is drinking of this heady stuff! Even the *am-ha...*"

The word *am-ha-aretz* almost slipped from his mouth, a word that meant the people of the land, the farmers, but that also had come to connote ignoramuses and country bumpkins.

"Even someone like this young man," the High Priest corrected himself quickly. "This is no time for such thoughts."

"Maybe it is times such as these that give rise to such thoughts," Rabban Gamaliel suggested.

"I know it isn't easy to live in troubled times," said Caiaphas. "Scripture is filled with hope, so why must we look so hard for Messianic hopes?"

"If," Gamaliel said, smiling, "the Messianic Kingdom is part of God's plan, as I believe it is, it won't go away even though we close our eyes to it."

"All it means to me is trouble, and I don't intend to have trouble," Caiaphas said. "We've had trouble before, remember?"

"Yes," said Gamaliel quietly.

"Judas the Galilean thought he was the Messiah, and he convinced some of our people," Caiaphas said. "How many did the Romans crucify because of him?"

Gamaliel felt the harsh, accusing gaze of Caiaphas.

"Two thousand!" Gamaliel answered.

"Was Judas the Galilean the Messiah?" Caiaphas asked fiercely.

Gamaliel did not answer.

"All right," Caiaphas smiled wryly. "Perhaps you can tell me how we will be able to recognize the real Messiah?"

Gamaliel stared thoughtfully at the floor. Then he looked up at Caiaphas and said quietly, "I have faith that God will give us a sign."

"Faith?" mocked Caiaphas. "I'm sure Judas the Galilean had faith. So did his followers. Anyway, I hope that all we will ever have to do is debate the matter, the way we have tonight, as a way to pass the evening."

Gamaliel smiled but said nothing.

"Rabban!" Judas asked suddenly, as all eyes turned toward him. "Who do you think will be the Messiah?"

Gamaliel smiled kindly at Judas. "Some say that every time a child is born in Israel he may be the Messiah," Gamaliel said. "I like to believe that."

Dinah suddenly smothered Judas with an embrace and kisses. "Yes, even my Judas!" she laughed, toying with the idea.

Judas quickly extricated himself and, anxious to change the focus of attention, said, "Or Jesus!"

They all smiled, politely admitting the possibility, though convinced of its improbability if not absurdity.

❋   ❋   ❋

Later that night, when they were alone, Judas turned to Jesus. "Do you know what I have always wondered about?" He asked.

"What?"

'How someone would know that he is the Messiah!"

Jesus grunted thoughtfully.

"I mean," said Judas, "would a person know it from the time he was born?"

"I don't think so," Jesus answered.

"How would he find out?"

"Like Moses," said Jesus, "like the prophets—a burning bush, a call in the night, a vision of holiness."

"A call from God?"

"Yes."

"When?"

"Any time, I imagine."

"Anywhere?"

"Anywhere."

"Oh."

'Only one thing is certain," Jesus said thoughtfully.

"What?"

"The call would be unmistakable," Jesus said.

They became silent and withdrew into their own thoughts...

"Come with me to Capernaum," Jesus said to Judas.

Judas fell in step beside him as they walked off together, leaving behind the city of Magdala and the cross that stood outside the city gate.

"It's been three years," said Judas, reminiscing. "A lot has happened since then."

"Yes, it has," said Jesus.

"How's your family?"

'My father, may his soul rest in peace, passed away," said Jesus.

'I'm sorry to hear that. May you be comforted."

"Thank you."

There was much to talk about, Judas sensed. He would wait until Jesus was ready to speak.

They continued walking in silence. It was near noon when they stopped at an orchard to rest and eat some of the fallen fruit.

"Judas," Jesus finally said when they had refreshed themselves, "I have found the key. The key is Love!"

"Love?"

"Yes, Love!"

Walking along, Judas listened as Jesus began to explain.

Every human being wants to be happy, Jesus began, and the question is how a person can be happy under all circumstances.

But what will make a person happy?

At the very heart of every human being is the need to be recognized, to be appreciated or, to put it another way, to be loved.

In fact, Jesus continued, this is at the very heart of every being, on every level of being, in the universe.

To be loved! To love!

What is love?

It is more than a feeling, an emotion. It is more than something that happens between a man and a woman or a parent and a child.

It is that, but also more, much, much more. It is something that goes on constantly and everywhere.

Love, Jesus said, is Giving and Receiving.

As you Give, you Receive; as you Receive, you Give.

Love is the fundamental nature of Life because wherever you look there is a Giving and Receiving going on constantly and forever.

Love is the fundamental law of life and everything else stems from it.

How wonderful it is! We are surrounded by love! We are swimming in a sea of love! We are giving and receiving, loving and being loved constantly and at all times, whether we are aware of it or not!

We must learn to become aware of it! We must learn to become more and more conscious of it!

This is our need—too love and be loved. But every moment, in some way, is a giving and receiving, a loving and being loved. This is the deep happiness that we can find, by knowing that we love and are loved in the deepest sense possible.

This is our task: to love one another!

But there is an even greater reason for joy. If love is basic to creation, then it is also basic to the Creator. If the law of love is basic to life, then the law of love is basic also to the source of life.

God is a God of Love, constantly and eternally giving and receiving Love!

Jesus went on to explain how we are part of God, linked to God, responsive to God, and how this is true of every being of creation, on every level of creation.

We do not belong to one another. We belong only to God.

Our need is for constant love. No human being can give us this kind of love constantly. Only God can.

Our need is for constant understanding. No human being can give us constant understanding. Only God can.

Our need is for constant reassurance. No human being can give us constant reassurance. Only God can.

Human beings fall short of the mark. God does not.

Human beings fail us. God does not.

Human beings die. God does not.

Our task is to serve God. It is our only task. It is the task of every being that has been called into life. There is nothing more meaningful that we can do. Every attitude, every action must be seen as a way of serving God.

That way our lives become important every moment.

Judas listened, his own spirit responding to the inner glow of Jesus' spirit.

"Do you see?" Jesus asked, eagerly searching his face.

Judas saw.

"We must make others see!" Jesus exclaimed, as if driven by some inner calling. "Once they see, it will change their lives, Judas! Once they see what alone can make them happy, once they see what really makes them happy, they will change, they will become happier human beings and better human beings. They will infect each other with love, Judas. One person and then another and then another! Jew and Gentile! Until the whole world has changed! A new heaven, a new earth! This, Judas, is the way to…"

"…the Messianic Kingdom!" Judas declared, trembling at the thought as he heard his own words.

"Yes," Jesus said with a quiet fervor. "Yes. This, Judas, is our task. We must make others see, so that it may come about."

Judas gazed at Jesus, a fearful question in his eyes and forming on his lips, yet one which he was unable to utter.

Both sensed the question and the answer.

"I have been away," Jesus said evasively. "I went to see John the Baptizer. As I stood in the Jordan, I suddenly saw the heavens open and the *Shekhinah*—the Spirit—like a dove, descending upon me, and I heard a voice from heaven saying, 'You are my beloved son in whom I shall be blessed.'"

"The sign!" Judas exclaimed. "You received the sign!"

Their eyes met and tested each other, but Jesus said nothing. Judas felt an excruciating joy and overpowering awe. He was afraid to breathe lest the spell be broken. He wanted to hear more, yet he was afraid to ask. He would wait until Jesus broke the silence, for truly he was unable to speak.

Jesus said nothing for the moment. He withdrew into the privacy of his own thoughts, recalling that day, and the days that followed, those days in the desert. He had wrestled with his soul…

❋   ❋   ❋

"So, you are the Messiah!" Satan had said. "Well, then, prove it to the world. Perform your miracles!"

And Satan had tempted him, taunting, "Let nature give abundantly of its fruits so that all may take of its bounty. If you are the son of God, tell these stones to become bread."

And Jesus had wondered if this was what men wanted of him.

"No," he thought to himself after a while. "No. Man cannot live on bread alone; he lives on every word that God utters."

And Satan had tempted him, taunting, "Show then a great miracle in the Holy City where everyone can see you. Go to the parapet of the Temple. Throw yourself down; for Scripture says, 'He will put angels in charge of you, and they will support you in their arms, for fear you should strike your foot against a stone.'"

And Jesus had wondered if that was the way he should reveal himself and, in one stroke, help usher in the kingdom of heaven.

"No," he had decided. "Scripture says again, 'You are not to put the Lord your God to the test.'"

And Satan had tempted him, taunting, "It was said that you would rule the nations. Rise up and conquer them! Israel is waiting! Israel is ready! Israel will win! And you will reign in glory! The way of the world and the pleasures of the world are yours!"

And Jesus had wondered if that was the course he should follow, until he saw that he must win not by might, nor by power, but by God's spirit.

And Jesus had said, "Begone, Satan; Scripture says, 'You shall worship the Lord your God and him only shall you serve!'"

And Jesus had decided to let Love speak for itself and all else would then come about in good time. Love was the miracle! Love would perform miracles!…

Returning to the present, Jesus regarded Judas, who seemed too frightened to speak.

"What is troubling you?" Jesus asked quietly.

"I'm afraid to say it!" Judas said, breathing hard.

"Say it!" Jesus commanded quietly.

Terror gave way to awe. "I believe," said Judas, "that you are the Messiah!"

Jesus regarded Judas silently with infinite love. "Please!" Judas pleaded. "Tell me if it is so! And if not, may our Father in heaven forgive me!"

"It is so," Jesus said softly.

The eyes of Judas filled with tears of joy as he declared, "Blessed are You, O Lord our God, King of the universe, who are good and dispenses good and who has revealed to us good tidings."

Then, bowing and stepping back three paces as in the presence of royalty, he added, "Blessed are You, O Lord our God, King of the universe, who has ushered in the days of the Messiah!"

Jesus smiled and said, "You are blessed, Judas Iscariot, for flesh and blood have not revealed this to you. It was revealed to you by our Father in heaven."

"Yes," Judas nodded. "I did not know it the last time I saw you."

"Our heavenly Father does not always reveal everything at once," Jesus explained.

"Have you always known, all along?" Judas asked.

"No," said Jesus. "Not until I found the key, Love."

"And the sign?"

"And the sign."

Judas nodded his understanding, full of wonder.

"Come!" said Jesus as they resumed their journey toward Capernaum. "Let us begin our work."

CHAPTER 3

Start of the Mission

The Sea of Galilee was calm that afternoon. Some of the boats had lain at anchor for cleaning and repairs and were being readied for the following day.

The boats of Zebedee and Jonah shared the same anchorage, since, in fact, the two families cooperated in all matters involving their occupation. They pooled each other's tools, knowledge and manpower at anchor and at sea. Their endeavors prospered.

Having returned from the midday meal, the sons of Jonah—Andrew and Simon—helped the sons of Zebedee—James and John—store the nets.

"The sea is calm today, we should have a good haul tomorrow," said Andrew.

Simon glanced over to their own boat where he saw his father at work tying up the sails.

"Father?" he called.

Jonah stopped and looked. "What?"

"Do you want us to come and help?"

"I'll call you if I need you," his father called back and went about his work once more.

"Don't you think you'd better go?" James asked.

"He'd say so," said Simon. "Anyway, he's got plenty of help."

It was true. Both Jonah and Zebedee had plenty of help.

"So why did you ask?" Andrew wanted to know.

"Well," mused Simon, "just…uh…to be polite."

They all laughed.

"Father must love him for being so devoted," Andrew teased. "I think I'll tell him."

Andrew pretended to leave and Simon grabbed him. "Don't you dare!" Simon exclaimed.

The two started to wrestle. Suddenly they heard their father calling. "What's the matter over there?"

Andrew and Simon stopped fighting. "Nothing!" called Andrew.

"Nothing," repeated Simon. "We were just playing around."

Jonah shook his head in mock despair and went back to work. Simon and Andrew looked at each other and laughed good-naturedly.

"There's only one thing worse than having a kid brother!" James snarled.

"What's that?" John asked belligerently.

"Well, I'd say…not having one at all," said James, ruffling John's hair as John punched him good-naturedly.

At that moment, Simon, who had been watching Caleb and Moshe, one of the crew, struggling with a sail, went over to him.

"Here, let me give you a hand," said Simon as he helped Caleb fold the stubborn sail.

"That's what I need, all right—a hand," Caleb remarked wryly. 'In fact, I could use a whole arm." His arm hung helplessly at his side.

"These sails are just too stubborn to handle," said Simon, trying to put Caleb at ease.

Caleb smiled bitterly. 'They're no trouble, with two good arms," he said. "You remember how it was when I had two good arms, don't you, Simon?"

"You were stronger than any two of us—so you're still doing a full man's work now," Simon said graciously.

"Thanks for trying to make me feel good," Caleb smiled. "It's been two years now like this, ever since the accident."

'Yes, I remember," said Simon softly.

"My brother always liked you."

"I liked him."

"I used to look after him, from the time he was a baby," said Caleb wistfully. "My mother always said, 'Caleb, you must look out for Jonah.' You know I tried to save him, don't you?"

"You did everything you could."

"Yes."

"It was a bad storm, a very bad storm," Simon said. "It's a wonder any of us are alive."

"That's right!"

"We thought you were all gone when the boat turned over."

"I held him up as long as I could!"

"We had a hard time getting to you."

"If I only could have held on a little longer," Caleb sighed.

"You were half-drowned yourself," Simon reminded him.

"Yes," Caleb remembered. "Yes. I couldn't hold on any more, I couldn't!"

"We were all helpless," Simon said.

'Maybe it was my arm, maybe I couldn't hold on any more because of my arm."

"It was numb when we got you out."

"Just like this," said Caleb. "Maybe that's why I couldn't hold on any more."

"That's probably it," said Simon.

"I just can't remember when it went numb, Simon. I keep wondering."

"You did everything you could."

"He kept choking me and pulling me down with him."

"It was a bad storm."

"It was terrible."

"God gives and God takes away," said Simon.

"Yes," said Caleb. "Blessed be the name of the Lord. Only, sometimes it's hard to say that."

"It's always hard to say," said Simon, "but it's all we can say." Caleb looked off into the distance. Suddenly he became aware of two approaching figures. Presently he recognized one of them. "Look who's coming!" He said to Simon, pointing toward the two men. "It's Jesus ben Joseph!"

"I wonder what he's doing here?" Simon asked.

"Hey, John, James, your cousin's coming!" Caleb called.

John and James stopped and looked in the direction of the approaching figures.

"Who's that with him?" Simon asked. Nobody seemed to know.

"Shalom!" John and James called out and waved.

Jesus waved back. "Shalom!" he called. Presently he and Judas came alongside the boat and stepped aboard.

Zebedee, who came over, stopped and embraced him. "Shalom, Jesus!" he said heartily.

"Shalom, Uncle Zebedee," Jesus replied. "How are you?"

"Fine, fine," Zebedee said. "And how is your mother?"

"Fine, thank you," said Jesus. "How is Aunt Salome?"

"Fine, just fine," said Zebedee. "She'll be glad to see you."

"This is my friend Judas, of Kerioth," said Jesus.

Judas smiled pleasantly. "Shalom!" said Judas.

"Shalom!" replied the others.

Jesus embraced his cousins and his friends one by one.

"Shalom, Jesus," said Caleb when Jesus had finished greeting Simon.

"Shalom, Caleb," Jesus said kindly. "I see you are still working as hard as ever."

"As hard as ever, but not as well," said Caleb. "I do the best I can."

Jesus smiled compassionately. "That's all our heavenly Father asks of us," he said. Then he turned to Judas and said, "These are my cousins, James and John. And these are my friends, Andrew, Simon and Caleb."

"Shalom," Judas said once more.

"Shalom," said the others.

"What brings you to Capernaum?" James asked.

"I thought it was time to pay you a visit," Jesus said.

"Good, good," said James. "Its been some time since you were here."

"Here, sit down," said John as he prepared a place for Jesus and Judas. "You've had a long walk."

"Thank you," said Jesus and Judas as they sat down.

"Did you hear about John the Baptizer?" John asked anxiously. "He's been arrested!"

"Yes," Jesus said, nodding his head slowly. "I heard."

"What do you think will happen now?" John asked.

Jesus looked at him and then said quietly, "The days are fulfilled. The kingdom of heaven is at hand. Repent and believe in the good news."

It was a strange answer, one that neither John nor the others had expected. John had been curious about the fate of John the Baptizer. Could Jesus have misunderstood the question? His answer had sent a shiver down his spine. John wondered if he had been the only one who had been affected that way. He looked at the others. They, too, seemed strangely affected by the remark. John suddenly realized that the words echoed those of John the Baptizer, who kept shouting, "Repent! For the kingdom of heaven is at hand!"

But Jesus had spoken so quietly that the delayed impact was almost deafening. Had the others caught the subtle change? John wondered if he was imagining things: "The days are *fulfilled*...the days are *fulfilled*...the days *are fulfilled*..."!

John regarded Jesus and searched his face eagerly for the answer. So did the others.

"What do you mean?" John asked finally.

Jesus now started to explain, as he had explained to Judas. They listened hungrily. A profound silence greeted him when he was done. Each one was afraid to speak, afraid of breaking the spell of the spirit that hovered over them.

Simon had been studying Jesus thoughtfully. He did not dare recall just now his initial thoughts, which had terrified him. His heart had pounded feverishly at the enormity of his thought, a thought which he suppressed now with all his might, lest he give foolish utterance to it. His feelings were all mixed up, but there was one thing he was certain of at this moment. He had known Jesus as a friend for a long time, but never before had he felt drawn to him like he did now. Suddenly, almost in spite of himself, he heard himself blurting out, "What would you have us do?"

"You must tell others what I have said," Jesus replied.

Caleb had been listening intently. He felt strangely affected by Jesus. He did not know what propelled him, but suddenly he rushed forward and fell upon his knees before Jesus. "Help me!" he pleaded. "Help me!"

The others looked bewildered, startled by Caleb's action.

"Do you believe that I can help you?" Jesus asked.

"Yes!" said Caleb fervently. "Oh, yes, yes!"

Jesus regarded the troubled man with the withered arm whose eyes looked pleadingly into his.

"Get up!" said Jesus, with quiet authority.

Caleb rose.

"Your sins are forgiven. Give me your hand."

Jesus held out his hand toward Caleb's withered arm. As it came to life, Caleb extended it slowly toward Jesus until their hands touched. Suddenly tears of joy welled up in Caleb's eyes.

"Blessed art Thou, O Lord our God, who creates wonders!" Caleb cried, addressing the great, invisible Lord of the universe.

"Your faith has made you whole," said Jesus. "Go in peace."

"I can move it again!" Caleb cried. "I can move it again!" He swung his arms wildly about as the others looked on in astonishment. Caleb ran off, unable to contain his joy. "My arm is well again!" he shouted. "Look! My arm is well again!"

Jesus regarded his cousins and his friends. "Come," he said, "and I will make you fishers of men."

Simon, Andrew, James and John left their nets at once and followed Jesus.

Word of what Jesus had done spread rapidly. Caleb saw to that. It was not surprising, therefore, that when it became known that Jesus had gone to Simon's house that many people came to see him, particularly those who sought his help. Their faith in his miraculous powers was confirmed further when they learned that he had also cured Simon's mother-in-law of her fever. Jesus cured many that day and night.

"Your faith," he told each one, "has made you whole."

The next day he withdrew so that the people could not find him. He had compassion for the halt, the dumb and the blind. But there were others who suffered, without visible signs. They, too, needed miracles. The whole world, he knew, needed a miracle—the Miracle of Love.

CHAPTER 4

The Lost Sheep

Business was slow today so Matthew, as he was wont to do under these circumstances, sat in the customs house by the lakeside meditating.

He was gaunt, looking older than his thirty-three years. At first glance his face looked tired, as if mirroring the fatigue of living. Once that might have been the case. The strains of that former life had left their mark. A closer look, however, showed the eyes to be anything but the tired eyes of an indulgent individual. True, the eyes were sad eyes, but they were the eyes of a man who had searched and suffered and, in doing so, had found serenity. Matthew's eyes were filled with compassion.

At times Matthew wished that his life might have been simpler, straighter. How much more pleasantly he might have fared. He had wealth, but it was not respectable wealth; he had friends, but they were not respectable friends. He lived a decent life, but he had not always lived decently.

His inward eye dwelt on the portrait of his life, ever scanning it for new meaning.

Matthew grew up with wealth and, in time, he inherited his father's money and business. Alphaeus, Matthew's father, was a tax collector after the manner of the times—he had bought the office from Rome at public auction and then fixed the rates arbitrarily so he could meet his commitment to the authorities and reap as big and as quick a profit as the traffic would bear.

He had a thriving business, taxing the daily hauls of the fishermen and all the goods that were sent out and were delivered to the city.

The fact that he was despised for his unscrupulousness did not bother Alphaeus at all. He had nothing but contempt for others anyway. He cared only for their money, not for their good opinion. Boys called him names and spat on him. Men spoke of him as a licensed robber, a wild beast in human shape. His word was not acceptable in a Jewish court of law, just as he was unacceptable to honorable men, for it was obvious to all that, in thought and deed, he denied men, God and Torah.

Alphaeus believed that, given enough money, you could buy the world. It was his article of faith. One did not earn respect or friendship or love—one bought it. Alphaeus raised Matthew by buying him.

Matthew never lacked anything when he was a boy. His father indulged his every whim. Alphaeus just smiled at the boy's wild and willful ways, so that no one could control him in time, not even Matthew's mother, who, long ago, had escaped into her own world of illusion and fantasy.

Alphaeus was openly pleased to see his son become a boisterous youth who explored the delicious pleasures of life early, secure in the knowledge that his father would get him out of trouble and right every wrong.

In time Matthew married and had children on a whim and because it was the thing to do. Some thought that he showed signs of maturing, but this lasted only until the novelty of marriage and parenthood wore off. Then Matthew, the man, became a spoiled, self-centered child again.

Matthew might have continued in this direction if it had not been for his wife's premature death. Suddenly, according to the mysterious ways of the spirit, Matthew saw his life—past, present and future—in a new light.

He saw the emptiness and hollowness of his existence and he saw his father as a false god who died with his death and who was undeserving of worship. In that moment, Matthew's heart opened and reached out for his Father in heaven.

It had been three years now, thought Matthew, since that turn of events. Once he discovered how spiritually parched he was, he started to drink deeply from the newly found fountain of his being. Night and day he meditated on God, learning how to pray, studying Torah, trying to walk in the ways of holiness, hoping to become acceptable in the sight of the Lord, yearning to become a blessing.

He changed his business ways and levied fair and honest taxes, much to everyone's surprise. While he was now regarded more sympathetically, his past still clung to him and people chose not to have anything to do with him. But Esther was drawn to him. Perhaps it was because she was plain and, at thirty, had never been married. Perhaps it was because she was the daughter of Moshe ben Haym, a pious dealer in precious gems. She offered her love to Matthew's yearning spirit. Matthew married Esther. God and Esther helped him in his grief over his former ways, and their effect on his son and daughter, whose troubled lives now were beyond his help and influence.

Matthew's circle of friends did not change much from what it was—the lost, the outcasts, the discards. They could not help but notice the change that gradually was taking place in Matthew, but since he talked little about it and since he seemed to become even kinder than before, his friends accepted him despite his eccentricities. Somehow they seemed drawn to him even more.

At first Matthew felt hurt because he was not accepted in the more respectable circles. After all, had he not changed, was he not willing to change, was he not making every effort to change? But gradually a new thought presented itself to him. Could it be, he thought, that this, too, was God's will? Could it be that God wanted him to stay where he was? Could it be that God wanted him to be a friend to the least—the outcasts and the discards? Could it be that God needed him where he was? The more Matthew thought about this matter, the more he became convinced that God had a purpose for him, vague as it still seemed.

Still, he had made some new friends—not many, two or three. James and John, the sons of Zebedee, had befriended him. Once he got to know them, he realized that their action was typical, for they had little regard for public opinion and they did not court public approval. They had detected a change in Matthew's life and they held out the hand of friendship and fellowship.

It was at Zebedee's house that Matthew first met Jesus. They had met and talked several times since then. Now he was in town again.

Matthew was startled when he received the first reports about Jesus. He went to see for himself and was amazed at what he heard and saw. He was puzzled by his feelings. This was the same Jesus whom he had talked with at Zebedee's house. True, he had been impressed with the young Nazarene. There was about him a spiritual quality and depth that was unusual for any man at any age. It was not so unnatural, therefore, for him to appear in public as he suddenly did. But it was strange, nevertheless. it was strange, having known him privately before, having seen him walk the same streets of Capernaum before, without attracting notice, and now, suddenly, becoming the talk of the town.

But why am I so agitated? thought Matthew. Why am I so troubled?

Matthew looked at the Sea of Galilee that had been there who knows how long. He looked at the fishing boats and the fishermen and he saw how they must have come and gone and pursued their daily tasks since time immemorial. he looked at the land around him and the people and he saw them living and dying, living and dying. He saw the changelessness of life.

And then he looked inside himself and he knew that men could change and life could change, and he knew that beyond the apparent, beyond the known, beyond the human, there was the mystery, the miraculous, the Messiah.

Matthew trembled as he thought about Jesus. He knows, thought Matthew. Jesus knows! Suddenly Matthew yearned for Jesus.

Am I mad? thought Matthew. I was mad before and I thought I was sane. The light I saw by was darkness, but I thought it was light. Is the light I see by now light, or is it, too, darkness? Does a sick mind replace one fever with another fever? Does anyone else see? Or do I see what no one else sees? Do I see?

Matthew was so absorbed that for a moment he did not know whether he was seeing or imagining Jesus coming toward him, a crowd trailing behind him.

"Shalom," said Jesus, as he approached Matthew.

"Shalom," said the tax collector.

Jesus searched Matthew's eyes. "Follow me," Jesus requested quietly.

Matthew stared at Jesus. Feeling, but not knowing why, Matthew rose and followed.

The dinner at Matthew's house that evening was a joyful affair. Although Matthew's friends were not the kind who would normally mix or even feel comfortable with their religiously more observant kinsmen, they came because they felt comfortable with Matthew and because of an overriding curiosity regarding this *maggid*, this wandering preacher, Jesus of Nazareth, who was creating such a stir.

Judas sat between the sandal-maker and the barber's fat wife.

So much had happened, thought Judas, since his fateful encounter with Jesus and his decision to follow him. Judas wondered where it would lead. But he did not try to figure it out. He trusted Jesus. He was sure that Jesus would lead them in the right direction, that he would do the right things at the right times, and that he would tell them what they needed to know and when they needed to know it.

After all, was he not the Messiah!

It was obvious to Judas. Was it obvious to anyone else? He wondered. Was it obvious to Simon and Andrew? Was it obvious to James and John? Was it obvious to Matthew? Did they know? Did they carry the same secret in their hearts? He had been told not to discuss the matter with anyone. Had they been told the same thing? If they knew, they weren't saying anything, even to each other. Judas would not say a word either.

But what about the others, the people? No one had said anything. Judas found it hard to believe that what seemed so apparent to him was not so at all to others. Maybe it was just as well this way, he thought. Obviously Jesus had known that it would be this way. It was part of the plan. if Jesus could wait, so could Judas.

Though it was not obvious to others who Jesus was, it was obvious that Jesus had gotten off to a good start. The people listened and were impressed, especially with his powers of healing. The leaders, so far, neither approved nor disapproved, but still withheld judgment. At least they had not bothered Jesus.

"Drink up!" The drunken, raucous voice of the sandal-maker startled Judas. The sandal-maker emptied his wine so that he would be ready for a full cup when the servant came with the flask.

"Thanks," said Judas evasively.

"You should be drinkin', not thinkin'," said the drunken one, laughing at his own joke.

"Noah!" his wife snapped. "Please!"

"What'd I do wrong now?" Noah bellowed, so that all heard.

"Keep your voice down!" his wife hissed.

Noah's big-boned wife was a perfect match for the big man, who glowered at her as he shrank from her.

"This is my wife, Sarah," Noah said to Judas.

"Shalom," said Judas.

Sarah nodded peevishly.

"You married?" Noah asked.

"No."

"Good," said Noah, smiling paternally. "Stay that way."

Sarah regarded her husband contemptuously.

Noah leaned over to kiss her with a slobbering mouth. Sarah pushed him away. "Behave yourself!" she ordered.

"See!" said Noah self-pityingly. "My name is Noah. Noah the sandal-maker."

'Yes," said Judas. "We were introduced earlier."

"Oh, yes, yes, earlier," Noah said, trying to recall who he was and where he was. "What's your name?"

"Judas."

"Oh, yes, Judas. Well, Judas, I hope you're enjoying the party."

"I am," said Judas.

But Noah wasn't listening any more. The servant had filled his cup and Noah was staring into it hard, searching the wine for meaning.

"Oh, pardon me!" exclaimed Leah with shrieking laughter. The fat wife of Nahum, the barber, had made a quick reflex move with her 230-pound body and, in so doing, had bumped into Judas.

"No harm done," said Judas politely.

"Oh, I'm terribly sorry!" she said, full of exhilaration, and, looking naughtily at the handsome young baker's assistant next to her, she giggled. "It was all Aaron's fault!"

Judas smiled tolerantly.

"Have you two met?" she asked coyly and, without waiting for an answer, she said, "This is Aaron, who works for Jacob the baker. And you are…?"

"Judas."

"Oh, yes, Judas. You're with him, aren't you?" she said, nodding in the direction of Jesus.

"Yes," said Judas and, turning to Aaron, he said, "Shalom."

"Shalom," said Aaron, looking bored and trapped.

"I'm just lucky to be between two such handsome men," Leah sighed.

Indeed, Aaron, as Judas, was a handsome youth in his late twenties. He was the youngest of eight children. The family was poor and the father had died early. Aaron went to work as a baker's assistant, but the prospects of eking out a meager living for the rest of his life disturbed him. He desired the easy, pleasurable life of the well-to-do. He craved luxury. He knew that he would never have the means for that kind of life. He did not have his own business. He would always have to work for somebody else. But he did have one asset—his good looks. He decided that these could be worth money to him. He discovered that some middle-aged matrons appreciated his attentions materially. He decided that eventually he would settle down and marry a rich spinster or widow, who was along in years. Everybody knew what he was doing. Some even knew with whom. Aaron didn't care.

"I hope I'm not taking up too much room," said Leah, trying to appear half her size.

"Everything's all right," Judas said politely.

Leah thanked him with a wisp of a smile. "It's all Aaron's fault," she said again, looking seductively at the baker, her layers of flesh quivering with excitement.

Aaron smiled wanly.

"I just can't resist him," she sighed flabbily.

Nahum, her husband, who had been talking to Asher, the fisherman, looked up suddenly.

"What's that, dear?" he asked sharply.

Leah's voice fluttered with flirtatious excitement. "I said I can't resist Aaron's...baking," she said.

Nahum shot Aaron a suspicious glance and then resumed his conversation with Asher.

"Do you think I'm getting too heavy?" Leah asked Aaron, winking furtively.

"You look all right," Aaron said dully.

Leah turned to Judas. "He's such a sweet boy," she purred, as she reached for another helping of food. "Eat some more—it's all so good."

Judas withdrew into himself once more as Leah became preoccupied with food.

The dinner was going well. The guests were making small talk and enjoying themselves. Simon, Andrew, James and John sat among the guests and mingled in their talk. Jesus sat next to Matthew. Jesus, too, was enjoying himself. Judas watched him laughing, talking, smiling, listening. It was obvious that Jesus felt comfortable with the guests, and they with him.

"Rabbi!"

Judas looked up and noticed Nahum, the barber, addressing Jesus.

"Yes?" Jesus asked.

"Asher and I were talking and, uh, I would be interested in your opinion." Nahum, a handsome man with still a full head of hair, spoke calmly.

"Jesus smiled. "What were you discussing?" he asked.

Since Nahum was not sitting near Jesus, he had talked louder than normal, causing others to take involuntary note of the conversation. It was the first serious question directed to Jesus that evening, and the guests stopped to hear what he had to say.

"Some of us have seen and heard you around town," Nahum said. "It just seems that you're expecting too much of people. You expect them to change. I don't think people change—much. They are what they are after a while, and that's the way they live and die. I don't think people want to change—they're tired, they want to relax at the end of the day, they've got enough problems trying to earn a living or manage the house. They don't want to change any-thing—either themselves or the world. They just want to be left in peace. You're looking for…miracles!"

"Yes," nodded Jesus. "I'm looking for miracles."

Some of the guests chuckled. Others smiled. The man knew how to arouse their curiosity. He certainly didn't mince words.

"We change all the time," said Jesus. "We get a day older every day, our feel-ings change about what's important and what's unimportant, our lives change. We are changing all the time. Who says we can't change?"

"I'm talking about the insides of a man," said Nahum.

Jesus smiled. "All right," he said. "Let's talk about the inside."

"It's not that men can't change," said Nahum. "Sure they can change—but they don't."

"Why not?" asked Jesus.

"Because they don't want to," said Nahum.

A few of the guests nodded their agreement.

"That's partly right," said Jesus.

"It's more than partly right," insisted Nahum. "Look, a drunkard knows drinking is bad for him. So does he stop? No. He goes on drinking. He just doesn't want to change."

"A drunkard drinks, a glutton eats, a lecher lusts—and the pious man prays," said Jesus.

The guests wondered what he meant. Some of them knew.

"Each has found a way of dealing with life," Jesus continued. "Don't you see what it's all about? Life! Living! It's not easy, is it, living? So we all find a way. We all find a way of getting from birth to death. We all find a way of handling our joys and our sorrows, our pleasures and our pains. We all find a way of embracing the world."

"I've always maintained there's nothing wrong with having a few drinks, as long as a person can handle it," Noah slobbered, blurry-eyed. He was too drunk to say more or notice his wife's angry looks.

Leah fidgeted nervously with her fingers as she felt compelled to speak. "Yes," said Leah, thinking out loud. "I always eat. I eat when I'm happy, I eat when I'm unhappy. I'm always eating."

"She sure does," Nahum said, wrily.

"There's only one trouble, isn't there?" said Jesus. "All the food in the world can't satisfy your hunger and all the wine in the world can't satisfy your thirst and all the lusting of the flesh can't give you love."

"We know that," said Leah sadly, "but we still keep doing what we do."

"You will keep doing what you do until you find a better way," said Jesus. "You cannot give up one way of life unless you have discovered a better way of life. You can find the Kingdom of Heaven if you look for it. You're like the merchant who was searching for fine pearls and who found one of very special value. So he went and sold everything he had and bought it. The Kingdom of Heaven is worth its price."

"I'll go along with you," said Asher, the fisherman. "You talk sense. Our scribes could learn a lesson from you. If they talked to us like you do, I'm sure more of us would listen."

"Oh?" Jesus said.

Asher smiled expansively. He felt strongly on the subject and was always ready to give his opinion whenever the matter came up.

"I've heard you speak a couple of times," he said. "You're saying exactly what I've been saying all these years, only you say it better, of course. Just ask Naomi."

Asher's wife nodded her agreement.

"The important thing about religion is to believe in God and act right," Asher continued. "You said it yourself—the two most important commandments are, 'Hear, O Israel, the Lord is our God, the Lord is One. And you shall love the Lord your God with all your heart, with all your soul and with all your might.' And the second one, 'Love your neighbor as yourself.' That's all you really need. I just can't go for all these long prayers and involved rituals that the Pharisees insist on. It's clutter!"

Jesus smiled patiently. "I'm glad you came to hear me," he said, "but you only got half the story…"

"No," insisted Asher, "that's exactly what you said that day!"

"Oh, yes," Jesus assured him quickly. "Yes, I did say that a few days ago, but I finished the story yesterday."

The guests laughed. Asher shrugged his shoulders in resignation.

"How was I to know that?" he said in mock despair. "I was working. If I had known, I would have come."

Jesus smiled. "I'll be glad to tell you what I said."

"Thank you," Asher said noncommittally.

"I said that you must not suppose that I have come to abolish the Law and the prophets," Jesus reminded his hearers. "I did not come to abolish, but to complete. So long as heaven and earth endure, not a letter, not a stroke will disappear from the Law until all that must happen has happened. if any man therefore sets aside even the least of the Torah's demands, and teaches others to do the same, he will have the lowest place in the Kingdom of Heaven, whereas anyone who keeps the Torah and teaches others so will stand high in the Kingdom of Heaven."

Asher looked disappointed.

"Well, I don't see why the prayers and rituals are necessary," Asher said. "They're meaningless, in fact, so far as I'm concerned."

No," said Jesus evenly. "They are not meaningless. Tell me, what does it mean to love the Lord your God with all your heart, with all your soul, with all your might, and your neighbor as yourself?"

Asher was at a loss for a succinct answer.

"You see, that's what our whole Torah is devoted to—to teach us the meaning," said Jesus. "As for prayers and rituals—prayers are paths, rituals are roads directing the heart toward the Kingdom of Heaven. Why go through the desert when you can travel over a good highway?"

Something stirred in Noah, something that reminded him of long ago. He tried to focus on Jesus and, for a moment, managed to put a sober thought into words.

"Some of us got off the highway long ago, if we were ever on it," he said, his eyes heavy in their sockets. "It's too late now to go back."

"No, it isn't," said Jesus. "Look at Matthew—see what he has done with his life. You know that God does not want the death of the sinner, only that he turns from his ways and lives. Our Father in heaven waits for us—until our dying day. He is like the man who had two sons. The younger said to his father, 'Father, give me my share of the property.' So he divided his estate between them. A few days later the younger son turned the whole of his share into cash and left home for a distant country, where he squandered it in reckless living. He had spent it all when a severe famine fell upon the country and he began to feel the pinch. So he went and attached himself to one of the local landowners, who sent him on to his farm to mind the pigs. He would have been glad to fill his belly with the pods that the pigs were eating; and no one gave him anything.

"Then he came to his senses and said, 'They can eat, and here am I, starving to death! I will set off and go to my father and say to him, 'Father, I have sinned, against God and against you; I am no longer fit to be called your son; treat me as one of your paid servants.'"

"So he set out for his father's house. But while he was still a long way off, his father saw him and his heart went out to him. He ran to meet him, flung his arms around him and kissed him. The son said, 'Father, I have sinned, against God and against you; I am no longer fit to be called your son.'

"But the father said to his servants, 'Quick! Fetch a robe, my best one, and put it on him; put a ring on his finger and shoes on his feet. Bring the fatted calf and kill it, and let us have a feast to celebrate the day. For this son of mine was dead and has come back to life; he was lost and is found.'

"And the festivities began. Now the elder son was out on the farm; and on his way back, as he approached the house, he heard music and dancing. He called one of the servants and asked what it meant. The servant told him, 'Your brother has come home, and your father has killed the fatted calf because he has him back safe and sound.' But he was angry and refused to go in.

"His father came out and pleaded with him; but he retorted, 'You know how I have slaved for you all these years; I never once disobeyed your orders; and you never gave me so much as a kid for a feast with my friends. But now that this son of yours turns up after running through your money with his women, you kill the fatted calf for him.'

"'My boy,' said the father, 'you are always with me, and everything I have is yours. How could we help celebrating this happy day? Your brother here was dead and has come back to life, was lost and is found.'"

The guests were strangely stirred. A distant hope flickered in their hearts. They looked at Jesus through tired, hungry eyes. If only for a moment, they felt a spark of life and they wondered whether there was still time to dream dreams and see visions.

❦   ❦   ❦

The following day, as Judas accompanied Jesus on their way to meet the others, they found them engaged in heated conversation with Samuel ben Yitzhak, and a handful of Pharisaic followers.

"Why is it that your master eats with tax collectors and sinners?" Samuel ben Yitzhak asked Simon. The Pharisee had not seen Jesus approach and was startled when he heard himself addressed from behind.

"It's not the healthy that need the doctor, but the sick," Jesus said. "Go and learn what that text means, 'I require mercy and not sacrifice.' I did not come to invite virtuous people, but sinners."

Before Judas could grasp what had happened, the sharp exchange was over. For a moment both parties stood facing each other. Then Samuel ben Yitzhak glowered, turned and walked off. Some others did likewise.

Judas regarded the other disciples and thought he detected his own mixed feelings in their faces. Obviously they had been challenged regarding Jesus. They seemed relieved when Jesus arrived and so effectively stopped all further debate.

Judas looked to Jesus for a reaction, but it was too late. The people were crowding around him, asking questions, waiting to hear what he had to say today. Judas took refuge in the crowd to think about what had happened. The words of Jesus had hit the mark and Judas was pleased with their effectiveness and truth. But he wondered now how they would be regarded. Had Samuel ben Yitzhak been curious only and puzzled by the actions of Jesus, and had he seen the truth and beauty of the answer and accepted it? Or had the hard tone of the answer detracted from its truth and caused a resentment towards Jesus which might have disturbing aftereffects?

Judas wondered. He looked around at Simon, Andrew, Matthew, James and John. If they had ever felt disturbed by what happened, they certainly did not look so now. They were listening to Jesus as he spoke to the people, and they looked pleased. Judas sighed with relief. Maybe he worried too much. Judas, too, listened and smiled.

"Shalom, Judas!" A familiar voice intruded on his thoughts. He looked around to see who had addressed him.

"Mary!" he exclaimed. "What are you doing here in Capernaum?"

"Same thing I did in Magdala," Mary said, laughing, enjoying his embarrassment.

"Did you come to stay?"

"Yes," she said. "I don't live far from here. Why don't you come over?"

"Now?"

"Why not? Or are you ashamed to be seen with me?"

She had not changed. She enjoyed baiting and trapping him.

"Of course not!" said Judas.

She smiled triumphantly as they walked off together.

🍁   🍁   🍁

Judas looked around as they entered Mary's place. She lived in style, no question about that. Mary watched him like a huntress stalking her prey. Then she approached him, stepped up to him seductively and put her arms around him.

"Well, Judas," she said alluringly, "do you still have that special feeling about me?"

Judas struggled with his feelings. It was impossible not to get aroused. He reached for her hands and released himself from her as gently as possible.

"Obviously Jesus arouses you more!" she declared, angry, irritated, flaunting herself in front of him.

Judas did not answer the loaded statement. "I would like you to meet him," he said evenly.

"Sure," she said wryly.

"I think if you got to know him…"

"I'd love to get to know him—right over there, on the couch!" she declared. Mary had won again. She relished the sensation. She had caught Judas off balance and made a fool of him.

"What do you two find to talk about?" she asked, needling him, pressing her advantage.

"Love," said Judas simply.

Mary smiled, coming in for the kill. "You should take a lesson from me one of these days and then compare the two."

Judas suffered the remark in silence.

"You know what's wrong with you and Jesus?" Mary asked rhetorically.

"What?"

"You're hiding!"

"From what?"

"From life as it really is!" she declared. "You're hiding behind God!"

"No, Mary," Judas said trying to explain.

Her eyes flashed with anger and she seized hold of her breasts. "This is life!" Mary shouted. "You want to change life into something that it isn't—something that's soft and warm and full of mother's milk! Well, Judas, the breasts of the world are dry! You'll get no milk other than what little comfort you can suck from my breasts!"

Judas considered her words quietly. "I don't believe that, Mary."

"Well you'd better believe it!" she declared. "You've looked at the world with your clothes on, Judas. I know what it looks like naked!" She advanced on him once more, seductively.

"You really think all men are alike, don't you, Mary?"

"Aren't they?" she asked mockingly.

"No."

"You mean some are different, like you?" she asked, stinging.

"Maybe."

Mary uttered a short, angry laugh. "Maybe you're not a man!" she spat out.

"And maybe you're not a woman!" Judas replied impulsively.

Mary's hand flew up and slapped his face. "Pig!" she screamed.

Judas was sorry for what he had said, but he was too upset to apologize.

"I'd…better go now," he said with controlled emotion.

"Don't just stand there!" Mary screamed. "Why don't you hit me back!"

But Judas had nothing further to say. he turned quietly and left. Mary followed him to the door, her eyes welling up with tears.

CHAPTER 5

Trouble

Rabbi Emmanuel approached the reading desk of the synagogue. He looked over his congregation, smiled and said, "*Shabbat shalom*—may Sabbath peace be with you."

"*Shabbat shalom*," answered the worshipers.

Rabbi Emanuel relished this moment and this feeling.

Shabbat shalom!

Today was a special day. Today was the Sabbath. It was a day of rest. it was a day of worship. It was a day of communion with God. It was a day of peace.

Not that every day was not a day of worship and communion, a day of talking and walking with God. But this was a special day—a day of rest for all men and all of Creation, a day of thought and worship and commemoration of the Creation.

It was a day of rest from the cares of the world. Emanuel had changed garments. He had put away his carpenter's tools from sundown to sundown.

Sabbath!

It was a day of peace, a day when everyone came to the synagogue and worshiped, a day when God's spirit crept even into the coarsest sensitivities, a day when all assembled under one roof and prayed with one voice.

Rabbi Emanuel thought of his friend and adversary, Samuel, the blacksmith, who sat there near the ark, rigid, hard, but a devoted scholar. Samuel's eyes scanned the congregation and he saw Jesus.

"A maverick," thought Rabbi Emanuel, and then he smiled to himself.

Here they were, all under one roof, held together by a common bond—*Torah*, Teaching! Then Rabbi Emanuel began, saying, "'And God spoke all these words, saying, 'I am the Lord your God, who brought you out of the land of Egypt, out of the house of bondage. You shall have no other gods before Me. You shall not make unto yourselves a graven image, nor any manner of likeness, of any thing that is in heaven above, or that is in the earth beneath, or that is in the water under the earth; you shall not bow down unto them, nor serve them; for I the Lord your God am a jealous God, visiting the iniquity of the fathers upon the children unto the third and fourth generation of them that hate Me; and showing mercy unto the thousandth generation of them that love Me and keep My commandments...

"'You shall not take the name of the Lord your God in vain; for the Lord will not hold him guiltless that takes His name in vain.

"'Remember the Sabbath day, to keep it holy. Six days shall you labor, and do all your work; but the seventh day is a Sabbath unto the Lord your God, in it you shall not do any manner of work...'"

Judas listened to the familiar words which became a background for his thoughts. He was sitting next to Jesus. Here he was, Judas Iscariot, sitting in the synagogue of Capernaum, praying in the presence of the promised Messiah!

Judas was staggered by the thought. How utterly incredible it all seemed. And yet how absolutely true it was.

But even more incredible, thought Judas, was the fact that no one had recognized Jesus for what he really was.

Judas looked around. He recognized Caleb, the man Jesus had cured, when he had called Simon and the others to follow him. The man's withered arm had been restored perfectly. Judas wondered how Caleb regarded Jesus. Judas noticed another man with a paralyzed arm next to Caleb. He thought of the many people Jesus had helped with their afflictions and he wondered how they thought of him. Judas wondered how others regarded Jesus.

Yes, thought Judas, that's how the people think of him—a wandering preacher, a rabbi and, at most, a prophet.

Judas smiled to himself. If they only knew!

He wondered how they would know and when they would know. In a way, he was annoyed that it wasn't obvious to them. At least the rabbi or some of the leaders might have been perceptive enough to know.

Judas smiled to himself as he savored the delicious secret. God truly was Father and King of all Creation, for nothing happened but that he willed it or permitted it. That is why the Messiah could walk on earth and the sons of men saw him without seeing and heard him without understanding—until such time that God was ready to give them understanding and open their eyes.

Judas wondered how it would happen. Maybe some day Jesus would address a crowd and someone suddenly would see the light and cry out, "Messiah! He is the Messiah, praised be the Lord!" And the people would take up the cry and the wonders would begin to happen.

Maybe it would be at a time like this and God would open the eyes of the rabbi and give speech to his tongue and he would turn to Jesus and declare, "Praised be he who comes in the name of the Lord, praised be the son of David, praised be the Promised One—praised be the Lord's anointed." And Jesus would rise and step forward and usher in the new heaven and the new earth.

Or Jesus would appear somewhere, sometime, and the heavens would open and the glory of God would descend upon him so that its radiance would illumine the world and a heavenly voice would declare, "Behold, the Anointed One," and some would ask, "Are you the Messiah?" And he would say, "Yes," but others would not ask, they would know, far and near, for the earth would be filled with the glory of the Lord.

Maybe it would not happen in any of these ways. Maybe it would happen some other way. But that it would happen, of this Judas was certain with each new event. He thought of the latest of these—the choosing of the disciples so that now there were twelve! Twelve disciples, one for each of the Twelve Tribes of Israel! He marveled that the people had not yet seen the significance. But then he smiled again inwardly, knowingly, as he glanced at the others, sitting there in the presence of Jesus, waiting.

Rabbi Emanuel made it a point to stay after the service and visit with the members of his congregation who assembled outside the synagogue, where they discussed the week's happenings and exchanged thoughts on all major and minor matters of their lives.

The rabbi walked over to where Jesus stood talking to some people.

"*Shabbat shalom*," Rabbi Emanuel greeted him.

"*Shabbat shalom*," replied Jesus. They smiled politely, curiously, each taking the other man's measure.

"It's nice to have you worship with us," Rabbi Emanuel said pleasantly.

"Thank you," said Jesus. "It is pleasant to be here."

"Rabbi!"

Both Jesus and Rabbi Emanuel looked around at the speaker. It was the man with the paralyzed arm whom Judas had noticed next to Caleb, in the synagogue.

'Yes, Ithiel," said Rabbi Emanuel, turning to him in a kindly fashion. "*Shabbat shalom.*"

"*Shabbat shalom,*" Ithiel said politely, as it was soon obvious that he wanted to speak with Jesus, whom he now addressed once more.

"Rabbi," he said fervently, "I know that you can perform wonders. Help me!"

Some of the people heard and stopped to see what Jesus would do. Jesus looked around. He studied the challenging eyes of Samuel the blacksmith, whom he had encountered publicly once before. He noticed, also, the concerned face of Rabbi Emanuel, whose eyes seemed to plead with Jesus to exercise tact and caution.

"Please, Rabbi!" Ithiel pleaded. "Please!"

Jesus looked at Ithiel and his eyes filled with compassion. "Come and stand out here," he said finally.

Ithiel obeyed.

"I put a question to you," Jesus said resolutely, addressing his listeners. "Is it permitted to do good or to do evil on the Sabbath, to save life or to destroy it?"

"Please!" pleaded Rabbi Emanuel. "Don't violate the Sabbath!"

"This is not a matter of life and death!" thundered Samuel, reddening with anger.

Jesus looked around at them all and then said to Ithiel, "Stretch out your arm!"

Ithiel did as he was told and his arm was restored.

Rabbi Emanuel was visibly upset and Samuel was beside himself with anger. So were others. They drew away from Jesus and became involved in a heated discussion of his sacrilegious deed.

Jesus did not stay to hear more. He left with his disciples. The Sabbath peace was shattered. As Judas followed Jesus, he wondered what would happen now.

❧   ❧   ❧

Emanuel ben Simon and Samuel ben Yitzhak were both Pharisees. Though the first earned his living as a carpenter and the second as a blacksmith, they were more than that. They were the leading scholars of Capernaum. Though they were both Pharisees, they belonged to the two different, major schools of

Pharisaic thought. Emanuel belonged to the School of Hillel and Samuel to the School of Shammai. The one was more lenient, the other was stricter, in the interpretation of the Torah. When in doubt, and as a rule, the Pharisees followed the more lenient School of Hillel.

That, too, was the reason why Emanuel and not Samuel served as rabbi of the local community. As was customary, every rabbi earned his living at some occupation or profession which he pursued full time, for it was said that "the Torah must not be used as a spade to dig with," meaning, it was not to be used for material gain.

The Pharisees had become a major force in Jewish life, which they had given a new dimension for the sake of survival in a changing world. They had developed synagogues everywhere, although the Temple in Jerusalem was still central for them as it was for all Jews, except the Samaritans. The Pharisees had developed an Oral Tradition, alongside the Torah, which was the Written Tradition. The Oral Tradition consisted of the interpretations of the Torah that had developed over the years, interpretations that the Sadducees refused to accept, choosing to stay strictly with what was written in the Torah. The Pharisees, who were more strictly observant than the people generally, hoped to guide others toward holy living through example rather than force. Their self-discipline in religious observance was meant to be a constant conditioning leading toward right attitude and action.

Samuel the blacksmith was still angry as he paced up and down in the home of Rabbi Emanuel, the carpenter.

"It was not a matter of life and death!" he fumed.

They had just come from the synagogue and their encounter with Jesus.

"Samuel," said Rabbi Emanuel, who, by nature, was the calmer of the two, "come and sit down. Let's eat first."

Samuel sat down reluctantly and began picking perfunctorily at some fruit, seething with feeling.

"It's a legitimate question—what one may or may not do on the Sabbath," Rabbi Emanuel reminded his friend.

"Of course it is!" snapped Samuel. "Of course one may even violate the Sabbath, if necessary. It was intended that a man should live by the Law, not die through it. But such violation may only involve a matter of life or death!"

'Of course," nodded Rabbi Emanuel.

"How long has our friend suffered from this arm?" Samuel asked sarcastically. "Five years, ten years…?"

"A long time, almost as long as I can remember."

"Is it unreasonable to assume, then, that he might have lived through another day?"

"No," smiled Rabbi Emanuel.

"Is it unreasonable to assume that our friend, 'the great healer' from Nazareth, could have waited one day?"

"He could have waited," the rabbi agreed.

"Why didn't he?" Samuel asked indignantly.

"Perhaps he acted in…fervor," Rabbi Emanuel suggested.

Inwardly he was surprised to be taking on the defense of Jesus. He agreed wholeheartedly with Samuel. There was no question but that he was right. But somehow Samuel, even when the two agreed essentially, caused Emanuel to sometimes defend the opposing point of view or suggest the extenuating circumstances. He realized that he did so for no other reason often than that Samuel was so absolute in his opinions.

"Oh," Samuel said sarcastically, raising his bushy eyebrow. "We're about to excuse him because he acted in fervor. What would happen if I murdered you out of a fervent belief that you were a bad influence around here and that my interpretations of the Torah were truer than yours? My defense—religious *fervor*, doing the will of God! What would happen?"

Rabbi Emanuel laughed. "I didn't realize how strongly you felt about me," he said, still trying to calm the atmosphere.

But Samuel was deadly serious. 'Fervor is no defense!" he said sternly.

"What about mercy?" Rabbi Emanuel suggested.

"Oh?" Samuel asked, arching his eyebrow. "You mean, his was an act of mercy?"

"Maybe that's how he saw it."

"Very nice," Samuel said. "Very nice. That makes me out to be merciless!"

"No, that isn't what I meant," Rabbi Emanuel said reassuringly.

"Then there is only one other conclusion to be drawn from this," Samuel suggested. "Namely, that the laws of Moses are harsh and that our Torah is merciless!"

"Our Torah is anything but harsh and merciless," Rabbi Emanuel said.

Samuel looked at him in mock surprise. "I'm glad to be reassured of that," he said wryly. "For a moment there I thought you suggested that our Sabbath laws were lacking in mercy. I must have misunderstood."

Rabbi Emanuel was amused rather than annoyed at Samuel's sarcasm. It was an ingrained part of the man and he used it effectively against friend and foe alike.

"A little more wine?" Emanuel asked kindly.

Samuel checked his cup. "Please, a little."

Emanuel filled their cups. "One other thing I don't want you to misunderstand," Rabbi Emanuel said.

'What is that?"

'His action was wrong and unjustified—he did violate the Sabbath!"

"I'm glad to know that," said Samuel. "I was beginning to wonder. You know I've been very patient regarding the Nazarene. You asked me to be tolerant and I've gone along with you until now. But this does it! I've had my fill of him!"

"What he did today was unnecessary," said Rabbi Emanuel soberly. "It may even have been defiant!"

"Who does he think he is?" demanded Samuel. "He goes around all over the place making big pronouncements: 'Do not suppose that I have come to abolish the Law and the prophets; I did not come to abolish, but to complete. I tell you this: so long as heaven and earth endure, not a letter, not a stroke will disappear from the Law until all that must happen has happened.'"

Rabbi Emanuel smiled at Samuel's imitation of Jesus.

"So what does he do?" asked Samuel rhetorically. "He goes and violates the Law himself. And then he has the nerve to call us hypocrites!"

Rabbi Emanuel laughed.

"It's not funny!" Samuel insisted.

'I know," said Rabbi Emanuel. "But you must admit that he's right sometimes. You and I have often talked about the habits of some of our 'respectable' friends. Some are pretty smug and self-righteous and they have a high opinion of themselves. They think God can't wait to see them, they're so sure of their reward in Heaven. If they only knew how God can wait!"

"Some will be in for a big surprise!" smiled Samuel. "Maybe that includes us?"

"It's a possibility," admitted the rabbi, smiling. "I guess we all think we're doing the right things, otherwise we wouldn't be doing them."

"Yes," said Samuel. "As for the fools and hypocrites among us, there are bad eggs in every nest. I'll be the first to admit that. It's too bad. But I don't recall God ever giving anything to fools and hypocrites, much less the *Torah*! He gave that to the children of Israel who have preserved the *Torah*, despite fools and hypocrites! Now, our friend Jesus, who is so ready to accuse others of hypocrisy, is not himself free from hypocrisy!"

"Well…"

"Look!" said Samuel. "You've seen it happen! We get involved in a discussion with him and if we don't see things his way, he starts calling us names! Oh, he says things like, 'Judge not, lest you be judged.' But what do you think he's doing? He says, 'Love your enemies.' We're not even enemies, and he doesn't even show us respect, much less love! I don't see him turning the other cheek. He's all for peacemakers and gentleness and mercy. Well, he comes on pretty hostile and belligerent at times. Oh, yes, what is it he likes to tell everyone: 'Do unto others as you would have them do unto you'? I think that's...lovely!"

Rabbi Emanuel smiled. Samuel had a way of capturing the irony of life.

"Heavenly fervor is often blind to its own contradictions," Rabbi Emanuel suggested.

"Oh," said Samuel slyly. "We're back to *fervor* again."

Rabbi Emanuel laughed. "No," he said, "I was just..."

Samuel got up and started pacing. "Stop trying to stretch the truth," he said. "We may pity him, but we cannot show this kind of tolerance any longer. If he were just a harmless, misguided individual, all right, I'd see what we could do. But he is preaching his ideas deliberately and trying to influence others. These are troubled times. I don't want well-meaning, innocent people to get hurt! Do you know what I mean?"

"Yes," said Rabbi Emanuel as he got up and stretched. "I know what you mean."

"Some of our 'leading citizens' are already talking," Samuel said. "'The friends of Herod' are buzzing. They don't want 'trouble.' Remember? And they're beginning to think that he's stirring up the people. One of these days they'll decide to take measures—quickly. And then a lot of people might get hurt!"

Rabbi Emanuel stared into the flame of a nearby oil lamp. "'Do you think he may be that kind of trouble?" he asked.

"Yes," said Samuel, coming close. "If he's *this* kind of trouble today, he'll be *that* kind of trouble tomorrow. Don't you see why? He's a law unto himself! He's unpredictable! He might do anything! Have you heard the way he talks?"

"Yes."

Again Samuel imitated Jesus, but this time Rabbi Emanuel didn't smile. "'I say to you this, and I say to you that,' it's always, 'I say to you,' and it's always directly from *avinu malkenu*, our Father, our King!" said Samuel.

Rabbi Emanuel faced Samuel. "Some regard him as a prophet," said the rabbi, "because he speaks after their fashion, rather than the way we speak today."

Samuel smiled cynically as he implored heaven with his eyes. "Exactly!" he said, as he stalked around dramatically. "I ask you, couldn't you talk like that? Or I? 'Thus says the Lord!' Of course we could! But that kind of talk went out with the prophet Malachi, some 450 years ago! Didn't it? Today we speak the language of scholars, not prophets!"

Rabbi Emanuel nodded his agreement.

Samuel stopped halfway across the room and regarded the rabbi thoughtfully. "There is only one other possibility," Samuel said. His tone was steady and unusually quiet.

"What?" asked the rabbi.

Samuel looked at him without flinching. "Perhaps he is the Messiah!"

Rabbi Emanuel felt the blood rushing to his temples. He was startled at the sound of the escaping thought.

"What's the matter?" asked Samuel.

"I'm just surprised," said Rabbi Emanuel, recovering his composure. "I mean, knowing your feelings about the Nazarene, that you would go so far."

Samuel regarded the rabbi steadily. "I will go wherever truth leads me," he said quietly. "One must consider everything!"

Rabbi Emanuel did not want to go on, almost afraid of the possibility of what Samuel had brought up. But now that the matter had been voiced, it had to be considered between them.

"Yes," said the rabbi, "one must consider everything. Well, do you think he is the Messiah?"

"No!" said Samuel emphatically.

"Why not?"

"The Messiah would not violate the Sabbath!"

'That's right," said the rabbi thoughtfully. "That's right."

"What about you?"

"H'm."

"Do you think he's the Messiah?" Samuel asked.

Rabbi Emanuel looked thoughtfully at Samuel before answering. "No," he said slowly. "No."

"Why not?"

Rabbi Emanuel smiled. "When the Messiah comes," he said, "he will appear in Jerusalem—not in Galilee!"

Both men sighed with relief.

"I'm glad we agree for a change," said Samuel. "But we must do something now about him. We must file charges."

"Yes, he violated the Law and I'd go along with you, ordinarily," said the rabbi.

"So that's it!" fumed Samuel. "You meant to be lenient all along and I was just taken in by you again! Well, I tell you..."

"Hear me out!" demanded Rabbi Emanuel. "Look at the larger issue in this case. He's got a few followers and sympathizers. A few people are always carried away by a man like this. If we pay too much attention to him, they'll make a hero out of him, especially if they feel that he is being punished unjustly by the authorities! Then we'll really have trouble!"

"What do you propose?" asked Samuel.

"Let's forget this matter," said the rabbi. "But let's not forget him! Let's confront him, challenge him and expose him, so that the people will not be taken in by him! You know they're with us! They're looking to us for direction. Let's give them a chance to make up their own minds. They'll make the right decision. Let's keep him on the run. He'll run out of followers soon!"

CHAPTER 6

Whore

Judas could not get Mary out of his mind. He had to see her again.

As he approached her house, a burly fisherman was leaving. One of her customers, Judas thought. He knocked on the door.

"Come in," Mary called phlegmatically.

"Shalom," Judas said, entering.

Mary was lying where the fisherman had left her. She looked and felt used. "Shalom," she said, indifferently.

"Do you have time?" Judas asked.

"For what?"

"Me."

Mary studied him. "What do you want?"

"I want to talk."

"That's not what I get paid for as a rule," she said, more a reflex action than with conviction. But there was no sting to the remark. It seemed almost as if Mary was relieved that the visitor was Judas rather than a customer. Judas sat down near her.

"Look at me, Mary," he said. "What do you see?"

"What should I see?" she asked.

"The same thing I see when I look at you."

"A whore?"

"No," said Judas, "a child."

The remark took Mary by surprise. Normally she might have laughed, but somehow the remark, spoken so compassionately, touched something deep inside her and she listened, as to a distant melody.

Judas continued. "A long time ago there was a child named Mary. She wanted what all children want—love. But the world—her world—somehow let her down. It hurt her. It showed her its hate, not its love. That child became a woman, and the woman decided to get even with the world for what was done to the child!" Judas reached for Mary's hand and took it. "I see the child in you, "Mary," he said. "Do you remember the child?"

Mary smiled sadly at Judas. "What's the point of remembering?" she sighed.

"It's never too late, Mary."

"Too late for what?" she asked cynically.

"Happiness."

Mary laughed a weary, hollow laugh. "Happiness!" she repeated mockingly. 'Is anybody really happy?"

"Yes," said Judas.

"Are you happy?"

"Yes," said Judas quietly. "When was the last time you were happy, Mary? Yesterday? Last week? Last month? Mary, happiness is possible every moment of your life, from this moment on!"

Mary regarded Judas skeptically. "What's it cost?" she asked.

"What's it worth to you?" he answered.

Mary did not reply.

"*Moshe rabenu*, Moses our teacher, gave us the answer long ago, Mary," Judas said. "'I have set before you life and death, the blessing and the curse: therefore, choose life, that you may live!'"

"I'm not exactly the pious type, Judas," Mary said mockingly. "You've come to the wrong address."

"We live at the same address, Mary!" Judas exclaimed.

"Come now," Mary laughed.

"Well, if not, we don't live very far apart," said Judas urgently. "Look, Mary, some people go through life believing or not believing, and nothing much troubles them. But you and I go through life the hard way—hurt, troubled, betrayed, filled with anger at the world, seeing what is, yearning for what it should be!"

Judas rose and paced thoughtfully back and forth as Mary watched him, strangely fascinated.

"Pious?" said Judas, laughing at the thought, as he confronted Mary. "I'm not the pious type, either—not in the ordinary sense. Truth, Mary, that's what I've been after. Truth!"

Judas knew that he had made himself vulnerable before Mary by baring his soul, but he was not afraid of her ridicule any longer. He spoke with humble yet firm conviction. Mary did not laugh.

"Jesus?" Mary asked.

"Yes, Jesus," said Judas, looking earnestly at Mary. "I may sound foolish, Mary, and you may laugh, but for the first time in my life, life makes sense to me. Life has taken on meaning, real meaning. He has handed me the key, Mary, and shown me how to unlock all the mysteries of life and of the human heart. Love, Mary, that's the key and the answer! I wish you would give love a try, Mary, real love. It's not easy, but it's…it's…happiness! I wish you would give yourself a new chance, a chance to be born again. I wish you would hear him because…because he's more than what he appears to be, Mary. He's someone very…special!"

Mary did not laugh at Judas. She had listened to the music from another world and, for a moment, had been moved by it. But now she felt the bonds of her own world pulling her back and she smiled a sad, distant smile as she rose to end this meeting.

"Is that what you came to tell me?" she asked, facing Judas.

"Yes," he said.

Mary started to reply when Judas interrupted her.

"There's one other thing I came to say," he said solemnly.

"What?" she asked.

"I love you, Mary," he said.

Mary, who long ago had stopped being shocked by anything in life, seemed astonished now. She searched his face and eyes in silence for a long time and, when she finally spoke, an unusual softness registered in her face and voice.

"You really mean that, don't you," she said.

"Yes," said Judas.

Mary smiled sadly. "Thanks," she said. "Funny, that means more to me than all your talk about God!"

"Don't let it," Judas said kindly, quietly. ""The world's love, at best, is imperfect, temporary, unreliable. But God's love is there for the asking beyond measure to all of us at all times. It's a matter of learning, Mary—learning to pray to Him, learning to obey His commandments, learning to believe in Him…"

"I think I could believe in you," Mary said, and once more she was surprised to hear herself say such a thing.

"You mustn't!" Judas said.

"Oh!" Mary said softly.

The instant he said it, Judas was sorry the remark had slipped form his lips.

Mary smiled sadly, gratefully. "Thanks," she said, slowly. "Thanks for trying. For once in my life, Judas, for a little moment, you made me feel decent and clean."

Judas wanted to say more but he could sense by Mary's look that she did not want to hear any more and that she wanted him to go.

For a moment Judas hesitated. He looked in her eyes. The next moment they were in each other's arms and Judas kissed Mary.

As Judas left the house, he saw Eliezer ben Jochanan approaching. The two passed each other in silence.

Eliezer ben Jochanan entered without knocking. He found Mary slouched in a chair. 'Got anything to eat?" Eliezer demanded without the formality of a greeting.

Normally Mary would have gone and fixed something for him. "There's food in the kitchen," she said indifferently.

Eliezer didn't like the tone of her voice or her moody, thoughtful preoccupation. He came over to her, placed his hand under her chin and forced her to look at him. "What's up?" he demanded.

Mary locked eyes with Eliezer, as if in mortal combat, before she finally spoke. "I'm quitting!" she said simply.

Eliezer regarded her incredulously for a moment and then laughed, as if he had just heard a side-splitting joke.

"Quitting?" he asked, when he had recovered sufficiently. "What's the matter—a bad day or something?"

Mary's resolve did not waiver under his ridicule. "Every day's a bad day," she said, with a quiet, leveling look and voice.

"What kind of talk is that?" Eliezer asked, flashing a rare smile that Mary had found irresistible on other crucial occasions.

"There's nothing to talk about any more, Eliezer. Good-bye!"

Eliezer's false smile hardened into a vicious grimace as he grabbed Mary's arm and yanked her to her feet.

Mary emitted a painful cry. ""Let go, you're hurting me!" she exclaimed, slapping Eliezer's face with her free hand.

Eliezer, wincing with pain, slapped her hard in the face and slammed her back down into the chair. "Whore!" he muttered.

This time Mary did not even cry out in pain. She just regarded Eliezer defiantly but said nothing. Their eyes met in a clash of wills but then, once more, Eliezer smiled disarmingly.

"What's the matter, Mary? You're not going sour, are you?"

'What if I am?" she asked cynically. "What's it to you?"

"What's it to me?" he asked, feigning innocent concern. "I love you, you know that!"

Mary's laughter had a sad, hollow ring to it. "You don't know what love is, Eliezer. We both don't know."

Eliezer bent over her to kiss her but she pushed him away.

"You got it bad, haven't you?" he said. "What's the trouble?"

"Being born," she said, with a touch of self-pity.

Eliezer slapped her again, evoking a sharp cry from Mary. "Snap out of it!" he demanded.

"I plan to," she said evenly. "This was my last day!"

Eliezer laughed, finding the situation utterly ridiculous. "What's gotten into you?" he asked. "Judas again?"

Mary was surprised at the unexpected strength she felt within her. "Yes!" she said fearlessly.

"Why did he come back?"

Mary smiled softly. "He came back to offer me life!" she said.

"Life?" asked Eliezer, sneering out of the left corner of his mouth.

'Yes," said Mary. "Life." She was surprised at her own confidence and calm. "He talked to me about love…"

"I'm sure he did," laughed Eliezer.

"No, Eliezer, not your kind of love—God's kind of love. He made me feel, for the first time in my life, that I really mattered in this world. He made me feel decent, clean. He treated me with dignity and respect. He said that it was not too late to change. He made me want a better life. He offered me happiness, Eliezer—real happiness!"

"And you believed him?"

'Yes, I believed him."

"That's nice," Eliezer laughed.

"What's wrong with that?" Mary asked, frowning.

"Nothing," said Eliezer, pacing up and down in front of her. "Nothing, except…"

"What?"

"What will you do?"

"Work!"

Eliezer laughed. "What kind of work can you do besides…"

"I can clean house!" Mary said.

"You? A servant? You can't even cook well!"

"I'll learn."

"Sure," Eliezer said wryly. "Sure, and how long will you keep it up? One week, two weeks, three weeks, maybe a month, until the boredom will get to you and you'll remember the comforts and the luxuries of this life and you'll come clambering back to it like a drowning man to the land!"

"I'll make out!"

"Who will hire you?"

"I'll go to another city." Mary got up as if to finish their conversation. Eliezer seized her arm.

"Once a whore, Mary, always a whore!" Eliezer hissed.

"Shut up!" Mary exclaimed, seething quietly. "And get out!"

Eliezer slapped her viciously. "Don't say that again—ever!" he snarled. Then he hit her again.

Mary stifled a cry and backed away.

"You know what'll happen?" Eliezer said, trying to sound reasonable. "Your past will catch up with you wherever you go. I don't want you to get hurt!"

"Thanks!"

"You don't believe me?"

"You just want me to stay so you won't lose a meal ticket," said Mary.

Eliezer laughed. "Meal ticket? You got it figured wrong, all wrong! I don't need you, Mary. There are always others. If you run out on me, I'll make a new connection—soon!"

"And I always thought that you cared about me!" Mary said wryly.

"I still do," said Eliezer unctuously. "I wouldn't be talking to you like this if I didn't. Look, I've seen what happens to girls who've tried it. They got hurt bad. It does something to them. They're never the same again, even when they come back. I want to spare you that."

Mary wondered whether he was right, and as she did, she knew that she wanted him to leave because she did not know how much longer she could resist the powerful attraction that she still felt and that had brought her under his spell.

"Don't try and stop me!" said Mary with more conviction than she actually felt.

"Look, Mary," said Eliezer reasonably, "this guy got you all upset. He really got to you, didn't he? Well, if he did, you're more stupid than I thought. He doesn't know you the way I know you. You and I, Mary, we're dirt and we've always been dirt. We don't breathe clean air like ordinary people, we don't live in the light of day. Our nostrils are filled with the foul smell of the dung heap in which we wallow. We move in the darkness of the night, hiding our shame from one another's view. We are the things that crawl in dank places, the maggots that tear at the flesh, the worms that slither on naked bellies over the stinking bodies of men. The air and the sun would kill you, Mary. Maggots are maggots, pigs are pigs and whores are whores!"

Mary cried out in anguish and hurled herself at Eliezer. "Get out!" she screamed. "Get out!" She scratched his face and bit his hands as Eliezer struggled with her as with a wild beast, trying to subdue her.

"You see!" he screamed, laughing hysterically as he seized her viciously. "You see what you are? You see?"

He dug his hands into her flesh until she screamed with pain, kicking her and choking her and beating her mercilessly before flinging her to the ground, where she lay in a heap, whimpering.

"This is what you really want, isn't it?" he screamed. "It makes you feel good all over, doesn't it? I've neglected you! It's been too long!" Eliezer let himself down in a chair and watched Mary, knowing that soon she would start crawling back to him.

Presently, Mary sat up and glanced at Eliezer, a wry smile playing on her lips. Eliezer returned the smile and waited.

Mary got up slowly, painfully, steadying herself against the wall. She fingered a piece of pottery, as if to keep from falling to the ground, but suddenly she seized it and hurled it at Eliezer, who screamed in pain as it crashed into his face. He leaped up, reeling, staggering after Mary, but Mary was already out the door, running blindly down the street as fast as she could, with Eliezer in pursuit.

She saw a crowd and headed for it, hoping to find safety there, just as Eliezer caught up with her. Mary wormed her way through the people who closed behind her, as she worked her way to the front. She looked back and saw that, for the moment, she was safe from her pursuer.

Now, for the first time, she became aware of a man's voice. She looked in the direction of the sound and noticed the stranger who had been addressing the crowd.

Before she really heard the words, she felt the calm, pleading earnest sound of the voice stirring her soul. The stranger's face seemed radiant with an inner light. Suddenly she felt his eyes upon her and she felt and saw love in those eyes as she had never felt or seen it before in the eyes of any man. She knew that she was looking into the eyes of Jesus.

"It is never too late," Jesus was saying. "'The Lord is our shepherd...' Suppose a man has a hundred sheep. If one of them strays, does he not leave the other ninety-nine on the hillside and go in search of the one that strayed? And if he should find it, I tell you this: he is more delighted over that sheep than over the ninety-nine that never strayed. In the same way, it is not your heavenly Father's will that one of His children be lost—for you are all His children. Look for Him, as He looks for you, and you will find Him. Return!"

Mary listened and as she heard, tears began to roll down her cheeks. The eternal child in her yearned for her heavenly Father's love. The face of Jesus swam before her blurred eyes and, suddenly, as he finished, she had a vision of God. At that moment, Mary ran forward and fell on her knees before Jesus. "Forgive me," she cried. "Forgive me! I have sinned!"

Jesus laid his hand gently on her head. "Get up now," he said compassionately. "Your sins are forgiven. *Shalom alechem.* Peace be unto you."

Mary rose and now, for the first time, she saw Judas standing nearby.

Jesus smiled at Judas and Mary. She smiled back gratefully. Then she walked over to Judas, who had been waiting for her.

"Whore!" snarled Eliezer at the back of the crowd, loud enough so that the stranger standing next to him heard.

"You know her?" asked the stranger.

"Know her?" scoffed Eliezer. "Everybody knows her!"

"I just arrived," said the stranger, as if apologizing for the fact that he did not know her.

"Whore!" snarled Eliezer again, fuming with anger, his face swollen. "You goddamn, bitchy, stinking whore!"

"Come on," said the stranger pleasantly. 'Sounds like you could stand a bottle of wine."

"Huh?" Eliezer said, startled, not really realizing that he had been talking to anyone.

The stranger smiled pleasantly. "Let's go have a little wine," he said. "I could use a drink, too."

Eliezer regarded the stranger suspiciously.

The stranger smiled candidly. "Look," he said. "I'll appreciate the company and it'll do you good to talk. Sometimes it's good to just talk things out. Sometimes it's also easier with strangers."

Eliezer felt receptive to the suggestion. "Thanks," he said. "My name is Eliezer ben Jochanan."

"*Shalom alechem!*" said the stranger. "I am Meier ben Jonathan."

"*Alechem shalom!*" said Eliezer. "Where are you from?"

"Jerusalem," said the stranger.

"What are you doing here?"

The man smiled evasively. 'Let's not talk business," he said. "Let's go and relax over a bottle of wine."

The idea suited Eliezer fine just now. He sensed that it was more than just a social invitation and that it had something to do with Judas, Mary and Jesus. He was ready to listen.

CHAPTER 7

Showdown

It was as Rabbi Emanuel had predicted. Jesus and his twelve apostles continued to speak publicly, trying to spread their message, but they were challenged more and more by various spokesmen for the community.

The people, too, tired of them after a while, as they tended to do with any situation, once its novelty had worn off. There were still those who were drawn to Jesus and his followers, but the mission, which was begun and received with such great enthusiasm, was slowing down rather than taking on greater momentum now.

"I just learned that Jesus plans to return home to Nazareth!" Rabbi Samuel informed Rabbi Emanuel one morning.

Rabbi Emanuel looked surprised. "Are you sure?" he asked.

"I heard it from one of his followers," Samuel said.

Rabbi Emanuel considered the matter thoughtfully.

"I think we've solved the problem!" Samuel suggested. "He's running home to stay!"

'You may be right," said Rabbi Emanuel as they smiled and sighed with relief.

The stay in Nazareth had proved unfortunate. The townspeople did not take Jesus seriously, but they did not run him out of town, as they had once before. Rather, his posturings now evoked pity for him and for his family. It was a good thing, said the people, that his father, Joseph, did not live to see this. Poor Mary.

Few came to be healed. Fewer yet were healed.

Jesus was disappointed and Judas recalled his remark: "A prophet will always be held in honor, except in his hometown and in his own family."

Jesus returned to Capernaum where he sent out the Twelve to carry his message. But the people were not as enthusiastic as before.

Judas, recalling this period, saw that Jesus had been bound for trouble, even without the Pharisees. Herod Antipas, the ruler of the region, had killed John the Baptizer, who had been a thorn in Herod's side. The people had listened to John, the outspoken preacher, who had dared to criticize Herod. Now they listened to Jesus. Herod knew that nothing good could come of it, and that it was only a matter of time before Jesus would cause embarrassment and trouble. He sent his officials to keep a close watch on Jesus and report his doings. Something would be done about Jesus, too, in time.

Judas remembered how uncomfortable things became. There were always some officials of Herod present now when Jesus addressed a group. Even if they said nothing, it was obvious that they were watching everything that went on and reporting every incident as they saw it.

What would have happened had Jesus not had another major run-in with the Pharisees nobody could say, not even Judas. The incident, however, was an important one, and Judas knew, looking back, that with it Jesus lost whatever sympathy and support still hung in the balance.

"Why do your disciples not conform to the ancient tradition but eat their food with defiled hands?" they asked Jesus.

Jesus could have turned the other cheek and given a soft answer, for the washing of hands was not mandatory under the circumstances, although the Pharisees practiced the custom and might properly expect it of a teacher and his disciples.

But Jesus declared bluntly, "Hear me, all of you, and understand: nothing that goes into a man from outside can defile him; no, it is the things that come out of him that defile a man."

The Pharisees had been outraged. He might call them hypocrites. But Jesus was a greater hypocrite. He paid unctuous homage to the Torah, claiming that he did not come to destroy, but to fulfill, saying that not a jot or tittle may be changed. And in the next breath he was ready to let men eat whatever they wished, including ultimately the unclean foods forbidden in the Torah. He did not come to fulfill, he came to destroy the Law of Moses!

This was what the Pharisees said. Jesus did not answer their charge. Judas did not know what the answer was. But now he knew why Jesus withdrew from the towns of Galilee and sojourned in the countryside.

When that proved too uncomfortable, Jesus left Galilee altogether and crossed into Phoenicia, heading for the areas of Tyre and Sidon, accompanied by his disciples and a small number of followers. The area, inhabited mostly by Gentiles, was no longer part of the land of Israel. Jesus felt safe here.

Judas felt sad as he reflected on recent times, recalling the change that had come over Jesus. Jesus, who had been so full of the divine glory, had become moody and uncommunicative. When he did talk, he spoke with unseemly anger and indignation. Judas recalled one such outburst in the presence of the disciples.

"Alas for you, Chorazin!" Jesus had said. "Alas for you, Bethsaida! If the miracles that were performed in you had been performed in Tyre and Sidon, they would long ago have repented in sackcloth and ashes. But it will be more bearable, I tell you, for Tyre and Sidon on the Day of Judgment, than for you, Chorazin and Bethsaida. And as for you, Capernaum, will you be exalted to the skies? No, brought down to the depths! For if the miracles had been performed in Sodom which were performed in you, Sodom would be standing to this day. But it will be more bearable, I tell you, for the land of Sodom on the Day of Judgment than for you."

Jesus could no longer hide his keen disappointment.

Jesus kept on the move. He left Phoenicia and traveled southeast, staying a while in the region of the Decapolis inhabited mostly by non-Jews.

But harder to bear than Jesus' anger and disappointment was his sadness. Judas felt a lump in his throat as he remembered a man who had come up to Jesus recently and said, "I will follow you wherever you go."

Jesus smiled at him sadly. "Foxes have their holes," he said, "the birds their roosts, but the Son of Man has nowhere to lay his head."

Once or twice Jesus made forays into Galilee, but he withdrew quickly. He kept away from the cities, even the Gentile cities of the Decapolis.

Finally he headed for Caesarea Philippi.

Philip, who ruled the area, was also a pawn of Rome, but he had proved to be a good and respected ruler, who had managed to stay in power some thirty years.

But the tetrarchy of Philip wasn't Galilee. It was inhabited for the most part by Gentiles, as evidenced by the many pagan shrines covering the landscape.

Nor could one forget that whatever virtues Philip possessed, and however safe it seemed in his territory, he was a friend of Rome who, as a token of his esteem for the Emperor, had rebuilt his capital Bethsaida and renamed it Bethsaida Julias, after Julia, the daughter of Emperor Augustus.

He had honored the Emperor further by building a city at Paneas which he had named Caesarea Philippi—Philip's Caesarea.

Judas came out of the farmhouse on the outskirts of town, where he was staying. He had seen Simon approach and he went to meet him.

"Shalom, Judas," Simon exclaimed.

"Shalom, Simon," Judas answered. He noticed Simon's troubled look and waited for him to speak.

"I have called a meeting for tonight," said Simon. "I would like you to be there."

"And the others?"

"Everyone I have talked to so far has agreed to come."

Judas searched Simon's face. It was unusually tense. "Will Jesus be there?"

Judas' question was unnecessary. He knew, as well as Simon, that Jesus was away for a few days. But he had to ask anyway, even though he sensed what the meeting would be about.

"No," said Simon with ill-concealed guilt. "Jesus will not be there. He is away for a few days."

"Good," said Judas.

"Then we can count on you?" Simon asked pointedly.

"You can count on me," said Judas.

Simon waited for him to say more, but Judas did not feel like talking.

"Good," said Simon finally. "Come to my place after you have eaten. Shalom."

"Shalom," said Judas as he watched Simon hurry away.

Judas had been worried about Jesus. But he was more worried now about the disciples. They had begun to whisper and grumble. Judas was glad that Simon had called a meeting for tonight. He was ready for a showdown.

❧   ❧   ❧

It was in the upper room of the house where Simon stayed that the Twelve Apostles were assembled this night.

Simon looked unusually somber as he regarded the others, whose eyes searched his features for the meaning of the gathering. Some knew. All sensed by the obvious absence of Jesus that it regarded him. The twelve men tried to avoid each other's gaze, for they were afraid to see in the other one's eyes the sense of conspiracy and betrayal each felt in his heart.

"I have called this meeting because I, and some of you I have talked with, feel we must talk things out," said Simon, addressing the group slowly and deliberately. "Jesus is away for a few days, as you all know. He does not know about this meeting—and he need never know about it unless, of course, we decide otherwise. There's been a lot of talking lately among twos and threes. I've done it. We've all done it. I think it's time we figure out where we stand and where we are going."

Simon spoke plainly enough. Everyone knew what he meant. For a while now they had been voicing various misgivings privately. But now that they were challenged to express them, nobody wanted to talk. Instead, each regarded some static object or became preoccupied with some other trivial concern.

"I know what you've been saying and thinking," said Simon. "Let's hear it! Nobody will criticize you." He looked around expectantly.

"I'll start," said Philip, smiling nervously as he felt the relieved eyes of the others upon him.

"Fine," said Simon. "Go ahead."

"Well," said Philip, wetting his lips, 'I don't mean to criticize Jesus. He has a lot of good ideas and I'm all for them. His ideas are right and all that..."

Philip looked around to see how he was doing. He didn't realize how hard it was to say in a group what he had frequently stated in private lately. He wished that the others could somehow sense what he wanted to say, without having to say it. He wished he had not been the first one to speak.

"Go on," Simon encouraged him.

"Well," said Philip, smiling nervously, hoping this way to make his unattractive thoughts more attractive, 'I feel that we haven't been as successful as I thought we'd be."

Simon and the others waited for him to say more. Philip would have been happy to let it go at that. He waited for others to say something. But nobody wanted to relieve him of the burden.

"In what way?" Simon asked.

"Well," said Philip, trying to be kind, "things were going along nicely at first—I mean, the way the people listened to Jesus. Remember? We really felt that suddenly things, the world, would get better. And when he sent us out, we felt that we had the power to bring it about. It was such a clear message! But only a handful of people continued to pay attention, until there were fewer and fewer and now, well, I wonder if there's any sense in...well, I mean, I wonder if...anyone...knows what we're doing any more."

A noticeable sense of relief spread over the group. Now it was out in the open.

"I think Philip has put it well," said Thomas, emboldened to speak. "But he didn't go far enough."

Relief gave way to a sense of tension once more.

"What do you mean?" asked Simon evenly.

'I mean Philip has explained pretty well what has happened, but he hasn't told us why it happened," said Thomas. "There's a lot behind what's been happening. You may not want to get into it."

"I think we should get into it," said Simon, with his usual frankness and directness. "Go ahead, tell us what's on your mind."

"All right," said Thomas, who tended to speak with a quiet, skeptical smile playing around his lips. "I'll only say this—we've stopped spreading the message. We're not going anywhere any more. We're on the run!"

John jumped up angrily. "I don't think that's true at all," he exclaimed. "Furthermore, I don't think this kind of talk is a good idea. It just undermines everything we're trying to do!"

"Maybe we can straighten out some wrong thinking by talking things out," said Simon. "You can't do it by ignoring it. Thoughts just don't go away like that. Go ahead, Thomas."

John stared fiercely at Thomas, who smiled apologetically.

"I don't mean to undermine our cause," Thomas continued quietly. "But I'm concerned about it, and I can't help seeing what I see. We have to face facts!"

'All right, what are they?" John demanded.

'Jesus was doing well at first," Thomas said quietly. "He didn't convince everybody, but he had a lot of followers and got to a lot of people with his ideas. All that changed! More than it should have! Why? I'll tell you why! They've decided he's an agitator, and they don't want to have anything to do with him any more!"

John laughed contemptuously. "Are you running scared?" he asked.

"No," said Thomas with quiet reasonableness. "But I think we must face facts, before we go any further, if we go any further!"

"'Agitator!'" John exclaimed contemptuously. "Sure he's an agitator! Moses was an agitator! Isaiah was an agitator! Amos, Micah, Hosea were agitators! Divine agitators—that's what they were, that's what Jesus is!"

"With one difference," said Thomas.

"What?"

'They did not violate the Law!" exclaimed Thomas.

"They cut to the heart of the Law!"

The agitated remark came from James, who could not remain silent any longer. All eyes turned towards him.

"The prophets had no patience with rituals," exclaimed James. "They had no patience with the letter of the Law. Amos said, 'I hate, I despise your feasts…I will not accept your sacrifices…But let justice well up as waters, and righteousness like a mighty stream.' Hosea said, 'For I desire mercy and not sacrifice, and the knowledge of God, rather than burnt offerings.' Those words didn't sit too well, either, with a lot of people. The prophets were concerned with the *spirit* of the Law!"

Bartholomew, who had been listening passively, suddenly spoke up. "Some of them, like Moses and Ezra, were as much concerned with the letter of the Law as they were with the spirit of the Law," he said. "You can't have one without the other, just as you can't have a body without a soul, or a soul without a body, at least, not on earth. They hold each other together."

"You didn't get the point I was trying to make," said Thomas, who had been anxious to speak again. "The letter of the Law leads to the spirit of the Law. The prophets only attacked those who observed the letter, but stopped short of the spirit. The prophets themselves did not violate the letter of the Law—or call for its violation! Jesus has!"

"When?" John demanded angrily.

"Before Thomas could answer, Simon spoke. "Let's not speak in anger," he said gently but firmly. "Let's remember that we are all friends, drawn together by a common cause, trying our best to understand and do the right thing."

"I'm sorry," said John, addressing Thomas.

"That's all right," said Thomas, whose realistic skepticism had a benevolent side-effect in that he was patient with people and slow to anger. "The violations are so obvious that I don't know why I even have to mention them: that time he healed on the Sabbath, when it wasn't a matter of life and death; and when he belittled the washing of the hands before eating, by saying what comes out of the mouth is more important than what goes into the mouth."

'He was trying to make a point!" said John.

"He went too far!" said Thomas. "Until then, he had the Pharisees with him!"

"Not all of them," said John. "They used to challenge him."

"What's wrong with that? We're challenging each other now. Maybe they weren't with him, every one, all the time, but they weren't against him!"

"May I say something?" It was Andrew who spoke, addressing Simon.

"Of course," said Simon.

"I'm more concerned about political trouble than trouble with the Pharisees," Andrew said cautiously. He looked around, hoping someone else would pick up the thought and develop it, but no one did, and he felt forced to continue.

"I don't mean to criticize Jesus," he said apologetically, "but it seems like he may be giving the wrong impression. I mean, the way the Sadducees and Herodians have been watching him…"

"They're so scared they watch everybody—including the dead!" exclaimed James.

Everyone laughed.

"They're afraid he'll start a revolution," Andrew persisted.

"Do you think he will?" James asked.

"No," said Andrew.

"Well, what are you afraid of?" James demanded.

"I just don't want them to misunderstand," said Andrew timidly. "It should be made clear that we are just teaching religious ideas and that we don't mean to make political trouble."

'Sure we mean to make trouble!" thundered John. "We mean to change the world!"

"That's not the way I understand Jesus," Andrew said timidly.

"Then you'd better drop out," John declared, "because that's where we're heading!"

"Let's not threaten each other," Simon cautioned.

"I'm not arguing Jesus' teachings—I believe in them as much as anybody here," Andrew declared defensively. "But I don't want us to get into trouble with the authorities—I mean, some of us have families, like Matthew…"

'Don't worry about me," Matthew said coolly.

"Just look at what they did to John the Baptizer!" Andrew said indignantly, so that it covered his fear.

"That's part of the price we must all be willing to pay!" John declared with typically reckless enthusiasm.

"Let's all calm down," said Simon. "Nobody has to die."

"I don't really see what all the fuss is about," said Thaddeus. "As for leaving Galilee, Jesus probably just wanted to spread his message to those other parts. Sure, most of the people here are Gentiles, but there are Jews here, too. He knows what he's doing."

Simon smiled kindly, patiently. Thaddeus was always the last one to notice that there was anything wrong.

"Things aren't going as expected, that's all I can say," said Thomas. "Don't you remember how he instructed us not to take the road to Gentile lands, but rather to go to the lost sheep of the house of Israel? So why has he taken us to the lands of the Gentiles, if not to get away from trouble? Certainly not to preach to the Gentiles. You heard what he said to the Phoenician woman, 'Let the children be satisfied first; it's not fair to take the children's bread and throw it to the dogs.' You've noticed how he's been keeping to himself and how he's tried to keep his whereabouts quiet."

"What are you trying to tell us, Thomas?" John demanded, with ill-concealed anger.

"I know I'm not making myself popular by questioning these matters," Thomas said candidly, "but I think we have to. Maybe we have to reappraise what's happened. Let's look at what's happened as if we were looking at these events from the outside. Before Jesus ever came to Capernaum, he was rejected at Nazareth. Then he came to Capernaum. In time, the Pharisees rejected him. The authorities became highly suspicious of him. When he went back to Nazareth, he was rejected a second time. Do you remember what happened when he came back to us? His mother and brothers came to get him. They were worried about his 'behavior.'"

John jumped up in anger. "Are you suggesting that maybe we should 'worry about his behavior' or perhaps desert him?"

A deadly silence filled the charged atmosphere.

"I think we should meet with him," said Thomas.

"And ask him what?" John demanded.

"His thoughts," Thomas said.

"Oh," said John sarcastically. "That's right! He's never shared those with us!"

"Please!" said Simon conciliatorily. "Please!"

Judas had been sitting quietly, observing, listening. There was no question but that doubt and uncertainty had crept into the ranks of the disciples. Judas tried to survey the extent of the damage. Simon, James and John were still solidly behind Jesus. That was obvious. So was Matthew and he, Judas. That made five. Thomas was openly critical. Right now he could not be counted on. Andrew was starting to run scared. Philip was shaky. That left Simon the Zealot, Bartholomew, Jude and James the younger. They tended to go along with Simon, John and James, but they were impressionable and could be swayed, especially by someone like Thomas. The Twelve now faced their moment of decision. It would either be total, clear and clean commitment—or nothing.

The sound of Simon's voice interrupted Judas' thoughts. "Judas," said Simon with an almost pleading quality to his voice.

"Yes?"

"You have not said anything," Simon said. "Is there anything you wish to say?"

The disciples regarded Judas expectantly, hoping that somehow he might point a way out of their perplexities.

"Yes," said Judas, after a long, thoughtful moment. "I do have something to say."

All eyes rested intently upon him.

"The whole matter rests on one question," said Judas gravely.

"Ask it!" said Simon.

'Who will answer it?" Judas asked.

Simon smiled. "Ask anyone you wish!" he said.

Judas nodded slowly. "All right," he said.

"Well?" asked Simon, slightly impatient. "What is the question?"

Judas looked about him before he spoke. Finally he asked, "Who is Jesus?"

An awed hush permeated the room. The disciples sat with averted eyes facing their own thoughts.

Judas let his eyes pass slowly from one to the other, looking for someone who would answer him, but no one met his gaze. Finally his eyes came to rest on Simon, whose body seemed to quake slightly upon perceiving itself to be the object of Judas' gaze. Gradually Simon's head rose and their eyes locked in a magnetic and hypnotic grip, which speech alone could break now.

When Simon spoke, he spoke from the very depths of his being. "I believe," he said slowly, awesomely, "that Jesus is the Messiah!"

A great calm now came over Simon so that the disciples, who were shaken to their very roots by the grand, terrible thought that finally found utterance, calmed down, too.

When Thomas spoke, his doubt cried out humbly for certainty. "Are you sure?" he asked.

Simon's eyes shone now with a divine certainty. "Yes," he exclaimed. "I'm sure, just as you have been sure, Thomas, from the very beginning—just as each one of us here has been sure. He has never said it, and we have never said it to one another, but each one of us sensed it, each in some special way, when he asked us to follow him! Do you remember? I have felt it many times since with him, and we have all shared the feeling and that unspoken thought. Tonight I speak it, I hope, for all of us!"

The eleven sat thoughtfully.

"We must know where everyone stands tonight," said Judas. "I think we should ask everyone the same question!"

"How do you feel?" asked Thomas.

"I agree with Simon," said Judas. "I know Jesus is the Messiah!"

"You know?"

Judas remembered his promise to Jesus not to tell. "I…believe," he said, correcting himself.

The others looked around uneasily.

"I know what's bothering everyone," said Judas. "If he is the Messiah—since he is the Messiah—why is he being treated this way?"

Judas looked around and noticed that this was the thought uppermost in their minds.

"It's simple," he said, with a casualness designed to put everyone at ease and make them receptive to these thoughts, thoughts that would appear so obvious that the disciples would wonder why they ever entertained any doubts. In his own mind Judas prayed to find the right words, keenly aware that the success of the cause now hung in the balance.

"That's right," he said. "It's really very simple. You and I know that Jesus is the Messiah. We have known it all along in our own hearts, as Simon said, from that miraculous moment that Jesus asked each one of us to follow him. Don't you remember what Jesus said just the other day? 'I thank Thee, Father, Lord of heaven and earth, for hiding these things from the learned and wise, and revealing them to the simple!' We are the simple to whom he has been revealed! Our Father in heaven has revealed to us the Messiah! To us, and to no one else—yet! That's the simple reason for it all, right now! We are the sharers of a great secret—that the Messiah is already among us, walking the earth, inspecting the children of men, like angels that appear as men. He has not said anything yet to anyone—not even to us—yet we have been told it by our heavenly Father, or how would we have known and felt these things and followed him? Despair? We should be full of joy tonight! For the time will come, and I feel it will be soon, when Jesus will say to us, and then to all the world, 'I am the Messiah, I am he who comes in the name of the Lord!' He knows the day and the time and the place! Then shall Isaiah's words be fulfilled, 'And it shall come to pass in the end of days that the mountain of the Lord's house shall be established in the top of the mountains, and shall be exalted above the hills; and all the nations shall flow unto it. And many people shall go and say, Come ye, and let us go up to the mountain of the Lord, to the house of the God of Jacob; and he will teach us of his ways and we will walk in his paths: for out of Zion shall go forth the Law, and the word of the Lord from Jerusalem. And he shall judge among nations, and shall rebuke many people: and they shall beat their swords into plowshares, and their spears into pruning hooks; nation shall not lift up sword against nation, neither shall they learn war any more.'"

There was no sound as Judas finished. Judas realized for the first time the fervent intensity of his devotion, which stemmed from a depth of being that he never knew existed. He looked about him and it was plain to him that their souls had been touched. The eyes of the disciples were alive once more with a divine joy and hope.

"Let us not falter," said Judas quietly. "Let us walk in the light of the Lord."

The others nodded.

"Amen!" said Simon, eyes glistening.

"Amen!" said the others.

Then Simon began to sing and the others joined him with a full voice and a joyful heart.

"Mi cha'mo'cha ba'elim adonai
Mi cha'mo'cha nedor ba'ko'desh
No'ra t'hi'lot osseh phe'leh."

"Who is like unto Thee, O Lord, among the mighty?
"Who is like unto Thee, glorious in holiness,
"Revered in praises, doing wonders?"

❦　　　❦　　　❦

"It is good to see you again," Jesus said, addressing the disciples in the upper room a few days later, upon his return.

"It's good to see you again, too, Rabbi," Simon said, speaking for all.

The peacefulness and the kindness that had radiated from him so often was again apparent. The gloom that had been apparent lately seemed gone, as if Jesus had come to grips with it and mastered it.

"You must all get away by yourselves from time to time and pray," he said, with his former gentleness. "Talk things over with your heavenly Father. It helps every time."

The disciples nodded their understanding. It was good to see him again.

"I am glad for your fellowship," he said. "I shall remember it. It is at difficult moments that our faith is put to the test."

"You need not worry about our faith," said Simon fervently. 'Everyone is with you."

Jesus looked around and saw affirmation in their eyes. What did those eyes know? What were they trying to tell him?

"Not everyone," said Jesus.

The Twelve look around with apprehension.

"We are all with you," Simon reaffirmed vehemently.

"Yes," said Judas. "All of us!"

Jesus looked at Judas and wondered what he was trying to tell him. Once he had told Judas that he was the Messiah. Judas alone knew. Had he told the others? No, thought Jesus, he could trust Judas not to tell.

"I know you are with me," Jesus said. "It is the others…"

"You have reached many already," Peter assured Jesus. "Many of the others believe in you."

Now suddenly Jesus had to know. "Who do they say I am?" he asked.

There was a long silence as the disciples regarded one another.

"Some say John the Baptizer," said Matthews.

"Some say Elijah," said James.

"Some say one of the prophets," said John.

Jesus nodded and looked around slowly, almost afraid and yet anxious to ask the next question. "And you?" he asked finally. "Who do you say I am?"

A terrifying silence hovered over the speechless disciples. The blood pounded through their veins and their eyes turned towards Simon. Jesus looked at Simon, who, for a moment, was afraid to utter the alarming words he so recently had spoken, in the absence of Jesus. Then, suddenly, his heart exploded into speech and he exclaimed, "You are the Messiah!"

The eyes of Jesus glistened with gratitude and love, as he saw Simon's words reflected in the eyes of all the disciples.

"Do not tell anyone," Jesus instructed them quietly. "The time is now at hand to go to Jerusalem!"

The eyes of the disciples sparkled in jubilation. They smiled at Simon and Judas. They had been right. Jesus was the Messiah!

❋   ❋   ❋

"We are leaving for Jerusalem!" Judas exclaimed excitedly, the first chance he had to see Mary. She regarded him quietly. Judas thought she did not understand and clarified the remark. "Jesus said it's time to head for Jerusalem!"

Mary Magdala looked away, saying nothing. Judas followed her as she proceeded to walk down the deserted country road. Presently she veered off into the field and headed for a peaceful spot. Judas studied her as she sat down, engrossed in thought.

She had always been beautiful, but she was more beautiful now than she had ever been. The external beauty of her being was now transfused with the beauty of her inner radiance, which gave a kindness and gentleness to her features, features that once were hard and harsh.

"What's the matter?" Judas asked presently.

"Nothing," she said evasively.

"Tell me," he said.

"All right," she said. "I had a very forward thought."

"What?"

"I'm trying not to be forward any more," she said anxiously.

"Go ahead," Judas said, smiling.

Mary regarded him earnestly. "I love you!" she said.

"I love you, too, Mary!" Judas said genuinely.

"Judas?"

"Yes?"

"Marry me!"

"Oh!"

"You wanted me to say what I was thinking."

"Yes."

Mary shrugged her shoulders defensively and broke into a thin, wry smile. "I should have known better," she said.

"No, Mary…"

"You don't really love me."

"I do love you!"

"But not enough to marry me."

"Enough to marry you, Mary," said Judas with unmistakable honesty. "If I were to marry anyone it would only be you."

"That's something, at least," Mary said, trying to cover her disappointment with a sad laugh and a slight smile.

Judas hurt inside and felt Mary's hurt, and he longed suddenly to marry her and ignore that inexorable urge within him that forced him to deny the yearning of his heart.

"I wish I could!" said Judas.

Mary realized that he was truly troubled. She took his hand. "Why can't you?" she asked gently.

Judas stared ahead of him as if trying to penetrate the mystery. "Jesus," he said softly.

Mary did not get angry this time. She loved them both too much now. "What about Jesus?" Mary asked.

"He needs me," said Judas.

"You have a right to lead your own life," Mary said.

"He has a mission!" said Judas.

"He will accomplish his mission with or without you," Mary suggested.

Judas thought about that. "Maybe," he said quietly.

"Well?"

Judas was puzzled by the ambiguities of his feelings. "I don't know, Mary," he said. "I don't know what my feelings are—my real feelings. I just feel that I must go with him. As if I'm being guided by something bigger than myself, perhaps even God! Maybe it isn't God at all. Maybe it's only me, maybe I need to feel that I have a mission in life!"

"Everyone has a mission in life, Judas," Mary said with gentle persuasion. "You know that better than I. I've learned it only recently. There's nothing ordinary about being ordinary, Judas. We've been sent here by God to lead extraordinary lives, each one of us. He wants us to be a blessing, he wants us to live in the beauty of holiness. When we see it that way, every minor moment of life becomes meaningful."

"I know that," Judas sighed heavily. "But I also know something you don't know."

Mary regarded Judas curiously. "About Jesus?" she asked.

Judas looked at her, surprised. "Yes," he said.

Mary regarded Judas quietly. "I know it, too," she said.

Judas was startled. "What do you know?" he asked.

"I know that he is the Messiah!" said Mary.

Judas looked shocked. 'Who told you?" he asked.

"No one!"

"How did you find out?"

Again a strange look came into Mary's eyes. "I had a dream," she said.

Something in her manner made Judas react in wonder and belief at the truth of her vision. "Then you understand," said Judas, relieved.

Mary regarded him with troubled eyes. "Please, Judas," she said. "Let's serve God in our own way, humbly, somewhere, here, in Galilee, anywhere you say. Please!"

His eyes told her that he couldn't.

"Don't go to Jerusalem!" she pleaded now.

Judas laughed gently. "Another dream?" he asked, smiling.

"No," she said, troubled, "just a feeling."

"I have to go, Mary!" Judas said with a bittersweet smile.

"Why?" she asked.

Judas looked at her with a deep love. "Just a feeling," he said.

Mary smiled bravely. "I understand," she said. "I will go with you."

They rose to leave.

Judas looked at Mary and smiled. "Thanks," he said. Then he pulled her towards him and kissed her.

CHAPTER 8

On to Jerusalem

Finally, thought Judas, finally we're on our way.

They had left Caesarea Philippi and returned to Capernaum. Jesus had considered going to Jerusalem through Samaria. He had sent James and John to check whether the Samaritans would permit them to pass through. It seemed like the safer route, since the territory was controlled by Pontius Pilate rather than Herod Antipas, who was no friend of theirs. Pontius Pilate might not be, either, but, unlike Herod Antipas, he did not seem to be aware of Jesus and his doings, so his territory seemed to be the safer to pass through. Pilate, of course, would become aware of them once they hit Jerusalem, but that was soon enough.

It was almost predictable that the Samaritans would not grant the Galileans permission to pass through their territory, as indeed they refused to do. Their unfriendliness was the result of deep antagonisms that had been molded over 700 years, to the point where the Samaritan Jews did not recognize the legitimacy of the Judean and Galilean Jews, symbolized by the Samaritan claim that their city, Shechem, and not Jerusalem, was the center of Jewish worship.

So Jesus decided to go by the usual, the only other, route. Jesus led his band through Peraea, part of the territory ruled over by Herod Antipas. They traveled on the east side of the River Jordan, through the forests of the Jordan Valley, which abounded in white poplars, tamarisks, castors, licorice and mallow trees.

The area was sparsely populated, owing to the intensive heat nine months out of the year.

Jesus and his band sang the pilgrim psalms as they walked joyfully toward Jerusalem.

> "O Israel hope in the Lord; for with the Lord there is mercy,
> and with Him is plenteous redemption.
> And He will redeem Israel from all his iniquities."

Strange things had happened, thought Judas. Stranger things were yet in store.

Try as he might, he could not imagine what would happen once they faced Jerusalem. He wondered how they would be received. He wondered how Jesus would act. He wondered what God had in store for them.

He looked at Jesus, leading them resolutely toward Jerusalem. There was a triumphant spirit about him these days that had spread contagiously to the others. At times, though, Jesus sounded a startling note that marred the joyful mood. Judas remembered the time Jesus discussed the journey to Jerusalem following the revelation at Caesarea Philippi.

"Let's go now!" Simon had said, with typical enthusiasm.

Jesus became melancholy and his eyes became sad and troubled. "We'll go soon enough," he said. "And when we get there, there will be trouble. The priests, the elders, the lawyers will cause me much suffering."

Judas remembered how Simon rushed up to Jesus and took his arm in great concern. "Heaven forbid!" Simon exclaimed. "No, lord, this shall never happen to you!"

The sad eyes of Jesus flashed suddenly with righteous indignation.

"Away with you, Satan!" he exclaimed. "You are a stumbling block to me. You think as men think, not as God thinks!"

Simon cringed at the rebuke. Judas remembered how he had felt sorry for Simon. It was an undeserved remark, for Simon loved Jesus and was concerned over him. But then Jesus, like all men, had his moments, thought Judas, and he had been troubled. One could forgive him a momentary, unkind outburst. He was sure that Simon had forgiven Jesus long ago, if not at that very instant.

"'Our soul is escaped as a bird out of the snare of the fowlers,'" sang Judas with the others. "'The snare is broken, and we are escaped. Our help is in the name of the Lord, Who made heaven and earth.'"

They were not the only pilgrims walking to Jerusalem, for there were many from all over making the Passover pilgrimage as commanded in the Torah.

Accompanying Jesus and the Twelve were Salome, the mother of John and James, and the three Marys—Mary, the mother of James, the less; Mary of Magdala; and Mary, mother of Jesus.

Judas wondered why Mary, Jesus' mother, had come along. Of course it could be said that she was fulfilling a religious duty, but then this wasn't really the case. Being a woman, she was excused from this duty, since her responsibility was toward the home.

Judas remembered Nazareth and how Mary had asked him to look after Jesus. It was a mother's concern for her son, one that increased rather than diminished with time. Judas recalled the last time he had seen Mary. She and the rest of the family had come to Capernaum shortly after Jesus had instructed the Twelve to go forth and spread his teachings. Mary and the family were sure now that Jesus was disturbed. He was going too far and unless they stopped him, he would get into serious trouble. Jesus and the disciples were eating when his family arrived. As usual, the room was crowded with people, so that it was impossible to get in.

"Your mother and your brothers are outside, waiting for you," someone said.

Judas remembered seeing Jesus tremble slightly, as if he sensed why they had come. But he betrayed no further emotion and, making no effort to welcome his family or see them, he looked about him and declared loudly, so that his mother and his brothers could hear, "Behold, these are my mother and my brothers! For whoever shall do the will of God, the same is my brother and my sister and my mother!"

Mary never got to see Jesus then or later, until she learned of his plans to go to Jerusalem. When they met, they greeted each other politely but with reserve. They did not talk much to each other along the way.

Judas wondered why Mary had come. Had God opened her eyes and shown her the Messiah in his glory? Or was she just a mother fearful for her son?

And they sang:

> "Lo, children are a heritage of the Lord;
> The fruit of the womb is a reward,
> As arrows in the hand of a mighty man,
> So are the children of one's youth."

Children!

The people came with their children when Jesus appeared in the small towns along the way, such as at this moment. They had heard of Jesus, the wonder-worker, and they crowded around him. They strained to reach him, pushing their youngsters forward, holding the babies high, imploring Jesus to bless their offspring.

"Come on, everybody, make room, let him pass!" Simon exclaimed as he and some of the disciples tried to clear the way. "We've got a long ways to go, we can't stay all day."

"Let the little ones come to me," Jesus said, making no effort to move. "Do not try to stop them, for the Kingdom of God belongs to such as these. I tell you that whoever does not accept the Kingdom of God like a child will never enter it."

Simon and the disciples figured they might as well wait patiently until the last of the children had been blessed.

Just as Jesus was ready to leave, a man of prominence asked, "Good Master, what must I do to win eternal life?"

"Why do you call me good?" Jesus said. "No one is good except God alone. You know the commandments: 'Do not commit adultery; do not murder; do not steal; do not give false evidence; honor your father and mother.'"

"I have kept all these since I was a boy," the man said.

Jesus gave the man a long, measured look. "There is still one thing lacking," Jesus said finally. "Sell everything you have and distribute to the poor, and you will have riches in heaven; and come, follow me."

The man's look fell visibly and his heart sank.

"How hard it is for the wealthy to enter the Kingdom of God!" Jesus declared. "It is easier for a camel to go through the eye of a needle than for a rich man to enter the Kingdom of God."

"Then who can be saved?" someone asked.

Jesus regarded them. "For men it is impossible," he said, "but not for God. To God, everything is possible."

With that, he and his disciples continued their journey.

"What's the matter?" Jesus said at one point, noticing Simon's preoccupation.

"I was thinking about what you said," Simon said tentatively.

"Yes?"

"About the rich man."

"Oh?"

"We gave up our belongings to become your followers." It was made as a flat statement, but it was tinged ever so slightly with the human desire for reward.

"I tell you this," said Jesus quietly, "there is no one who has given up home, or wife, brothers, parents or children for the sake of the Kingdom of God, who will not be repaid many times over—in this age, and in the age to come, have eternal life."

Simon and the disciples mulled the words and kept on walking, thrilling more and more at this prospect which appeared imminent.

Presently James and John, the Sons of Thunder, worked their way forward to Jesus, flanking him.

"Master?" John asked with ill-concealed excitement. "We should like you to do us a favor!"

Jesus looked from one to the other. "What is it you want me to do?" he asked.

James tried to keep his voice down so he wouldn't be overheard by the others. "Grant us the right to sit in state with you, one at your right and the other at your left!" he asked eagerly.

Jesus kept walking. He smiled wryly as he looked into the distance. "You don't understand what you are asking," he said, as if talking to himself. "Can you drink the cup that I drink, or be baptized with the baptism I am baptized with?"

"We can!" John and James said eagerly.

Jesus continued speaking as if he had never heard their answer. "The cup that I drink you shall drink, and the baptism I am baptized with shall be your baptism. But to sit at my right or left is not for me to grant. It is for those to whom it has already been assigned."

But James and John had been overheard.

"What's the idea, pleading special favor!" Simon said indignantly, expressing their common feelings, when he thought Jesus was out of earshot.

But Jesus heard and stopped walking, waiting for the Twelve to catch up. He smiled understandingly and regarded them patiently. "You know that in the world the recognized rulers lord it over their subjects, and their great men make them feel the weight of authority. This is not the way with you. Among you, whoever wants to be great must be your servant, and whoever wants to be first must be the willing slave of all. For even the Son of Man did not come to be served, but to serve."

James and John lowered their eyes.

"Sorry," mumbled Simon.

Jesus smiled gently and they resumed their journey.

Strange, thought Judas, strange. "The cup that I drink you shall drink, and the baptism I am baptized with shall be your baptism." Judas wished Jesus didn't talk that way. It only created doubts and fears. They had had enough of that. It was important now to maintain the enthusiasm of the disciples—they would need every ounce of it once they got to Jerusalem.

What would happen once they got to Jerusalem? Judas wondered. How would they be received? What would Jesus do? Would he reveal himself openly, or would he be recognized—by whom?—as the Messiah and be declared so officially? Would there be trouble first—is that what Jesus meant? And then, after the trouble—what kind of trouble?—what, how? What about Rabban Gamaliel, what about Caiaphas, the High Priest, what about Pontius Pilate, the Roman governor—how would they react? How did they fit into the picture? How would—God—usher in the Messianic Age? Judas realized that he did not know and that Jesus had never really explained the details. Did Jesus know or did he trust God to guide him, as now, one step at a time? Suddenly the immensity of it all hit Judas and he turned his own heart to God in prayer as he joined the others, singing:

"I will lift up mine eyes unto the mountains:
From whence shall my help come?
My help cometh from the Lord,
Who made heaven and earth.
He will not suffer thy foot to be moved;
He that keepeth thee will not slumber.
Behold, He that keepeth Israel
Doth neither slumber nor sleep.
The Lord is thy keeper;
The Lord is thy shade upon thy right hand.
The sun shall not smite thee by day,
Nor the moon by night.
The Lord shall keep thee from all evil;
He shall keep thy soul.
The Lord shall guard thy going out
And thy coming in,
From this time forth and for ever."

As the band entered Jericho, teeming now with pilgrims on their way to Jerusalem, Jesus approached a sycamore tree and, looking up, noticed a man sitting in its branches.

"Shalom!" exclaimed the man.

Jesus stopped and regarded him curiously. "Shalom," said Jesus.

The man smiled sheepishly, realizing that he presented a somewhat foolish sight. "I wanted to get a good look at you," he said apologetically.

"You know who I am?" Jesus asked.

"Yes, Rabbi," the man said cautiously.

"What's your name?"

"Zacchaeus."

"Shalom, Zacchaeus," Jesus said, smiling. "I don't presume you climb trees for a living."

Zacchaeus laughed. "No, Rabbi, I'm superintendent of taxes around here."

Jesus detected a note of shame in his voice. "Quick, Zacchaeus, come down, I must come and stay with you today."

For a moment Zacchaeus did not move, doubting what he had heard. Then suddenly he came alive and clambered down as fast as he could. "Welcome to my house!" he exclaimed joyfully as he brushed himself off and approached Jesus. "You do me a great honor."

Jesus smiled at the little man and then followed him inside, together with his disciples.

"What do you think of that?" murmured the people in the crowd who had watched the incident. "He has gone in to be the guest of a sinner."

Zacchaeus turned to Jesus and said, "Here and now, sire, I give half my possessions to charity. And if I have cheated anyone, I am ready to repay him four times over."

Jesus smiled and said to him, "Salvation has come to this house today—for this man, too, is a son of Abraham, and the Son of Man has come to seek and save what is lost."

⁂

Bartimaeus, the blind beggar, son of Timaeus, sat along the road to Jerusalem on the outskirts of Jericho. It was his daily post and he could not remember how long he had come here, because time had become vague and blurred to his mind's eye. He had come here since the time of his blindness, which seemed to go back long, long ago, as if to the time of his birth. Bartimaeus measured his life now in relation to the three holy pilgrimages, for these were good times for beggars, for there were many people who passed by on the way to the Holy City and they were generous towards beggars.

Leaving Jericho, Jesus and his band approached on their way to Jerusalem. They were singing and the voice of Jesus rose above the voices of the others:

> "Unto thee I lift up mine eyes,
> O Thou that are enthroned in the heavens."

The words reached Bartimaeus, who became strangely affected by the sound of the voice.

"Who is that?" he asked of anyone within earshot. But the other beggars just grunted their ignorance and some passing pilgrims were too preoccupied with their journey to pay attention.

The singing continued.

> "Behold, as the eyes of servants unto the hand of their master,
> As the eyes of a maiden unto the hand of her mistress;
> So our eyes look unto the Lord our God.
> Until He be gracious unto us."

Jesus and his band were now close by.

"Who is that?" Bartimaeus demanded once more anxiously, thrusting out is arm, seizing the cloak of an unsuspecting pilgrim who happened to pass at that moment. "Who is that?"

"Jesus of Nazareth," grumbled the man, glad to have overheard this bit of information earlier, for it satisfied the bold beggar, who let go of him, but who now began to shout:

"Son of David, Jesus, have pity on me!"

Some of the passing pilgrims were shocked at the beggar's wild words. Son of David! It was a title reserved for the Messiah!

"Be quiet!" some of the men said reproachfully.

But Bartimaeus only shouted all the more. "Son of David, have pity on me!"

Jesus and his band were now even with him, and Jesus stopped. "Call him!" he ordered.

Soon Jesus was surrounded by the pilgrims who had stopped to see what was going on. Judas, who was nearest Bartimaeus, turned to the beggar and said gently, "Take heart. Stand up. He is calling you."

At that, the blind beggar threw off his coat, sprang up and came to Jesus.

"What do you want me to do for you?" Jesus asked.

"Sir," said Bartimaeus plaintively, "I want my sight back!"

At that moment, a profound feeling passed between the two. "Have back your sight," Jesus said quietly. 'Your faith has cured you."

Suddenly Bartimaeus saw again and tears came to his eyes. "Blessed be Thou, O Lord our God, King of the Universe, who createst miracles daily!" the others exclaimed, awed by what they had seen.

Jesus continued his journey and Bartimaeus followed him, praising God with his whole being.

It has begun, thought Judas. It has begun! He has started to reveal himself! Son of David! They heard and he answered! He did not deny it! God! God! It has begun!

It was not far now to Jerusalem. Soon the sights of the Holy City would be a reality. They had started their ascent at Jericho, which lay 250 feet above sea level. Twenty-three more miles and they would stand 2,378 feet above sea level, on the Mount of Olives, from where they would behold the Holy City and the Holy Temple.

It was Sunday when Jesus and his band arrived at Bethpage, near Bethany, which lay three miles southeast of Jerusalem, on the slope of the Mount of Olives.

Judas was aware of the number of pilgrims that had attached themselves to their band in the course of their journey through the towns of the Jordan Valley and along the road from Jericho. Some had been there when he was called "Son of David," and they had told others. Could it be? To God all things were possible. They decided to go along and see.

Judas had been watching Jesus. Except when he led the singing, Jesus did not talk. He seemed intensely preoccupied with the nature of events that shortly lay ahead.

Even the others had become more and more quiet the closer they came to Jerusalem. For some time now they had made no effort to speak with Jesus. They had also stopped speaking with one another. Judas felt tense inside and he sensed the same tension in the others.

They had entered Bethpage. Suddenly Jesus stopped. "Let us rest a while," he said.

It had been a long uphill march and the rest was welcome. But Jesus did not sit down. He looked off toward a nearby village and then motioned for John and James, who got up again just after having made themselves comfortable.

"Go to that village," he told them, "and just as you enter, you will find tethered there a colt which no one has yet ridden. Untie it and bring it here. If anyone asks, 'Why are you doing that?' say, 'Our Master needs it and will send it back here without delay.'"

Judas, who had sat down a distance from Jesus with the rest of the disciples, wondered what Jesus wanted with John and James and where they were going, but he did not have to wonder long. Soon he saw them return, leading a donkey.

Jesus rose. Presently he was surrounded by his disciples and the rest of the pilgrims.

Jesus noticed that James and John had placed their coats over the colt for him. He thanked them with a fleeting smile. Then he mounted the animal.

The symbolic, silent drama suddenly exploded with a joyful sound of pilgrims crying, "Hosanna! Blessed is he that comes in the name of the Lord. Hosanna in the highest!"

The pilgrims scrambled ahead of Jesus and spread their garments in the road, as before kings. They cut down branches of trees and the tall green grass and they waved them and they threw them before the approaching Jesus, calling, "Blessed be the kingdom of David, our father…Hosanna to the Son of David…Hosanna! Blessed is he that comes in the name of the Lord! Hosanna in the highest!"

Jesus smiled joyfully, deeply moved by this moment.

As he approached the descent from the Mount of Olives, the band in their joy sang, "Blessings on him who comes as king in the name of the Lord! Peace in heaven, glory in highest heaven!"

One of the pilgrims, who thought the others were going a bit too far in their enthusiasm, turned to Jesus and said, "Master, reprimand your disciples."

But Jesus answered, 'I'll tell you, if my disciples keep silence, the stones will shout aloud."

He knows what he is doing, thought Judas. It is happening now. He recalled Zechariah's words, "Rejoice greatly, O daughter of Zion: shout, O daughter of Jerusalem: behold, the king cometh unto thee: and upon a colt the foal of an ass."

The signs were again unmistakable. Jesus was making it clear and plain who he was.

Jesus stopped as he gained his first view of Jerusalem. The others stopped, too, and looked, and their hearts soared within them with the memories and dreams and visions of their people, and they sang a song of David:

"I rejoiced when they said unto me:

'Let us go unto the house of the Lord.'

Our feet are standing within thy gates, O Jerusalem;

Jerusalem, that art builded

As a city that is compact together:

Whither the tribes went up, even the tribes of the Lord,

As a testimony unto Israel,

To give thanks unto the name of the Lord,

For there were set thrones for judgment,

The thrones of the house of David.

Pray for the peace of Jerusalem;

May they prosper that love thee.

Peace be within thy walls,

And prosperity within thy palaces,

For my brethren and companions' sakes,

I will now say: 'Peace be within thee.'

For the sake of the house of the Lord our God

I will seek thy good."

There lay the City of David in all its splendor, there stood the Temple in all its holiness, waiting for the realization of Israel's ancient hope, waiting for the fulfillment of prayer and prophecy, waiting for the Messiah.

And Jesus wept.

Jerusalem was now teeming with pilgrims who had come to observe the commandment of the Lord, as it was written in the Torah:

"Three times thou shalt keep a feast unto Me in the year. The feast of unleavened bread shalt though keep; seven days thou shalt eat unleavened bread, as I commanded thee, at the time appointed in the month of Abib—for in it thou camest out from Egypt; and none shall appear before Me empty; And the feast of harvest, the first fruits of thy labors, which thou sowest in the field; And the feast of ingathering, at the end of the year, when thou gatherest in thy labors out of the field. Three times in the year all thy males shall appear before the Lord God."

And so they came in spring, summer and autumn, to give thanks at *Passover* for the deliverance from Egypt, and at *Shavuot* for the Giving of the Torah, and at *Succot*, for the safe journey to the Holy Land, a land flowing with milk and honey.

And the city of 75,000 inhabitants bulged with pilgrims so that the population tripled, numbering 225,000 men, women and children who, as now, came to carry out their Covenant with God.

It has been 1,200 years now since the Lord spoke unto Moses and Aaron in the land of Egypt, saying:

> "And this day shall be unto you for a memorial, and ye shall keep it a feast to the Lord; throughout your generations ye shall keep it a feast by an ordinance forever. Seven days shall ye eat unleavened bread...And ye shall observe the feast of unleavened bread; for in this selfsame day have I brought your hosts out of the land of Egypt; therefore, shall ye observe this day throughout your generations by an ordinance forever. In the first month, on the fourteenth day of the month at even, ye shall eat unleavened bread...And it shall come to pass when your children shall say unto you: 'What mean ye by this service?' That ye shall say: 'It is the sacrifice of the Lord's Passover, for that He passed over the houses of the children of Israel in Egypt, when He smote the Egyptians, and delivered our houses.'...And Moses said unto the people: 'Remember this day, in which ye came out from Egypt, out of the house of bondage...' And thou shalt tell thy son in that day, saying: 'It is because of that which the Lord did for me when I came forth out of Egypt.'"

And Israel remembered: "I am the Lord thy God, who brought thee out of the land of Egypt, out of the house of bondage."

And in evil times Israel prayed for deliverance. And Israel hoped for the Messiah. And Israel remembered these things, especially at Passover. And Rome knew—and feared—that Israel remembered. That is why Pontius Pilate, the Roman procurator of Judaea, left his official residence at Caesarea in Samaria on the Mediterranean Sea, and came with his soldiers to Jerusalem, doubling the military contingent quartered in the Tower of Antonia at the northwest corner of the Temple area.

That Tower, with its access and passageways and walled walks overlooking all parts of the Temple area, served as a silent reminder of Rome's watchful eye and mighty arm and iron fist!

The Temple!

It was said that he who had not seen it had never seen anything beautiful. It stood majestically atop Mount Moriah, proclaiming the majesty of God.

It had risen from humble beginnings. It had started as the Tent of Meeting, the Tabernacle of the Congregation established by Moses and Aaron 1200 years ago during the wanderings in the wilderness. It accompanied the Israelites during those wanderings, and after, for 200 years, when David established his kingdom and brought the Holy Ark to Jerusalem and instructed his son, Solomon, saying:

> "It was in my mind to build an house unto the name of the Lord my God, but the word of the Lord came to me, saying, 'Thou hast shed blood abundantly, and hast made great wars. Thou shalt not build an house unto my name, because thou hast shed much blood upon the earth in my sight.
>
> "'Behold, a son shall be born to thee, who shall be a man of rest, and I will give him rest from all his enemies round about. For his name shall be Solomon, and I will give peace and quietness unto Israel in his days.
>
> "'He shall build an house for My name, and he shall be My son, and I will be his father, and I will establish the throne of his kingdom over Israel forever.'
>
> "Now, My son, the Lord be with thee and prosper thee, and build the house of the Lord thy God, as he hath said of thee."

And Solomon did. And the majestic Temple of Solomon stood atop Mount Moriah for 410 years, until it was razed by Nebuchadnezzar, the Babylonian conqueror, who destroyed Jerusalem and carried Israel into captivity.

And the captives sang their lament, remembering:

> "By the rivers of Babylon,
>
> There we sat down, yea, we wept,
>
> When we remembered Zion…
>
> If I forget thee, O Jerusalem,
>
> Let my right hand forget her cunning.
>
> Let my tongue cleave to the roof of my mouth.
>
> If I remember thee not;
>
> If I set not Jerusalem
>
> Above my chiefest joy!"

Challenged to survive without a homeland and a Temple, Israel created the synagogue, for Israel discovered that the ladder of Jacob reached heaven from anywhere on earth.

Israel survived. Israel returned. Israel built synagogues and rebuilt the Temple.

The second Temple stood 350 years until its foreign defilement by Antiochus Epiphanes, who aroused the wrath of the Maccabees. Spearheading the successful revolt, they restored, purified and rededicated the Temple, commemorated ever since by the Feast of Lights, the Festival of Freedom, Chanukah, the Festival of Rededication. Israel, which was now in bondage to Rome, remembered its glorious freedom under the Maccabees two hundred years ago.

The temple stood as a silent reminder of that glory and of that freedom.

It was the same Temple and yet, in appearance, it was not the same. It had been given its present look by Herod the First, the tyrant-king of Judea who died shortly after Jesus was born. Irreverent towards man and God, Herod, who worshipped power, turned to things of stone for his immortality, believing that he could deceive man and God. He built frantically everywhere. His crowning glory was the restoration of the Temple. He set 18,000 men to work. The edifice had been forty years in the making and had been finished, for all practical purposes, only recently, long after Herod's death.

This, then, was the House of the Lord. Yet Israel knew that neither the Inner Holy of Holies, nor the Temple itself in all its greatness and splendor, could contain the Lord. For the God of Israel could not be contained. The heaven was His throne and earth His footstool. Holy, holy, holy was the Lord of hosts! The whole earth was full of His glory!

And Israel prayed:

> "The earth is the Lord's, and the fullness thereof; the world, and they that dwell therein. For He hath founded it upon the seas, and established it upon the floods. Who shall ascend the mountain of the Lord? And who shall stand in His holy place? He that hath clean hands and a pure heart; who hath not taken my Name in vein, and hath not sworn deceitfully. He shall receive a blessing from the Lord, and righteousness from the God of his salvation."

Israel loved the Torah, and remembered God's words:

> "I give you good doctrine; forsake ye not My Teaching. It is a tree of life to them that grasp it and of them that uphold it, every one is rendered happy. Its ways are ways of pleasantness, and all its paths are peace."

And Israel believed that the day would come when the peoples of the world would join the pilgrimage to Jerusalem as the prophet Isaiah had said:

> "And it shall come to pass in the last days, that the mountain of the Lord's house shall be established in the top of the mountains, and shall be exalted above the hills; and all nations shall flow unto it.
> "And many peoples shall go and say, 'Come ye, and let us go up to the mountain of the Lord, to the house of the God of Jacob; and he will teach us of His ways, and we will walk in His paths.' For out of Zion shall go forth the law, and the word of the Lord from Jerusalem."

How would this come about?

Through the Messiah!

The current writings were full of such talk. The Book of Jubilees, the Ethiopic Book of Enoch, the Psalms of Solomon. These spoke clearly and unmistakably of the Messiah who would come to redeem Israel and establish God's kingdom.

Some turned to the Torah and the prophets and the Holy Writings for word of the Messiah. Isaiah, Jeremiah, Ezekiel, Haggai, Zechariah, Micah. Men searched the words for new meaning and found in them the promise of a messiah, The Messiah.

Some, reading the prophecies, checking the current writings, said he would be an earthly being. Some said he would be a heavenly being. Some said he would be of the House of David, some said he would be David himself. Some said Israel itself would be the Messiah in the household of nations, some said the House of Israel would give birth to the Messiah. Some said the Messiah would reign over the nations. Some said the Messiah would clear the way for God's reign over the nations. Some said God Himself would be the Messiah.

Some said he would come in peace. Some said he would bring war. Some said he would come to judge Israel. Some said he would come to judge the nations of the earth. Some said he would cause Israel to rule over the nations. Some said he would rule over all the nations. Some said he would destroy the heathen nations and drive the foreigners from the land. Some said he would destroy the wicked and redeem the righteous of all nations. Some said he would drive the impious heathen from Jerusalem. Some said he would cause the nations to come to Jerusalem. Some said he would come with power. Some said he would trust in God. Some said he would come in heavenly splendor and glory. Some said he would enter Jerusalem on an ass.

Some said he had already come—that he was Zerubbabel, Cyrus, Alexander. Some said he had not yet come. Some said he would come some day in the future. Some said he was already among them. Some said he would come with the end of the Roman Empire. Some said the end had come.

How it would happen, they did not know. That it would happen, they knew. For God had made a covenant with Abraham so that his seed would be a blessing to the nations. God had chosen Israel as his people, and Israel had chosen God. Israel had chosen to serve, not to rule, to be a blessing, not a curse. Israel had made a covenant with God and man. They had sealed that covenant at Sinai.

Israel knew that in His way and in His time, God would fulfill His promise of the Heavenly Kingdom on earth.

Jesus and his band entered the Temple area by the Fountain Gate, singing:

> "Behold, bless ye the Lord, all ye servants of the Lord,
>
> That stand in the house of the Lord in the night seasons.
>
> Lift up your hands to the sanctuary,
>
> And bless ye the Lord."

"Who is that?" some of the people asked as Jesus passed through the crowds.

"This is the prophet Jesus from Nazareth in Galilee," some told the others.

"It's the Messiah!" some whispered, hardly trusting their eyes.

Some just wondered and waited.

Jesus entered the huge rectangular court of the outer Temple, which served as a public place and which was open to anyone, even Gentiles. Here people strolled and visited and transacted business, out in the open area or under the renowned porticoes with their triple aisles and thirty-six-foot high columns of Solomon's Porch on the east, and the ninety-two-foot high Corinthian columns of the Royal Porch on the south.

Beyond this area of the outer Temple stood the inner Temple, which was off limits to Gentiles on penalty of death. It stood fifty feet higher. Thirteen gates opened into it. Here were the two courts—the Court of Women and the Inner Court.

The Inner Court contained numerous halls, including the Hall of Cut Stone, where the *Great Sanhedrin* met. In this court, too, stood the great altar of burnt offerings, behind which rose the Temple itself—three hundred feet wide, three hundred feet long, and three hundred feet high. It contained three stories of rooms and offices, thirty-eight in all, but beyond that it contained the Sanctum with its shewbread, its seven-branch candlestick and its gold-covered incense altar, where incense was placed twice a day.

Beyond this, almost dark and perpetually silent behind a final curtain, stood the Holy of Holies, which was empty except for a bare rock on which the High Priest, once a year, set the incense on Yom Kippur, the Day of Atonement.

Jesus, like other pilgrims, had arrived today to purchase the lamb on the tenth of Nisan as prescribed in the Torah. The animal would be delivered on the afternoon of the fourteenth, in time for the sacrifice, but this was the day it had to be purchased. They would pay their money and they would get a receipt. But first they had to see the money-changer who converted the various monies of the land and from other lands into the currency of Judea.

Judas approached one of the money-changers. Jesus had asked him to handle the transaction, since he was more familiar with local customs. Jesus and the disciples watched and waited.

The place was noisy with activity. Despite this, Judas' voice suddenly rose above the din. "What's the big idea?" he demanded. "This money is worth more than that!"

"Look," said the money-changer, "I don't have time to argue. I'm busy. Take it or leave it!"

"Last year...," began Judas.

"That was last year!" The money-changer snapped. "Do you want it or not?"

Judas nodded and shot him an angry look. He felt helplessly enraged. They were taking advantage of the situation, and there was nothing anybody could do about it. Judas grabbed the money and went to buy a lamb.

The man who quoted him the price looked startled as Judas pounded the table. "What kind of a thief are you!" Judas shouted. "This is double what it should cost!"

"Easy, easy," said the man, trying to placate Judas. "Maybe where you come from..."

"I come from right here—and I know the price of lamb!"

"Look, I know how you feel," said the man. "If it were up to me, this wouldn't happen. But everything's gone up. Everything costs more, too, so what can I do?"

"Everyone's taking advantage of the situation!" Judas thundered. "Look, I'm a butcher, I know what the price of lamb should be!"

But the man was tired of arguing. "Why don't you shop around!" He sneered.

Suddenly, before Judas had a chance to respond, he felt someone charge past him.

It was Jesus. He took hold of the man's stand and toppled it, and then he rushed at the money-changer and pushed over his table, so that the coins clattered to the ground. The crowd cheered him on, as he lashed about him, upsetting a number of other stands. Finally he stopped and looked challengingly about.

"The Torah says, 'My house shall be called a house of prayer,' but you are making it a robbers' cave!"

Jesus turned his back on the merchants as the people cheered and followed him and assembled to hear what he had to say.

❀   ❀   ❀

Caiaphas rushed from his office in the Inner Court of the Temple to look for Rabban Gamaliel. He sighed with relief to find him outside the Hall of Hewn Stone. Gamaliel had just finished talking to someone and was about to go inside when Caiaphas called him.

"Rabban! Rabban Gamaliel!"

The rabbi stopped when he heard Caiaphas' voice and waited for him. "What's the matter, Caiaphas? You look worried," he said pleasantly.

"Trouble!" Caiaphas puffed. "Big trouble!"

"Oh?"

"Just a little while ago in the Outer Court somebody attacked the sellers and money-changers. A Galilean..."

"Oh, yes, Jesus of Nazareth," Rabban Gamaliel said quietly.

"You know about it?" Caiaphas, asked, astonished.

"Yes."

"How...?"

"I have my sources, just as you," Gamaliel said politely but pointedly.

"Well, something has to be done about it!"

"I agree with you!"

Caiaphas looked surprised and pleased. "Oh?" he asked tentatively.

"Yes, I intend to bring the matter before the Sanhedrin."

"Good! Good!" Caiaphas said, pleased.

"We need some stricter laws—regulating commerce during the holidays!" Gamaliel said.

Caiaphas looked disappointed. "But what about him?" he demanded.

"I'd say he was a bit impulsive," Gamaliel said with a slight smile. "But I must admit his heart was in the right place."

"We just can't let him get away with it! Look at what it's done for him! The way the people...Do you know what they're saying about him?"

"Yes, yes," said Gamaliel, trying to calm the agitated High Priest.

"Well...?"

"All the more reason to proceed cautiously, don't you think? If he has suddenly become that popular with the people, let's not arouse them further and worsen things."

"You're right," said Caiaphas as he thought over Gamaliel's words. "You're right. Who is he, anyway?"

Gamaliel gave him an amused smile. "You should know," he said.

"I?"

"You met him once."

"Never."

"A few years ago, at the home of Nathan ben Reuel," Gamaliel reminded him. "We had dinner there. He's a friend of Judas, whom he came to visit."

Caiaphas tried to recall. "Oh, yes," he said finally. "That one! Well! A friend of Judas, h'm?"

"Yes."

"We must do something!" Caiaphas said determinedly.

"Let's hear what he has to say," said Gamaliel softly.

Caiaphas searched Gamaliel's face as he pondered the suggestion. Gamaliel smiled enigmatically.

"Yes," said Caiaphas, smiling inwardly. "Yes, let's hear what he has to say. Shalom, Rabban."

"Shalom, Caiaphas."

Gamaliel, regarding the retreating figure of Caiaphas, looked troubled.

☙   ☙   ☙

Pontius Pilate had heard the news, too. He was transacting the various affairs of state form his seat in the Tower of Antonia when the commander of the guard entered and hurried towards him.

Pilate, lean, hard, unsmiling, was instantly alert. He watched the soldier approach, salute and wait for permission to speak. Pilate leveled cold, piercing eyes at the man and nodded slightly. The soldier came right to the point.

"A disturbance broke out in the outer Temple. A Galilean attacked the money-changers and sellers of animal sacrifices. The people cheered him on. When he was through they followed him to hear what he had to say. He talks about a kingdom of heaven."

"What else does he say?" Pilate demanded.

"We did not stop to listen too long. We felt you should be informed immediately."

"Damn these Jews!" Pilate said, glad for an occasion to relieve his chronically sour disposition. 'Did you get his name at least?"

"Yes!" exclaimed the guard, relieved. "Jesus, of Nazareth."

Pontius Pilate stared thoughtfully at the soldier without really seeing him. The prolonged silence made the man feel extremely uneasy.

"That will be all," Pontius Pilate said presently, with a grim smile. "Keep an eye on him!"

The commander of the guard saluted and withdrew quickly.

Jesus, too, had withdrawn to Bethany for that day.

CHAPTER 9

Lying in Wait

The next day, Monday, Jesus was back in the Outer Court of the Temple area. Many had come to listen, for word had spread about him. Judas and the disciples, too, stood in the crowd surrounding Jesus.

"The Kingdom of Heaven, therefore, should be thought of in this way," Jesus explained. "There was once a king who decided to settle accounts with the men who served him. At the outset there appeared before him a man whose debt ran into millions. Since he had no means of paying, his master ordered him to be sold to meet the debt with his wife, his children and everything he had. The man fell prostrate at his master's feet.

"'Be patient with me,' he said, 'and I will pay in full.'"

"And the master was so moved with pity that he let the man go and remitted the debt.

"But no sooner had the man gone out than he met a fellow servant who owed him a few pounds. And catching hold of him, he gripped him by the throat and said, 'Pay me what you owe.'

"The man fell at his fellow servant's feet and begged him, 'Be patient with me, and I will pay you.'

"But he refused, and had him jailed until he should pay the debt. The other servants were deeply distressed when they saw what had happened, and they went to their master and told him the whole story. He accordingly sent for the man.

"'You scoundrel!' he said to him. 'I remitted the whole of your debt when you appealed to me. Were you not bound to show your fellow servant the same pity as I showed to you?'

"And so angry was the master that he condemned the man to torture until he should pay the debt in full.

"And that is how my heavenly Father will deal with you, unless you each forgive your brother from your hearts."

The faces and the hearts of the people glowed with understanding. Some nodded to one another.

"Rabbi?" someone asked.

Jesus looked in the direction of the voice, nodded his recognition and waited for the question.

"When will the heavenly kingdom come?" asked the man, adding pointedly. "Is the moment at hand?"

Jesus trembled slightly. He looked about him and paused thoughtfully. Then he said, "Be alert, be wakeful. You do not know when the moment comes. It is like a man away from home. He has left his house and put his servants in charge, each with his own work to do, and he has ordered the door-keeper to stay awake. Keep awake, then, for you do not know when the master of the house is coming. Evening or midnight, cock-crow or early dawn—if he comes suddenly, he must not find you asleep. And what I say to you, I say to everyone—keep awake."

An undercurrent of excitement swept the group as they wondered if the words meant what each thought they meant, for the words were loaded with meaning.

A voice suddenly boomed forth from the crowd, demanding, "Tell us by what authority you are acting like this. Who gave you this authority?"

Judas felt a warning fear in his stomach. Even before he looked around to see the questioner, he knew that the man was not a casual observer. The voice had the ring of authority. Judas did not recognize the man but he felt that he had been sent to challenge and to test Jesus. Judas felt intuitively that there were others present now, too, for the same purpose. He'd be able to tell soon by their questions who they were and who had sent them. Judas was tense but tried to relax, with faith that this was all part of God's plan. He hoped Jesus would meet the test.

Judas regarded Jesus anxiously. For a moment their eyes met and they reassured each other. Then Jesus turned to the questioner and the others who had started to move and mumble restlessly.

Jesus answered, "I have a question to ask you, too! Tell me, was the baptism of John from God or from men?"

Judas smiled with relief at the clever way Jesus had turned the issue, for now the questioner turned to one of the other men and said, "If we say, 'from God,' he will say, 'Why did you not believe in him?'"

And the other man said, "And if we say, 'from men,' the people will stone us, for they are convinced that John was a prophet."

The questioner then turned to Jesus and said, "We cannot tell."

Jesus said, "Neither will I tell you by what authority I act."

Judas recognized the man who spoke. He was a Pharisee, one of the leaders of the community. He was no friend of Gamaliel but of Caiaphas, and of Rome.

"Master," he said, addressing Jesus, "you are an honest man, we know. You teach in all honesty the way of life that God requires, truckling to no man, whoever he may be. Give us your ruling on this: Are we or are we not permitted to pay taxes to the Roman Emperor?"

Jesus smiled wryly, aware of the malicious intention and said angrily, "You hypocrites! Why are you trying to trip me up? Show me the money in which the tax is paid."

Someone handed him a silver piece.

"Whose head is this, and whose inscription?" Jesus asked.

"Caesar's," someone said.

Jesus turned to the speaker and the crowd, saying, "Then pay Caesar what is due to Caesar, and pay God what is due to God."

The answer took everyone by surprise. Judas smiled with relief. He noticed, though, that some of the people were leaving. He wondered why. It disturbed him.

Then another man spoke, obviously a Sadducee, with Caiaphas pulling the strings. Caiaphas seemed afraid of Gamaliel, because the question was meant to discredit Jesus in the eyes of the Pharisees. Caiaphas would stump Jesus on the resurrection of the dead. If Jesus denied it, he'd be out of favor with the Pharisees and Gamaliel. If he believed in the resurrection, he was bound to fumble the answer, being a dumb Galilean. This, too, would discredit him with the Pharisaic scholars and, for that matter, the Sadducees. The people, too, would get the point—and the whole thing would blow over by the time Pontius Pilate got wind of it, as he would, inevitably. Caiaphas was in good standing with Rome and this would prove it again. It was a tricky question.

"Master," said the Sadducee, "Moses said, 'If a man should die childless, his brother shall marry the widow and carry on his brother's family.' Now we knew of seven brothers. The first married and died, and as he was without issue, his wife was left to his brother. The same thing happened with the second, and the third, and so on with all seven. Last of all, the woman died. At the resurrection, then, whose wife will she be, for they had all married her?"

Jesus answered, "You are mistaken, because you know neither the Scriptures nor the power of God. At the resurrection men and women do not marry, but are like angels in heaven. About the resurrection of the dead, have you never read what God himself said to you? 'I am the God of Abraham, the God of Isaac and the God of Jacob.' He is not God of the dead, but of the living!"

The people smiled at the clever way Jesus handled that one.

A group of Pharisees had been listening. One of them came up now and asked, "Which commandment is first of all?"

Jesus replied without hesitation, 'The first is, 'Hear O Israel: the Lord is our God, the Lord is One. And you shall love the Lord your God with all your heart, with all your soul, and with all your strength.' The second is: 'Love your neighbor as yourself.' There is no other commandment greater than these."

The Pharisees looked pleased, for this was what their great teacher Hillel had taught only a few years earlier.

"Well, said, Master," the Pharisee answered. "You are right in saying that God is one and beside Him there is no other. And to love Him with all your heart, all your understanding and all your strength, and to love your neighbor as yourself—that is far more than any burnt offerings or sacrifices."

Jesus smiled and said, "You are not far from the kingdom of God."

At this moment Jesus happened to look through the Beautiful Gate into the Inner Court, the First Court, where stood the thirteen trumpets for the Temple offering. Some of the rich had been offering their gifts and suddenly Jesus noticed a poor widow dropping two coins into the receptacle.

The crowd had been following Jesus' gaze and saw what he saw.

"I tell you this," he said. "This poor widow has given more than any of them. For those others who have given had more than enough, but she, with less than enough, has given all she had to live on."

A feeling of fury suddenly overwhelmed him, as it had done so often when confronted with the injustices perpetrated against the meek and helpless of the world, and all that pent-up feeling exploded once more as he denounced the good with the bad, declaring, "Beware of the scholars who love to walk up and down in long robes, and have a great liking for respectful greetings in the street, the chief seats in our synagogues, and places of honor at feasts. These are the men who eat up the property of widows, while they say long prayers for appearance's sake. And they will receive the severest sentence.

"Alas for you, scribes and Pharisees, hypocrites! You pay tithes of mint and dill and cumin. But you have overlooked the weightier demands of the Torah—justice, mercy and good faith. It is these you should have practiced, without neglecting the others. Blind guides! You strain off a midge, yet gulp down a camel!

"Alas for you scribes and Pharisees, hypocrites! You clean the outside of cup and dish, which you have filled inside by robbery and self-indulgence! Blind Pharisees! Clean the inside of the cup first. Then the outside will be clean also.

"Alas for you, scribes and Pharisees, hypocrites! You are like tombs covered with whitewash. They look well from outside, but inside they are full of dead men's bones and all kinds of filth. So it is with you: outside you look like honest men, but inside you are brim-full of hypocrisy and crime.

"Alas for you, scribes and Pharisees, hypocrites! You build up the tombs of the prophets and embellish the monuments of the saints, and you say, 'If we had been alive in our fathers' time, we should never had taken part with them in the murder of the prophets.' So you acknowledge that you are the sons of men who killed the prophets. Go on, then, finish off what your fathers began!

"You snakes, you vipers' brood, how can you escape being condemned to hell? I send you therefore prophets, sages and teachers. Some of them you will kill, others you will flog in your synagogues and hound from city to city. And so, on you will fall the guilt of all the innocent blood spilt on the ground, from innocent Abel to Zachariah, son of Berachiah, whom you murdered between the sanctuary and the altar. Believe me, this generation will bear the guilt of it all.

"O Jerusalem, Jerusalem, the city that murders the prophets and stones the messengers sent to her! How often have I longed to gather your children, as a hen gathers her brood under her wings. But you would not let me. Look, look! There is your Temple, forsaken by God. And I tell you, you shall never see me until the time when you say, 'Blessings on him who comes in the name of the Lord.'"

The crowd was stunned.

The people who, only a little while ago, had sided with him in their hearts, as this simple Galilean bested the scholars and authorities, were disturbed now in their feelings.

But the authorities knew now how they themselves felt, and they withdrew, just as Jesus withdrew, to Bethany.

Judas stayed behind.

Judas, too, was stunned. All he could figure was that Jesus had not expected this kind of reception. Or had he? He had used strong words. Very strong words. What had he hoped to gain? What would happen now? Judas tried hard to think clearly. Why had he stayed behind?

"He sure let 'em have it, didn't he?" a short fat man said nearby, chuckling over the incident. "I liked the way he talked."

"He sure lost me!" said a thin one.

The conversation drifted over to Judas, who now found himself eavesdropping.

"What do you mean?" asked the Fat One.

"The way he lashed into the scribes and Pharisees!"

'Some of them deserve it, that's all I can say!" the Fat Man bristled.

"Some of them, sure," said the Thin Man. "But the way he talked, none of them are any good!"

"Look," reasoned the Fat Man. "He's talking like a prophet—they always talked like that!"

"Well," said the Thin Man, "I don't like it! You know that the Pharisees are the best friends we have. And the way he talked about the Temple—'forsaken by God.' That's pretty arrogant, if you ask me."

"Look, he talks like the prophets," said the Fat One, adding confidentially, 'Some say he's more than a prophet!"

The two exchanged knowing glances.

"I was almost ready to believe that," said the Thin One. "The way he talked! I felt real strange inside, as if…you know. He touched my heart and almost made me want to cry. I felt hope! And then this kind of talk…"

"What's wrong with it? I tell you…"

"I'll tell you what's wrong with it," said the Thin One. "It sounds big but it's cowardly. It doesn't take much guts to attack the scribes and Pharisees and Sadducees. In fact, it's nerve…"

"It's not!" interrupted the Fat One. "There's nothing impudent about it. Somebody's got to tell them off—they're not angels. Besides, look at the way they tried tricking him. I can't blame him."

"They, they?" said the Thin One angrily. "Why does it have to be everybody all the time? Okay, so the Saducess tried to trick him, but the Pharisees, except for that one, were very courteous and approving of what he had to say. Anyway, you never let me finish…"

"About what?"

"His lack of guts!"

"What do you mean?" asked the Fat One.

"If he really is who some think he is, he should denounce Rome and drive Pilate out of here!"

"What makes you think he won't?" the Fat One asked.

"The way he double-talked!"

"What do you mean?"

'The slippery way he said, 'Render unto Caesar the things that are Caesar's,' et cetera, et cetera, et cetera. He was sure hedging on that one. I would expect him to tell Caesar where to get off in no uncertain terms!"

"Look, maybe he will, and more!" said the Fat One, winking knowingly.

The Thin One stared at him for a moment. "What do you mean?"

"Sometimes," said the Fat One, "you gotta play it smart, the way he did. You know, keep 'em from suspecting anything. So what's he do? He pretends to be all upset about the Pharisees and the scribes and the Sadducees, and what not, and that's just fine with Pilate, because he couldn't care one bit. So, the Romans don't worry. But it's just clever strategy. When the right moment comes, POW!—he'll let the Romans have it!"

"Well…"

"Look," said the Fat One eagerly, "do you see this?" He uncovered the folds of his robe, revealing, for an instant, the glistening blade of a dagger which he quickly covered up again. "I'm not the only one who's got one of these," he said conspiratorially. "There are a lot of us, waiting for the signal!"

The Thin One was intrigued. "How do you know he'll give it?" he asked.

"I have it on good authority!"

"Whose?"

"I can't tell you," said the Fat One.

"Are you sure?"

"Sure I'm sure," he smiled. "Remember what he said?"

"What?"

"'Keep awake!'"

"Oh!" said the Thin One.

'He's dumb, like a fox!" the Fat One said, and winked.

"Maybe you're right," said the Thin One, and smiled.

They walked off and disappeared in the crowd.

Having heard all there was to hear, Judas was about to leave, too. Suddenly he heard someone call him by name.

"Judas!"

He turned in the direction of the voice. It was Barabbas.

Judas was startled. "Shalom!" he said.

"Shalom!" said Barabbas, and smiled. "You look surprised."

"It's just that…"

"Don't explain," said Barabbas, smiling. "Besides, this is a terrible place to talk. Let's go to my place."

'Well, I…"

Barabbas stopped smiling. 'Come!" he said, with quiet, compelling forcefulness.

Judas felt drawn to obey.

❀   ❀   ❀

Pontius Pilate waited impatiently, his fingers drumming on the arm of his chair. He was alone in the room, as he had ordered. Suddenly the door opened and the person he had waited for entered.

It was a strange sight. To all appearances the man looked undistinguished, like an ordinary Israelite. As he drew closer, he removed the covering that veiled part of his face. Pilate smiled, despite the urgency of the situation.

"Hail Caesar!"

Pilate returned the salute. "Hail Caesar!" he answered.

"I came as fast as I could."

"Good, Flavius."

It was the man who had befriended Eliezer ben Jochanan, Mary's pimp, the day of her dramatic encounter with Jesus in Magdala.

"What's the situation?" Pilate asked.

"He's been teaching in the Temple area. He has a lot of potential followers. The people are sympathetic. They're ready! The leaders seem more skeptical. The Sadducees have tried to discredit him, without noticeable success. The Pharisees test him, but they are not unfriendly. He attacked them publicly, which may have alienated some, but, at best, they're just laying off. The situation looks threatening."

"You are sure?"

"He claims to be the Messiah!"

"Has he said so?" Pilate asked.

"Through his actions, ever since Jericho. It's coming to a head now, and Rome is the target. It's been spelled out clearly in their writings. Not the Temple, not the Saducees, not the scribes or Pharisees, but Rome is to be destroyed, and driven from the land! You are Rome! The Messiah will destroy the heathen and drive them from the land. It's part of his 'Divine Mission'!"

"The people are armed!" Pilate declared.

"Yes."

"I will deal with him!"

'He is staying in Bethany. Shall I..."

"No," said Pilate thoughtfully. "I have a plan. This time things will go flawlessly. I didn't handle these Jews right on a couple of occasions when I first came here. Those were exercises for this one! So you see, Flavius, mistakes can be very valuable, if we are willing to learn from them. This time I will make no mistakes. Within a week Jesus of Nazareth will be forgotten. He will be a memory only to his mother!"

"Shall I proceed as planned with the other matter?"

"Can you trust..."

"...Eliezer ben Jochanan? He has been paid well. And I can trust his hate!"

"Proceed!"

The audience was over. Flavius saluted. "Hail Caesar!"

"You have served your country well. You shall be well rewarded. Caesar shall hear of it. Hail Caesar!"

Flavius beamed appreciatively and left.

❦   ❦   ❦

"So," beamed Barabbas. 'The moment's finally at hand!"

Judas did not know how to answer. He looked away from Barabbas and stared at the floor. They were alone in the room.

"Come now," laughed Barabbas. "You and I don't have to play games!"

"I'm not playing games," Judas said defensively.

"Look!" Barabbas said firmly now. "I've been getting my reports. I've been watching his progress. I know who he is and what he has come to do. I have not made contact till now because I wanted to be sure. I am sure now. I want you to tell him that he can be sure of us."

"Us?"

"The people have their daggers on them, night and day, and there are enough of us to take on the Romans," Barabbas said feverishly. 'We have come armed. We are ready for his signal—any time!"

Judas was staggered by what he heard. "He has no intention of using violence!" he finally stammered out.

Barabbas smiled tolerantly. "Did he give you that assurance?" he asked, amused.

"He has preached love, giving, forgiveness," Judas said fiercely. "He has preached peace. Never once did he say anything about war!"

"Did he give you that assurance?" Barabbas again pressed.

"No, but…"

"Then tell him we are ready."

'He's not interested!" Judas exclaimed.

"Do you know his thoughts?"

"No."

"God has always sent him the right answers. Perhaps this is the word he is waiting for now. Perhaps this is part of your role, to carry the message to him. Can you refuse this role? Look, all you have to do is tell him what I said!"

"I didn't expect this!"

"What did you expect—that Pilate would step aside peacefully? Look, just don't worry about the details. Let God worry about those."

Judas looked troubled.

"Look, Judas," Barabbas said patiently. "Don't worry. Things will work out. It's all part of God's plan."

But before they had a chance to continue, their attention was distracted by the rhythmic sound of footsteps which were close by and which suddenly seemed to come to a halt outside the house.

Before Judas or Barabbas could react, a handful of men spilled into the room. They were Roman soldiers, except for Eliezer ben Jochanan.

"Shalom, Barabbas!" he said, in order to identify Barabbas.

Barabbas looked at the soldiers who were poised to seize him. The situation was hopeless. Suddenly he leaped at Eliezer ben Jochanan. "Traitor!" He screamed, as he whipped the dagger out of his belt and drove it into the man's heart.

A split-second later the soldiers had disarmed and subdued the Zealot leader. Eliezer looked up incredulously, clutching the dagger feebly. Then he fell back and lay still.

Judas had not moved. He tried to blend into the wall but he felt utterly exposed.

"What about him?" one of the soldiers asked, indicating Judas.

"We've got our man," said the one in charge. "Let's go."

The next minute they were gone.

Judas could not move or stop trembling. Things were happening so fast suddenly that it was hard to grasp everything fully. The corpse convinced him of the reality of the situation. Suddenly he wanted to get out. He had to find Jesus.

Judas rushed out of the room and bumped into Flavius, who had watched the arrest from a strategic position.

"Eliezer?" Flavius exclaimed, mistaking Judas for the informer.

"In there!" Judas exclaimed, terror in his eyes.

"Oh!" said Flavius as Judas rushed away. Flavius smiled, pleased. He recognized Judas as one of the disciples. He had moved in the nick of time. But he knew from Judas' look that something had gone wrong. He moved quickly to the house and looked inside. He saw Eliezer lying on the floor in a pool of blood, obviously dead.

There was nothing now that Flavius could do for the informer, even if he had wanted to. Flavius shrugged his shoulders.

Well, he thought, the man had served his purpose. It was just as well this way.

Flavius left and melted into the crowded street.

CHAPTER 10

Rome Speaks

Caiaphas was on his way to see Pontius Pilate. It was Tuesday. Caiaphas planned to bring up the "incident" involving the "irregular" arrest of Barabbas the previous day.

But that, of course, was not the chief reason for seeing the Roman procurator.

Caiaphas was on his way to ask for his vestments which he needed to officiate during the Passover ceremonies. Pilate kept them under lock and key in the Tower of Antonia. It was his way of controlling the High Priest, the spiritual and political head and symbol of the country, so that he, in turn, would control the people—and do Rome's bidding.

For a fleeting moment, as he went to beg for his vestments, Caiaphas felt keenly reminded of the truth and indignity of the situation. But he had lived with it now longer than any High Priest before him, since the late Herod I began manipulating the high priestly office. There had been a new High Priest every four years, and Caiaphas was the thirteenth. Unlike the others, he had lasted some dozen years now, going back even prior to Pilate.

When he was honest with himself, Caiaphas admitted that he enjoyed the power, prosperity, privileges and prestige that went with the position. But aside from such selfish motives, Caiaphas felt deserving of his position. He reasoned that through his talents at diplomacy, he was giving his people and his country what other High Priests before him were unable to achieve—stability. Once the High Priest had held office a lifetime. Now he ruled only at the discretion of the political superior. Caiaphas hoped to extend what had become a privilege into the fact of a lifetime. He had forgotten, or overlooked, one other difference between the old and the new—these days the office of the High Priest was no longer hereditary. It was for sale!

Caiaphas had sent word earlier seeking an audience with Pilate. He had no difficulty getting past the various Roman guards. Besides, they knew who he was. His visits were familiar to them.

After being announced, Caiaphas entered the room and approached Pilate.

"Peace!" he exclaimed, bowing to Pilate. "Shalom!"

"Hail Caesar!" Pilate exclaimed, smiling faintly. "Sit down, sit down!"

"Thank you, Governor," Caiaphas said as he sat down.

He noticed that they were alone and that Pilate seemed to be in a good, perhaps even pleasant, mood. Caiaphas, who wasn't sure how or whether to bring up the matter of Barabbas at all, felt encouraged now that he might be able to discuss it at the proper moment.

"It is the time of the Passover," said Caiaphas, knowing that Pilate liked to come to the point. "I would like to respectfully request, if it please your Eminence, the release of my vestments so that I may officiate over this festival in the tradition of my people."

"Of course, of course, my friend and High Priest Caiaphas," Pilate said cordially. "They've been under lock and key, since the last time. They're in perfect order. You'll find nothing amiss. Sometimes it strikes me as such a needless arrangement, between you and me, which it obviously is, a mere formality."

Caiaphas smiled and bowed graciously.

"I am glad to have enjoyed such a long and pleasant relationship with your country and I have tried to be of service to both our peoples," Caiaphas said ingratiatingly.

"You talk as if you're about to resign," Pilate chided with mock seriousness.

"Oh, no, no," Caiaphas exclaimed, laughing nervously. "I trust that this relationship will continue a long time."

"I trust it will," said Pilate. "How long have you held office now?"

"Going on a dozen years, longer than any of my predecessors," Caiaphas said proudly. "They held office for four years, on average, since the reign of Herod I."

"A great man—Herod the Great—and a great friend of Rome!"

'Indeed," Caiaphas agreed.

"Did you consider him cruel?" Pilate asked.

'I was a child…"

"On the basis of what you have heard."

"It has been said he was a tyrant," Caiaphas said.

"Some of your people have said that, yes," said Pilate. "What do you say?"

Caiaphas knew that the question was more than casual, though Pilate still spoke pleasantly enough.

"I say that kings cannot be subjects, and subjects, kings."

Pilate looked pleased.

"I like that," he said. "Yes, I like that. What holiday is this again?"

While Caiaphas was pleased with the compliment, he was annoyed by the question. He was sure Pilate knew as well as he. It was a custom of his, though. It was not so much the question as the contempt contained in it that annoyed the High Priest.

"Passover," said Caiaphas politely, hiding whatever feelings he had.

"Oh, yes, yes," said Pilate. "And that commemorates what again—the birth, death and resurrection of your god, isn't it?"

Caiaphas felt outraged at the delicious cruelty of the question, but he knew better than to speak out in righteous indignation.

"We believe in one God, the uncreated Creator of Heaven and Earth who was, who is and who will be for ever and ever, from eternity to eternity. Passover, your Eminence, commemorates Israel's deliverance from Egyptian bondage through Moses, God's servant. It is our festival of…freedom!"

"You make it sound like a challenge!" Pilate said challengingly.

"That was not my intention, Governor, truly it wasn't," Caiaphas said appeasingly.

"I felt that you were drawing a parallel between Egypt and Rome!"

"I beg your humble pardon if I gave that impression," Caiaphas scraped. "I meant only to recount a historical fact."

"And the resultant moral of political freedom!" Pilate declared.

"For one purpose only, to attain religious freedom," Caiaphas replied quickly. "And that is how we view the holiday these days. The main concern of our people is religious, not political, and, so long as we enjoy religious freedom, we are not concerned about the political conditions of the time. To be plain, we are grateful to Rome for permitting us religious freedom."

"It is reassuring to have your reassurance in this matter," Pilate said, smiling slightly.

"May I remind you that you have always enjoyed that," Caiaphas said, hoping to strengthen his case.

"Pilate needs no reminding!" the Governor snapped angrily. "Dead friends are no shield against living foes."

"You have my loyalty."

"Good."

Caiaphas thought of Barabbas. Perhaps, under the circumstances, it was best to drop the matter.

"What's on your mind?" Pilate asked incisively.

Caiaphas dismissed the matter quickly.

"Nothing," he declared eagerly. "Nothing at all."

"How we have strayed from the matter that brought you here!" Pilate said insincerely. "The vestments certainly are at your disposal."

"Thank you, Governor," Caiaphas said, relieved. "I shall have them picked up today, let's say about…"

"One small matter," Pilate interrupted casually.

"Yes?" Caiaphas asked generously.

"Jesus."

"Jesus?"

"Get rid of him!"

Caiaphas stared in stunned disbelief at Pilate, who stared back with cold, stony eyes.

"What do you mean?" Caiaphas asked, trembling.

"You have four perfectly good ways—stoning, burning, slaying or strangulation," said Pilate emotionlessly. "Any one will do."

"Kill him? How?"

"I've just told you how!"

"Why?"

"Because I said so!" thundered Pilate. "I do not render an accounting to Jews—only to Caesar!"

"But the legalities!"

"Don't bother me with Jewish details, Priest!" Pilate exclaimed, his voice menacing. "That's for you to figure out. Or do I have to do everything myself?"

Caiaphas seized this straw desperately.

"Perhaps it would be better if you handled this…important…matter. It would be quicker!" Caiaphas suggested overeagerly.

"Like Barabbas?"

Caiaphas did not recognize the trap.

"Yes," he said eagerly. "Like Barabbas!"

"Why were you asleep?" screamed Pilate.

"I…we…," stuttered Caiaphas.

'If I hadn't been kept informed by my own people and if I hadn't moved quickly, there'd be blood in the streets today—yours and mine!" Pilate exclaimed. "It was up to you to handle that matter! That's what I've got you for! What do you think I'm interested in—how impressive you appear or how well you pray? I want to know what goes on and I want you to handle trouble before it is trouble, your way!"

"I'm sure he won't give us trouble," said Caiaphas. "I'm convinced Jesus…!"

"You'll make certain!" exclaimed Pilate.

Caiaphas stood silent, motionless.

"Rome," said Pilate sarcastically, "prides itself on respecting the spiritual integrity of its territories. It is out of such respect that I turn the matter over to you. I am aware that my hasty actions, on occasion, do not meet with the full understanding or approval of your people. I know that the arrest of Barabbas has not received popular support or understanding. I do act impulsively from time to time. Therefore, I turn this other matter over to you, so it will be possible to observe the legal proprieties. I am keenly aware of Jewish concern for justice."

Caiaphas crumbled.

"I will send for the vestments," he said spiritlessly.

"Tomorrow!" Pilate said.

"Tomorrow?" Caiaphas asked.

"After your next visit—tomorrow!" Pilate said with unmistakable finality.

"Tomorrow," Caiaphas said, capitulating.

'Hail Caesar!" Pilate said cynically, dismissing Caiaphas.

"Shalom," said Caiaphas.

He turned and walked out sadly. It was Passover, but his spirit was enslaved. He was in bondage to Pharaoh.

The *Great Sanhedrin* had been in session since the morning sacrifice. It met regularly in the Hall of Hewn Stone, within the inner Temple area, in the extreme north of the priests' hall. Though there were forerunners and though some traced the institution to the time of Moses, it was established in its present form some 170 years ago with the Hasmonean dynasty, following the Maccabean War of Liberation. Then the *Great Sanhedrin* served as the supreme political and religious body of the land.

The Pharisees had assumed permanent control of the institution some 100 years ago, and though the *Great Sanhedrin* was stripped of its political authority during the recent reign of Herod I, it was still the chief legislative body in all religious matters. In exceptional cases it acted as a judicial court. The *Great Sanhedrin* defined the law for the small twenty-three-man religious sanhedrin in the land, but it was not an appellate court for them.

Violations coming under the religious law were tried by these smaller *sanhedrin*, whose twenty-three members had the power of imposing the death sentence.

Jerusalem's small *sanhedrin* was composed of twenty-three members of the *Great Sanhedrin* sitting for judicial rather than legislative purposes. Heading the *Great Sanhedrin* was Rabban Gamaliel, who was speaking now.

"I propose," said Rabban Gamaliel, addressing the seventy-one members, "that a study be made by the appropriate committee with a view to corrective legislation governing unethical holiday price practices, especially in the Temple precincts. Discussion?"

There was general agreement.

"So ordered," Gamaliel ruled. He was about to proceed to the next order of business when a Temple messenger entered and approached him, whispering a message to him. It was obvious that Gamaliel did not appreciate the interruption, but the matter seemed serious, judging from the fact that he turned to the senior member present to preside in his absence.

Gamaliel left the Hall of Hewn Stone and headed for the High Priest's quarters. Caiaphas was pacing up and down nervously, as Gamaliel entered.

"I'm sorry for interrupting your meeting," said Caiaphas, "but the matter couldn't wait. Will you have something to eat?"

'No, thank you," Gamaliel said, noting the mere formality of the offer. It was obvious that Caiaphas was too agitated to think about food and anxious to get on with the discussion.

"Sit down," Caiaphas said.

Gamaliel sat down as Caiaphas continued pacing.

"Something must be done, about Jesus!" Caiaphas exclaimed.

So that's it, thought Gamaliel.

"Oh," he said. "Why?"

Caiaphas could barely control himself and speak reasonably.

"He's a threat to the nation's security!" he said angrily.

"What do you have in mind?" Gamaliel asked quietly.

"May I speak bluntly?" Caiaphas asked.

"Please do."

"Death."

'Oh," said Gamaliel, laughing wryly. "What a delightful idea. I'm sure you'll find him happy to oblige. Have you informed him yet of your thoughtful plan?"

"Please!" said Caiaphas impatiently. "This is no laughing matter…"

'I'm sure he won't find it very funny!"

"It's serious!"

"Obviously!" said Gamaliel. "You do seem to have very strong feelings in the matter."

Caiaphas sighed deeply.

"Not I," he said softly. "Pilate!"

"Oh!" said Gamaliel, surprised.

"I just came from him," said Caiaphas.

"Now there's a charming idea," said Gamaliel sarcastically. "Perhaps he suggested how, too?"

Caiaphas misunderstood.

"He didn't specify—he left the choice up to us."

"What a just and understanding man!" Gamaliel said angrily. "What's your pleasure?"

Caiaphas, who was agitated enough over the whole issue, now erupted over Gamaliel's biting remarks, which became unbearable.

"Don't act so pious!" he shouted, getting red with anger. "If it weren't for you, this would never have happened!"

Gamaliel was taken aback by the unexpected attack.

"Me?" he asked.

"You—all of you! That's what comes of not leaving the Torah alone, as it was meant to be! No, you wouldn't listen to us. 'The Sadducees this' and 'the Sadducees that'—we were too strict, we were too literal, we refused to change with the times, we were so anxious to preserve the letter of the law that we killed its spirit! So what did you Pharisees do? You interpreted and re-interpreted and interpreted again! You bent and stretched and turned and twisted until you could find anything and everything in Scripture—including the Messiah! You've infested the people with a Messianic madness! Their minds are on fire with fantasy, and there is fever in the land! Jesus is your madness, not ours! You breathed life into him! Now you can snuff him out!"

Gamaliel bridled his feelings. He was terribly calm, and he stared at Caiaphas with cold, deadly eyes.

"What would you propose?" he asked evenly.

Caiaphas was still breathing heavily.

"Haul him before the *Great Sanhedrin*!" he said harshly.

Gamaliel sneered.

"May I remind the High Priest," he said, "that the *Great Sanhedrin* can only sit in judgment in cases involving the ruler of a region, the king or the High Priest. The court can consider treason. Jesus fits none of these classifications. Oh, yes, one more. We can try a false prophet, but I would remind the High Priest that the age of prophecy ended with Malachi, some four hundred years ago. Besides, Jesus has made no such claim."

Gamaliel's manner irritated Caiaphas, especially since he knew that when it came to matters of the Law, he was no match for the scholar.

"All right, forget the Great Sanhedrin," Caiaphas said angrily. "Haul him before the small *sanhedrin*, then."

"It's not that simple," Gamaliel mused, as if seriously considering the subject. "We have other matters on the calendar. Besides, it takes time to prepare for a trial. Anyway, we would need two consecutive days for the trial, when the death penalty is involved—one day for the trial, the following day for deciding the issue, since this is not permitted the same day as the trial. What with the holiday coming up, we could not take a chance of running out of time. As you know, it is against the law to have the Sabbath or a holiday intervene between the two days involved."

"You could still make it, if you tried!" said Caiaphas impatiently.

"On what charges?" Gamaliel asked.

You can find something to get him on!"

Gamaliel laughed bitterly.

"Let's see, now," he said wryly, pretending to consider various charges. "Plucking corn on the Sabbath? He didn't do that, his disciples did. His indifference to the laws of purity? At worst this would make him a Pharisee in bad standing, but no harm done, otherwise. Healing on the Sabbath? A controversial point, true! Perhaps you could get him on this, if you could produce witnesses. But since it happened in Galilee…! What else is there? Oh, yes, he does forgive sins. So do the Essenes, and so have I, on occasion. It does wonders for people! Some say he drives out devils with the aid of Beelzebub. Try and prove that some time! He doesn't fast! Not everyone fasts on the minor fast days. He leads men to idolatry? Hardly!"

"What about the way he attacked the Temple?" Caiaphas exclaimed angrily.

"Bad, bad!" said Gamaliel. "Very undiplomatic! It puts him in such bad company as Jeremiah and Ezekiel. Anything else?"

"Make it blasphemy or something!" declared the High Priest.

"Perhaps you have better sources than I!"

"What do you mean?"

"No one has ever told me that he has gone around cursing God or pronouncing the Ineffable Name. Perhaps you can enlighten me!"

Caiaphas bristled.

"He causes people to think he is the son of God, the Messiah! Isn't that enough?"

'Yes," Gamaliel said with a sad, gentle smile.

"Well?" asked Caiaphas.

"We have never punished anyone for that," Gamaliel said quietly, "and we are not about to start now."

"Perhaps you consider him the Messiah!" Caiaphas said sarcastically.

"It's not a question of what I consider him to be," Gamaliel said fiercely. "It's a question of justice—whether he is actually the Messiah or just a poor disturbed soul. Just between you and me, none of the above charges, even if they were true, would be punishable by death, for the most part. Lashes, maybe, but not death. If you want something to tell Pilate, tell him that the Torah is a tree of life, not death!"

"You are very eloquent in front of me!" said Caiaphas sarcastically. "But problems are not solved with eloquence, only with action. Remember that we are dealing with Pilate, and Pilate is not squeamish about spilling blood. On previous occasions he did not act so diplomatically. This time he has given us a choice: Jesus, or who knows how many! Let's talk reason now rather than rhetoric—it's better to let one person die than cause a whole nation to perish!"

Gamaliel met Caiaphas' gaze squarely. His look and his words expressed the unbridgeable difference between them.

"Then let us all be killed, rather than deliver one soul of Israel!" Rabban Gamaliel said with quiet fervor.

The two men had nothing more to say to each other. Gamaliel left Caiaphas to his troubled thoughts.

CHAPTER 11

Judas

It was Wednesday. They had been here four days now, thought Judas, as his eyes took in the activity in the outer Temple area. He was only half-listening to Jesus, who was addressing a group of listeners.

Judas was sure, almost from the way he spoke now, that Jesus was aware of the waning interest in his words. He had caused a lot of excitement the first two days. He still had listeners, but not as many any more.

Judas wondered why. He felt that the authorities had had something to do with it, in part. People are cautious, by nature, he thought. They may like what they hear, but if it comes to them in an unaccustomed way, they'll look for permission before they'll embrace what they like. If the leaders say no, the people back off. At best, the authorities had left Jesus alone; at worst, they had challenged him. The people took their cue from this.

Something more was involved, though, Judas felt. Those who had turned away and those who were still sympathetic wondered the same thing that Judas was wondering—how and when was something going to happen? Not just talk, but action! Big action! That would be the turning point for all concerned, regardless of the many changeable moods of the moment.

"But what do you think about this?" Jesus was saying. "A man had two sons. He went to the first and said, 'My boy, go and work today in the vineyard.' 'I will sir,' the boy replied, but never went.

"The father came to the second and said the same. 'I will not,' he replied, but afterwards he changed his mind and went. Which of these two did as his father wished?"

"The second," someone answered.

Then Jesus replied, "I tell you this—tax-gatherers and prostitutes are entering the kingdom of God ahead of you. For when John came to show you the right way to live, you did not believe him, but the tax-gatherers and prostitutes did. And even when you had seen that, you did not change your minds and believe him."

At that moment Judas felt someone tap him on the shoulder.

"Judas!"

Judas looked around and recognized Joseph ben Yehuda, one of the Levites of the Temple, whom he remembered.

"Joseph!" Judas said, surprised. "Shalom!"

"Shalom!" said Joseph.

Judas felt strange. He wondered what Joseph wanted. He did not have to wait long.

"Caiaphas wants to see you," the Levite said.

"Caiaphas!" Judas exclaimed, shocked at the thought.

"Yes."

"Why?"

"He did not tell me."

"When?"

"Now."

Judas trembled. His mind raced furiously. It's about Jesus, he thought. I know, it's about Jesus. What does he want with me? I don't have to go, nobody can make me go. I'll refuse. That's what I'll do—I'll refuse. He won't come after me. He won't force me to come. I'll say no, that's all I have to do. I'll say no.

Joseph looked at him curiously. "Come," he said. "I'll take you."

Maybe I should go, thought Judas. Maybe I must go. Maybe I'm meant to go. Yes, maybe that's what God has in mind for me. Maybe that's part of the plan. Maybe it was all a deception—that other stuff—to throw Rome off balance. Maybe something's in the works. Maybe they know who Jesus really is. Maybe they're making contact now! That's it, thought Judas, that's it! It's the next step!

"All right," he said to Joseph, smiling enigmatically. "Let's go!"

The two slipped away quietly. At that moment Jesus noticed Judas disappearing.

❧   ❧   ❧

Caiaphas greeted Judas cordially as he entered the room. "Shalom, Judas," he said. 'It's good to see you again in Jerusalem."

"Shalom," said Judas tentatively, trying to penetrate the High Priest's enigmatic look.

"Sit down, sit down," said Caiaphas, waving Judas to a chair.

Judas sat down and the High Priest sat down opposite him. "You've been away a long time," said Caiaphas, trying for friendly informality.

"Yes," said Judas.

'Have you seen your parents since you've been back?"

"No," said Judas, slightly on edge, wondering if this was the purpose of the meeting.

"You must go see them—they've missed you," said Caiaphas, adding almost casually, "Have you been with Jesus all this time?"

Judas' heart skipped with excitement. We're coming to the point quickly, thought Judas. Good.

"Most of the time," he said. "I worked in Magdala at first."

"Good, good," said Caiaphas sympathetically. "Sometimes it's good to get away from home for a while, hard as it may be and difficult as it may be to understand. Parents have a hard time sometimes understanding, don't they?"

"Yes."

"Well, between you and me, Judas, I have a feeling that what you did was meant to be—and your parents will understand that, too, soon!"

Judas listened eagerly as Caiaphas shot him a significant look before continuing. "Sometimes we do things for whatever reason and only in time do we realize the importance and the far-reaching consequences of our actions. Sometimes what we do for purely limited, personal reasons becomes part of...the Divine Plan. Do you follow me?"

"Yes," said Judas, hardly daring to breathe.

"You and Jesus were meant to meet—can you believe that?"

"With all my heart!" Judas declared, his emotions welling up within him.

"I believe that, too, Judas," said Caiaphas, "and I believe we were meant to meet today. Now. Here. We are meeting for nothing less than to do God's will. It is an enormous trust!"

"I will do my best," Judas said softly.

"Good," said Caiaphas gravely. "This is the great moment of your life, Judas—the moment you have been preparing for all these years, without ever knowing it. You may have sensed it without ever knowing when or how it would happen. True?"

"Yes," said Judas quietly. "I have always felt that...God...had something special in mind for me."

"He has, Judas. God needs you. I...we...Israel...your people...your nation...OUR people...need you!"

Judas felt the divine spark responding within him. He was too moved for words.

"You must be our link!"

"With Jesus?"

"With Jesus!"

"Night or day!" exclaimed Judas jubilantly. "I will not rest or sleep until the final hour!"

Caiaphas regarded him curiously. "It must be done discreetly," Caiaphas said, studying Judas.

"Of course!" smiled Judas.

Caiaphas leaned close to Judas and locked eyes with him. "Do you understand what I'm saying?" Caiaphas asked slowly.

"Yes," said Judas, trembling. "You are acknowledging privately what you could not yet declare openly—that Jesus is the Messiah! I am to act as the link between you and Jesus, in preparation for that official moment that will establish his reign. It is a matter that must be handled discreetly, lest we arouse the suspicions of Rome!"

Caiaphas regarded Judas silently. Judas began to feel uncomfortable waiting for the High Priest to speak, which he finally did.

"Rome is suspicious," Caiaphas said significantly.

"Then we must be doubly careful," Judas said.

"We dare not take chances!" the High Priest said.

"Right!" Judas agreed.

"You must listen carefully now, Judas."

"Yes."

"We must have Jesus!"

Judas was stunned and puzzled. "...'have' Jesus?" he asked.

"Yes."

"What do you mean?"

Caiaphas' eyes burned into Judas. "We must take him into custody," Caiaphas said soberly.

"Custody?" Judas repeated mechanically, wondering whether he heard correctly.

"The safety of the nation is at stake!" Caiaphas said. Whatever warmth and friendliness had been in his voice was gone now.

Judas' mind spun dizzily. "Then you don't really believe he's the Messiah?" Judas asked, shocked at asking the question, shocked at the prospect of an answer whose possibility he wanted to dismiss from thought.

"I am willing to believe that Jesus is well-meaning," Caiaphas said. "Ordinarily I would let it go at that, but these are not ordinary times. I am forced, therefore, to take extraordinary measures!"

Judas could not speak. He looked white as death.

"We are not children, Judas! We cannot afford to play games! Life is too serious for that! Children play dead, and then they jump up and run away and laugh again. When men play at life, they play for keeps. When they kill, they kill; when they die, they die! Nobody rises from the dead for another chance at the game!"

Judas wished he were dead.

"Pilate will make a bloodbath of Jerusalem!"

"Pilate?" mumbled Judas.

"He has indicated that he will show restraint if…"

"…Jesus is turned over to him?" Judas exclaimed, aghast at the thought.

"Yes."

"He'll kill him!" Judas shouted. He rose from his chair, trembling, and paced around. Caiaphas caught up with him. He held him by the arm.

"Listen! Listen to what I'm telling you!" said Caiaphas. "He'll kill him anyway, one way or another! First he'll go after him and you and the others! Then he'll come after the rest of us and he won't stop until the streets run red with blood! Is that what you want? It will happen! When it does, could your soul bear the burden, living or dead?!"

Judas looked stunned. "He's the Messiah," he muttered flatly. "Don't you believe he's the Messiah?"

For a moment Caiaphas felt sorry for Judas. Suddenly he had a thought. "Perhaps he is, Judas, perhaps he is!" Caiaphas said, pretending to consider the possibility. "If he is, this, too, perhaps is the way things were meant to happen."

Judas tried to fathom the eyes of Caiaphas.

Caiaphas smiled reassuringly. "You will lead the guards to Jesus. We will make arrangements for his arrest. I will call a hearing. After the investigation he will be turned over to Pilate. Don't you see?"

"What?" Judas asked, trance-like.

"God does not act according to our ways, we must act according to His," said Caiaphas. "Perhaps this is His way, and maybe a safer way! Rome, knowing that Jesus will be arrested, will put its suspicions to rest. I, and the others, will have a chance to meet Jesus and speak with him freely. If he is who you say he is, there is nothing to worry about. God will reveal him to us, and to Pilate! I am humble enough to consider that, Judas. I am willing to have that faith in God. Are you?"

For the first time in what appeared like eternity, Judas saw a glimmer of light and felt a new hope.

"Maybe," he nodded. "Maybe."

Caiaphas hugged him around the shoulders. "Think about it the rest of the day," he said, sure now of Judas. "Tonight come to my house. You only have till tonight!"

Caiaphas led Judas to the door. As it closed behind him Caiaphas sighed with relief for the first time since he had seen Pilate.

❦   ❦   ❦

"Rabban Gamaliel!"

Rabban Gamaliel, who had just left the Great Sanhedrin, stopped and looked in the direction of the caller.

"Judas!" he exclaimed. "Judas ben Nathan! Shalom!"

"Shalom, Rabban," said Judas, pleased but tense.

"It's good to see you again," said Gamaliel. "Why don't you come by the house one of these days…"

"Rabban, I must see you!" Judas said anxiously.

Gamaliel noticed the troubled voice. "All right," he said, regarding Judas searchingly. "Come by tonight."

"It can't wait, Rabban! I must see you now!"

"Well…" Rabban Gamaliel started to protest.

"It's a matter of life and death!" Judas blurted out.

Gamaliel knew the sound and look of despair. "All right," he said quietly. "Come with me."

Gamaliel led him to one of the unoccupied chambers nearby. Rabban Gamaliel sat down and folded his hands thoughtfully before his face as he watched Judas pace up and down like a caged animal.

"You must give me an answer, Rabban!" Judas said suddenly without standing on ceremony. He sat down on the edge of a bench close to the Rabbi. "I must have an answer!"

"I shall try my best," Gamaliel said gently.

"Tell me plainly—yes or no!" Judas exclaimed feverishly.

"What is the question?"

"Jesus!"

"Jesus?"

"Is he the Messiah?" Judas asked hoarsely.

Gamaliel saw terror in his eyes. The Rabbi pondered the question, wondering at the implications of his answer.

"Yes or no, Rabban! Tell me, frankly, plainly—yes or no! Now!" Judas demanded.

Gamaliel regarded Judas with eyes full of sadness and compassion. "I do not believe him to be the Messiah," he said gently.

Judas' mouth twitched, his face ashen with despair. "Why?" He asked hoarsely.

"I know what he means to you," Gamaliel said, trying to soften the shock.

"Just tell me why!" Judas demanded, impatiently.

Gamaliel nodded and stroked his beard. "Why?" he said. "Why! Where is the new heaven and the new earth? Where do you see the wolf lying down with the lamb? Have the nations beaten their swords into plowshares, their spears into pruning hooks? Have they stopped hurting and destroying? Have they come up to the mountain of the Lord, to the house of the God of Jacob and said, 'Teach us of His ways and we will walk in His paths'? Is the earth full of the knowledge of the Lord? Where is it—the new heaven and the new earth?"

"We must help him bring it about!" Judas exclaimed.

"God?"

"And Jesus!"

Gamaliel regarded Judas thoughtfully. "What makes you think he can do it?" he asked.

"He teaches Love!" exclaimed Judas fervently. "Love can change men's hearts!"

'Is that why you feel he is the Messiah—because he teaches Love?" Gamaliel asked compassionately.

"Yes!" exclaimed Judas. "Love can change the world!"

"I'm glad you believe that, Judas…"

"It's how we can bring about the new heaven and the new earth!" Judas said eagerly. "He has brought us a new Truth…!"

Gamaliel smiled sadly. "No, Judas, not a new Truth, just an old, old Truth in new bottles. When the young discover Truth it is always new, like the world. They feel, they think, they see, as if no one had ever felt, or thought or seen before. And no one has, quite that way. But the world isn't new, and Truth isn't new, and Love isn't new! God spoke in Love to Abraham, Isaac and Jacob, and they spoke with Love to God. God chose Israel in Love to be a blessing to the nations. God gave us the Torah in Love. God has been a God of Love since He passed before Moses and said: 'The Lord, the Lord God, merciful and gracious, long-suffering and abundant in goodness and truth, keeping mercy unto the thousandth generation, forgiving iniquity, transgression and sin.' His mercy far exceeds his justice towards us, yet since He is a God of Love, He is a God of Mercy AND of Justice, for mercy without justice is mockery, and justice without mercy is misery.

"God's Love? The prophets burned with God's Love! 'Let justice run down as waters, and righteousness as a mighty stream!' 'He has showed thee, O man, what is good: and what doth the Lord require of thee, but to do justly, and to love mercy, and to walk humbly with thy God.' 'I desire mercy, and not sacrifice; and the knowledge of God more than burnt offerings.' 'Justice, justice shalt though pursue!'

"Love, Judas? It is all God has ever talked about, it is all He has ever asked of us! To love the stranger, for we were strangers once in the land of Egypt; to love our neighbor, for he is as I am and you are; to have one manner of law by which all men are judged—rich or poor, high or low, strong or weak; to love the sinner, but not the sin; to love the evil-doer, but not the evil.

"God has asked us to love Him by loving our fellow man through our actions in the world of men, this world. God has loved us through His anger as well as His pleasure, His harshness as well as His gentleness, His sternness as well as His kindness, His firmness as well as His permissiveness, His 'Thou shalt not' as well as His 'Thou shalt.' God, who is Love, has created us in His image, in Love, that we may be holy, as He is holy, that we may live so our lives sanctify His name, that we may love so that we may be a blessing to Israel and that Israel may be a blessing within the household of nations. 'And thou shalt love the Lord thy God with all thy heart, with all thy soul and with all thy might!'

"Love, Judas? The Torah is a love story, Judas, the greatest love story ever written! It is a love story between God and Israel, between God and you, between God and me, between our Father in heaven and His children here on earth."

Judas looked at the floor and sighed. "Then you think Jesus is an impostor?"

Gamaliel noticed the quiver that ran through Judas as he pronounced the possibility.

"No," Gamaliel said sadly. "He is not an impostor. He is a reverent soul, fervently in love with God and men. He is a God-intoxicated man, possessed of a sublime innocence. He wants earth and heaven to reach out and touch and kiss. No, Judas, he is not an impostor. He is a Jew!"

Judas searched Gamaliel's face. "What will happen to him?"

"If you have any influence with him," Gamaliel said gravely, "tell him to leave as soon as possible."

"What about Passover?"

"He must leave now," Gamaliel said urgently. "And if he won't leave, you must leave, quickly!"

They looked at each other like two men trying to fathom each other's thoughts, as if knowing more than either one could reveal to the other.

"Rabban?" Judas asked softly.

"Yes?"

"Isn't it possible that he really is the Messiah?"

Gamaliel contemplated the idea.

"Isn't it possible," Judas urged, "that God may still reveal him to be the Messiah at the proper moment?"

"It is possible," Gamaliel nodded, "to God all things are possible."

"Thank you, Rabban," Judas said, as he rose to go.

Gamaliel nodded and smiled gently. "Shalom, Judas. Peace!"

"Peace!" Answered Judas.

He left. Avoiding Jesus, who was preaching in the outer Temple area, Judas hurried to Bethany.

❧   ❧   ❧

"Shalom!" exclaimed Caiaphas, bowing to Pilate.

'Hail Caesar!" Pilate answered, betraying no emotion.

"I have come to request the ceremonial robes," Caiaphas said artlessly.

"Then you have taken care of the matter?" Pilate asked matter-of-factly.

Caiaphas knew that Pilate was referring to Jesus. He dared not lie. 'In a way, yes," Caiaphas began.

"It's a lie!" Pilate said in a deadly quiet voice.

"No, your Eminence…"

"Is he dead?"

"No…"

"Then you are lying!" Pilate screamed.

'Please, let me explain…" Caiaphas pleaded.

"I ordered you not to come back until you took care of the matter as I commanded!" Pilate thundered. "Don't you pay any attention to me? Do you think that I'm talking for my health? Do you think I'll forget and you can do whatever you feel like doing once you leave here? Doesn't Rome get any kind of respect around here? Well, I'll have to see to it that there'll be some improvements—if it takes a different High Priest every month for a year!"

Pilate was purple with rage.

"Please, please," pleaded Caiaphas. "Let me explain. I can explain…"

"All right," Pilate sneered cynically. 'What's your explanation?"

"I have a plan to take care of Jesus!"

"A plan!" mocked Pilate. "Why haven't you carried it out, then?"

"I cannot work it through the religious Sanhedrin," Caiaphas said subserviently. "The Pharisees see no religious grounds on which to conduct a trial, especially one involving the death penalty. Besides, they say there is not sufficient time for such a trial before the holiday, even if there were grounds."

"Grounds!" Pilate screamed. "Some madman decides he's King of the Jews and he's ready to set up his kingdom, God's kingdom, I don't give a damn whose kingdom, and they say there are no grounds? I'll give them grounds! Rome has grounds! That's all the grounds they need!"

"I have a simpler solution," Caiaphas said placatingly. "May I explain?"

"Please do!" Pilate said sarcastically.

"Let us forget the religious Sandhedrin," Caiaphas explained with all the persuasiveness he could muster. "I have already started confidential negotiations to have Jesus delivered to me through one of his disciples. It must not be done during the day, but at night, because of the people…"

"Tonight?"

"No, tomorrow night, after the Passover meal."

"It may be too late."

"No," said Caiaphas. "The people will be too busy tomorrow preparing for the Passover meal to think of anything else. If anything is to happen, it will happen the following day. By the time the people find out, it will be too late already."

"Why not tonight?"

"It cannot be done."

"Are you sufficiently convinced of this plan to risk your office and your life?"

"I am," Caiaphas said without flinching.

Pilate smiled wryly. "Once you have him, then what?" he asked.

"My advisory council, the *political sanhedrin*, which, as you know, consists of men I have appointed, with your approval, and who have nothing to do with the *religious sanhedrin*, will investigate Jesus, find him guilty and then hand him over to you for sentencing and execution, as is customary with political offenders."

Pilate laughed contemptuously. "So," he thundered. "You want Rome to do the dirty work and take the blame, eh?!"

"May I remind the Procurator that it is Rome that wants his death!" Caiaphas said, with ill-concealed anger.

"May I remind you of your position!" Pilate thundered.

"I'm sorry," Caiaphas apologized and bowed. "May I suggest that by my action I will share the responsibility, which will cause the people to accept the matter without...incident."

Pilate laughed harshly, rose and paced up and down. "Caiaphas, you are a coward!" Pilate exclaimed. "You are all cowards! If you were otherwise, you could say, 'Life, Death,' as naturally as a child says, 'mother, father'! That's the difference between ruler and subject, and that's why Rome rules and you obey! You invited Rome to rule, remember? You have had Roman order—*Pax Romana*, Roman peace—instead of Jewish chaos for one hundred years now! Does anyone thank us? No! We are cursed and criticized! The people and the 'leaders' scheme against us! You call us thieves, tyrants, oppressors! Do you know why? Because the weak are too weak to tolerate strength. They must tear strength down to give their weakness the appearance of strength. They point to the frailties of others, to hide their own frailties. They pray for failure to give comfort to their own failures. You are flies, trying to sting the strong to death. You are too stupid to know that when the strong die, the weak die also. Bring him to me! When a fly leaves the dung heap and lands on your arm, you kill it, before it stings!"

Pilate had stopped face to face with Caiaphas.

"I will deliver him," Caiaphas said deferentially.

They embraced silently. Suddenly they heard approaching footsteps. As they stepped away from each other, the door opened, revealing Jesus and the other Apostles.

"Shalom!" said Judas and Mary, greeting the group.

"Shalom!" Jesus and the Apostles replied.

"I wish to visit my parents," Judas said, addressing Jesus. "I will return later tonight."

Jesus regarded Judas strangely, nodding slightly without speaking. Judas pretended not to notice the strange look. He nodded to Mary, smiled slightly and hurried away.

It was time to see Caiaphas.

CHAPTER 12

Pax Romana—Roman Peace

"Moses then summoned all the elders of Israel and said to them, 'Go pick out lambs for your families, and slaughter the Passover offering.

'Take a bunch of hyssop, dip it in the blood that is in the basin, and apply some of the blood that is in the basin to the lintel and to the two doorposts. None of you shall go outside the door of his house until morning.

'For when the Lord goes through to smite the Egyptians, He will see the blood on the lintel and the two doorposts, and the Lord will pass over the door and not let the Destroyer enter and smite your home.

'You shall observe this as an institution for all time, for you and for your descendants. And when you enter the land which the Lord will give you, as He has promised, you shall observe this rite.

'And when your children ask you, "What do you mean by this rite?" you shall say, "It is the Passover sacrifice to the Lord, because He passed over the houses of the Israelites in Egypt, when He smote the Egyptians, but saved our houses.'

"The people then bowed low in homage. And the Israelites went and did so, just as the Lord had commanded Moses and Aaron, so they did."

It was Thursday afternoon and the Temple area swarmed with pilgrims who had come to sacrifice the Passover—one male lamb, one year old, without blemish, for every family or group.

It was a day of slaughter for many lambs.

Three full services were held consecutively to permit the participation of all the pilgrims, who were divided into three groups.

Jesus and his disciples managed to be in the first of the three groups, now assembled in the Inner Court, whose gates remained closed for the duration of the first service, while the other pilgrims waited in the outer area.

This was the time the pilgrims could redeem the lambs they had paid for on arrival Sunday. Qualified laymen performed the slaughter, but the blood was caught by a priest.

Rows of priests with gold and silver cups stood lined from the Temple slaughtering area to the altar, passing the cups along to the last priest, who sprinkled the blood on the altar.

Choirs of Levites, accompanied by brass instruments, sang the six psalms of the *Hallel*, in the course of each service. They were singing now:

> *Hallelujah.*

Judas looked and listened. He, Jesus, the others, were part of the crowd, a crowd of thousands who had come to worship and sacrifice.

> *Praise, O ye servants of the Lord.*

Judas felt hemmed in on all sides. The lines of worshipers moved slowly though the slaughterers worked swiftly, surely. Judas was glad that they had come early. At least they were near the head of their line and near the altar.

> *Praise the name of the Lord.*

Judas marveled at the efficiency of this vast operation. No sooner did he hand over his receipt than a helper handed the lamb to the slaughterer.

> *Blessed be the name of the Lord*
> *From this time forth and forever.*

Judas noticed the lamb's helplessness and fear. He heard the terror in its voice. Strange, he thought, how he had never noticed these things before. He had slaughtered many lambs in his lifetime. He had never let himself think about them before. Suddenly he heard their cry.

> *From the rising of the sun unto the going down thereof*
> *The Lord's name is to be praised.*

The lamb shook and trembled. Judas felt its helplessness and fear and terror. He felt sorry for the lamb. He wanted to touch it and comfort it. Suddenly he had a wild desire to tear it out of the slaughterer's arms and save it. But the knife was near the throat now and the people pressed round about and there was no place to hide or turn or run.

> *The Lord is high above all nations,*
> *His glory is above the heavens.*

Now the knife slid swiftly, cleanly, mercifully across the animal's throat. The bleating stopped. The deed was done. The priest caught the blood as it emptied into the gold and silver cup which was handed from priest to priest to the nearby altar, to be sprinkled over it, becoming one with the blood of many sacrifices.

> *Who is like unto the Lord our God,*
> *That is enthroned on high.*

The lamb hung lifeless now on the stake on which it had been placed. Here it was skinned, its abdomen cut open, the fatty portions taken out, placed in a vessel and offered by the priest on the altar.

> *That looketh down low*
> *Upon the heaven and upon the earth?*

When the lamb was clean, it was taken down. Judas stepped forward to receive it.

> *Who raiseth up the poor out of the dust,*
> *And lifteth up the needy out of the dunghill.*

Judas held the lamb gently and looked once more toward the altar. He spotted Caiaphas and for a moment their eyes met. Then Judas joined Jesus who, too, had been watching sadly and quietly all along.

> *That He may set him with princes,*
> *Even with the princes of His people.*

Jesus and his followers made room now for others. The bleating of the lambs, the stench of the sacrifices, and the songs of the Levites mingled and filled the air.

> *Who maketh the barren woman to dwell in her house*
> *As a joyful mother of children.*

Behind the altar and the Temple, the Tower of Antonia stood silently, like a sentinel.

> *Hallelujah.*

Soon it would be sundown and time for the *seder*. It would be time for the Passover meal…

🍁   🍁   🍁

The *seder* table was set traditionally: the lamb, whole and roasted; the three mazzot, the unleavened bread of the Exodus from Egypt; the bitter herbs; the *haroset*; the parsley; the salt water; and the wine.

Only the cup of Elijah was missing from the center of the table. He was the forerunner of the Messiah, invited to every Passover meal in the hope that sometime, somewhere, he would come into some Jewish home to prepare the way for the Messiah. Tonight, here, there was no need for the cup of Elijah, because Elijah had come already in the form of John the Baptizer and the Messiah was present, surrounded by his disciples.

Jesus raised the cup of wine and the others did likewise, saying: "Praised be Thou, O Lord our God, King of the universe, who has sanctified us by Thy commandments. As a token of Thy love, O Lord our God, Thou hast given us occasions for rejoicing, festivals and holidays for gladness, this Feast of the Unleavened Bread, the season of our liberation from bondage in Egypt. Thou hast quickened within us the desire to serve Thee, and in joy and gladness, hast bestowed on us Thy holy festivals. Praised be Thou, O Lord, who hallowest Israel, and the festivals."

Together they said: "Praised be Thou, O Lord our God, King of the universe, who hast kept us in life, sustained us, and enabled us to reach this season."

They drank the first cup of wine.

Jesus took the parsley, dipped it in salt water and passed a piece to each of them, saying; "These greens are a symbol of the coming of Spring. Before partaking of them, let us say together, 'Praised be Thou, O Lord our God, King of the universe, who createst the fruit of the earth.'"

They ate the parsley.

Jesus now held up three *mazzot* and said, "Behold the *mazzah*, symbol of the bread of poverty our ancestors were made to eat in their affliction, when they were slaves in the land of Egypt! Let it remind us of our fellow men who are today poor and hungry. Would that they could come and eat with us! Would that all who are in need could partake with us of this *Pesah* feast.

"Let us here resolve to strive unceasingly for that blessed day when all will share equally in the joy of *Pesah*—when poverty will be no more and when all mankind will enjoy freedom, justice and peace. And let us say, 'Amen.'"

"*Ma nishtana halaila hazeh, meekol halaylot*," asked the youngest of the disciples, symbolic of the child that asks the question. "Why is this night different from all other nights?"

And Jesus answered, according to the tradition: "Indeed this night is very different from all other nights of the year, for on this night we celebrate one of the most important moments in the history of our people. On this night we celebrate their going forth in triumph from slavery into freedom."

He continued reading from the scroll. "'I am glad you asked the questions you did, for the story of this night was just what I wanted you to know. Although the *Haggadah* we are reading tells this whole story, and if you listen carefully you will surely learn it, I should like to tell you here, in a few words, the answers to your questions.

"'Why do we eat only *mazzah* tonight? When Pharaoh let our forefathers go from Egypt, they were forced to flee in great haste. Now, they had prepared dough for bread to take on their journey, but the Egyptians pressed them to hasten out of the land. So they snatched up their dough and fled, and had no time to bake it. But the hot sun, beating down on the dough as they carried it along with them, baked it into a flat, unleavened bread which they called *mazzah*. That is why we eat only *mazzah* on *Pesah*.

"'Why do we eat bitter herbs on *Pesah* night? Because our forefathers were slaves in Egypt, and their lives were made bitter. That is why we eat bitter herbs on *Pesah* night.

"'Why do we dip the herbs twice tonight? You have already heard that we dip the parsley in salt water because it reminds us of the green that comes to life again in the springtime. We dip the *maror*, or bitter herbs, in the sweet *haroset* as a sign of hope; our forefathers were able to withstand the bitterness of slavery because it was sweetened by the hope of freedom.

"'Why do we recline at the table? Because reclining at the table is a sign of a free man, and since our forefathers were freed on this night, we recline at the table.'

"Now let us recite the story of *Pesah* as we find it in the Torah..."

Judas and the others listened attentively. They had heard this story every year of their lives, just as it had been told every year in the life of Israel since the Exodus.

Ma nishtana halaila hazeh, meekol halaylot?

Why is this night different from all other nights?

Jesus continued, "'In every generation, every Jew should feel as though he himself took part in the Exodus from Egypt; as the *Torah* tells us: 'And thou shalt tell thy son on that day, saying, "It is because of what the Lord did for me when I came forth out of Egypt."' In this generation, too, we should feel as though we, ourselves, went free when our forefathers left Egypt.

"'We should therefore sing praises and give thanks to Him who did all these wonders for our fathers and for us. He brought us from slavery to freedom, and from sorrow to joy, from mourning to festivity, from darkness to light, and from bondage to redemption.

"'Let us express our grateful joy, let us sing a new song before him. HALLE-LUJAH!'"

Jesus waited until the cup of wine was refilled for the second time before starting the responsive recitation of the psalms.

"*Ma nishtana...Why is this night different from all other nights?*"

Judas remembered the other nights...his mother, his father, the preparations for the lavish meal, the guests, he, Judas, in his best clothes. How old was he when he attended his first seder? Four, five, six? He couldn't remember. All he could remember was how he had practiced for weeks—*ma nishtana halaila hazeh*—how he had learned it by heart, how he waited for his turn and how his heart leaped when the moment arrived and everyone looked at him and waited, and how he spoke the words without making any mistakes, as he was afraid he might do, and how everyone listened and how they smiled and praised him when he was done. He remembered the wine, and how they let him drink all four glasses, small glasses to be sure, but four glasses neverthe-less. He remembered how hungry he used to get during the service waiting for the start of the meal, and how they used to let him nibble on *mazzah*, and how crunchy it was and how dry his mouth got. He remembered how hard it was to keep his eyes open and how hard he tried not to fall asleep and how sometimes he fell asleep and how proud he was when he managed to sit through the whole service. He remembered how he got bored listening to words that he did not understand, he remembered how the service always took so long and seemed so endless.

And tonight, Judas wished it would take forever and never end.

Jesus lifted the cup and said, "Praised be Thou, O Lord our God, King of the universe, who createst the fruit of the vine."

"Amen," said the others as they drank the second cup.

"It is time now for the washing of the hands," said Jesus.

John rose to get the pitcher and basin, but Jesus stopped him. "Sit down," he said. "I will do it."

"But, Rabbi," John started to protest.

"Please, John, thank you, but I wish to do it," Jesus said kindly.

The others looked at one another strangely.

Jesus poured the water into the basin, took the towel and went from one to the other while they washed their hands. Then he washed his own. Then they said together: "Praised be Thou, O Lord our God, King of the universe, who hast sanctified us with Thy commandments and bidden us wash our hands."

It was the only washing required at this point. The disciples waited for Jesus to put the basin aside and sit down once more. He proceeded now to wash their feet.

Simon was the first one. He was obviously shocked, as were the others. "You, Lord, washing my feet?" he exclaimed.

Jesus looked at him enigmatically. "You do not understand now what I am doing, but one day you will," he said.

Simon protested. "I will never let you wash my feet!" he said.

"If I do not wash you," Jesus replied, "you are not in fellowship with me."

Simon looked puzzled. "In that case," he said eagerly, "don't just wash my feet, but my hands and head as well!"

Jesus smiled at him reassuringly. "A man who has bathed needs no further washing," he said. "He is altogether clean. And you are clean, though not every one of you is."

Simon and the others wondered what he meant by these strange words. Judas felt that they were meant for him.

When Jesus was done, he put the basin away and returned to the table. He took the upper and the middle *mazzah* and distributed a piece of each to all present, who joined him saying, "Praised be Thou, O Lord our God, King of the universe, who bringest forth bread from the earth. Praised be Thou, O Lord our God, King of the Universe, who hast sanctified us with Thy commandments and bidden us eat unleavened bread on Passover.

"May the sweet *haroset* which we eat with these bitter herbs be for us a symbol of the hope of freedom which enabled our ancestors to withstand the bitterness of their slavery."

It was time now for the meal.

The disciples waited for Jesus to give the word, but he seemed strangely silent. The whole evening had been strange. Everyone had sensed it. Strangeness had hung in the air, like the painful estrangement that comes from high expectation and disappointed hope.

Jesus sat, his head bowed, as if wrestling with his soul. Then he looked around from one to the other, smiling sadly, and said, "How I have longed to eat this Passover with you before my death!"

The word struck terror into the group, leaving the disciples speechless.

"For I tell you," continued Jesus, "never again shall I eat it until the time when it finds its fulfillment in the kingdom of God."

The Twelve were too confused to speak. They watched Jesus fill his cup with wine, saying, "Praised art Thou, O Lord our God, King of the universe, who createst the fruit of the vine."

Then he took the *mazzah* and said, "Praised art Thou, O Lord our God, King of the universe, who hast sanctified us by Thy commandments, and bidden us eat unleavened bread at Passover."

It was strange. Everything was strange. For had he not offered these same blessings only a few minutes before?

He held up the cup and said, "Take this and share it among yourselves. For I tell you, from this moment I shall drink from the fruit of the vine no more until the time when the kingdom of God comes."

He passed the cup around and they drank.

Then he broke the *mazzah* and handed a piece to each of them. "This," he said, "is my body."

It was too much. The disciples hardly dared look at him, wondering if the words were true or untrue, and disturbed in either case.

Had they looked, they would have noticed the agitation in his face. They didn't have to look. He could not hide the agitation from his voice. "Mark this," he said. "One of you will betray me! One who is eating with me!"

Judas blanched. "Betray!" he whispered, terrified. He looked around wildly, thinking he had shouted it. But the others, too, had been seized by terror and they looked around wildly, incredulously.

"Who could it be?" they asked. "Who could it be?"

Judas, too, mumbled, "Who could it be?"

But Jesus said no more.

Betrayal! thought Judas to himself. Betrayal! No, no, that's not it at all! How could Jesus say that? Didn't he know better? Judas wanted to jump up from his seat and explain everything to everybody. I'm not betraying Jesus, he wanted to say. I'm helping him! I'm the agent! I'm the instrument! I'm making the final confrontation possible! I'm setting it all up so that the Messiah can usher in God's heavenly kingdom!

Judas knew better than to jump up and say such things. They might not understand! God did not want anyone to know at this point, except Judas and Jesus.

Judas looked at Jesus. Jesus met his gaze.

Don't you understand? Judas pleaded with his eyes. I know now that you know! Surely God has told you! It's not a betrayal! You know better than that! Surely you know better than that! You must know better than that! It's the great moment, the moment of revelation, the new heaven, the new earth, and I'm paving the way for you. I'm not here to destroy you, I've come to save you, I won't betray you, I'll redeem you! I am *your* messiah! Don't you see?

But Jesus just regarded Judas with sad, accusing eyes and then he looked away. "The Son of Man is going his appointed way," said Jesus, "but alas for the man by whom he is betrayed."

Like children seeking reassurance that pain really isn't pain, and trouble really isn't trouble, and tears hide smiles, the disciples turned quickly from these troubled words, seizing instead the faint syllables of hope. Had not Jesus talked strangely before? It was just a mood.

"It must be near now!" exclaimed John.

"What?" asked Simon, trying to come to grips with his own feelings.

"The Kingdom!" exclaimed John eagerly.

The others listened hungrily.

"Oh?" Simon asked.

"Of course!" exclaimed John. "He as much as said so—the next time he sits down with us to drink and eat…!"

"That's right!" interrupted James eagerly. "He has jut said it after blessing the wine. He said he won't be drinking again until the kingdom of God comes!"

Simon looked puzzled.

"When is the next meal?" asked John triumphantly. "Tomorrow night—we eat, we drink in the kingdom of God!"

For the first time that evening, Simon smiled. "Of course!" he said. "That's it!"

The faces of the others lit up with joy.

"Just remember," John said happily. "I get to sit next to him..."

"You sit on his right and I'll sit on his left," his brother James reminded him.

"Wait a minute," Simon objected.

But before they had a chance to reopen the old argument, Jesus interrupted them. "In the world, kings lord it over their subjects," said Jesus, sadly, because they had such a hard time understanding. "And those in authority are called their country's 'benefactors.' Not so with you. On the contrary, the highest among you must bear himself like the youngest, the chief of you like a servant. For who is greater—the one who sits at table or the servant who waits on him? Surely the one who sits at table. Yet here am I among you like a servant."

Had he not waited on them and washed their feet?

"You are the men who have stood firmly by me in my times of trial," he said. "And now I vest in you the kingship which my Father vested in me. You shall eat and drink at my table in my kingdom and sit on thrones as judges of the Twelve Tribes of Israel."

They smiled. Each one felt that John had been right. It wouldn't be long now. The great moment was almost at hand. The disciples were happy that Jesus was done with talk of betrayal and death. It was one of those moods that had come over him from time to time. Everyone had his moods. Well, they had stood by him in times of trial. For that matter, these last days in Jerusalem hadn't been the easiest. They hadn't measured up to expectations. In fact, they had been something of a disappointment. Each of the disciples had found it best to keep his own counsel, especially regarding their doubts. Could it be that Jesus wasn't...? They dared not speak of it. They hardly dared wonder.

"Simon, Simon," said Jesus. "Take heed: Satan has been given leave to sift all of you like wheat. But for you I have prayed that your faith may not fail. And when you have come to yourself, you must lend strength to your brothers."

'Lord," replied Simon fervently. "I am ready to go with you to prison and death!"

Jesus smiled sadly, gratefully. "I tell you, Simon," he said, "the cock will not crow tonight until you have three times over denied that you know me!"

Simon's eyes filled with terror and anguish as he shook his head, denying such an unspeakable thought.

Jesus continued. "When I sent you out barefoot without purse or pack, were you ever short of anything?"

"No," they said.

"It is different now," Jesus explained. "Whoever has a purse had better take it with him, and his pack, too. And if he has no sword, let him sell his cloak to buy one. For Scripture says, 'And he was counted among the outlaws,' and these words, I tell you, must find fulfillment in me. Indeed, all that is written of me is being fulfilled."

"Look, Lord!" said Simon, revealing his own sword and that of Simon the Zealot. "We have two swords here."

The disciples were surprised.

"Enough, enough," nodded Jesus. "Come now, let us eat."

He served them portions of the lamb, being careful not to break its bones.

They ate silently. For the first time, each man felt alone, his soul weighed down with confusion and fear.

"Rabbi?" Judas asked when they had finished eating.

Jesus nodded.

"May I go now?" he asked hoarsely.

Jesus nodded expectantly. "Do quickly what you have to do," Jesus said.

"As I told you earlier," Judas stuttered, 'my parents asked me to spend part of the seder with them."

Jesus made no comment. Judas looked away. "Shalom," he mumbled.

"Shalom," said Jesus.

"Shalom," said the others.

Judas hurried out.

The disciples accepted the explanation and gave no further thought to Judas. They were too involved with their own thoughts. They were too confused to wonder.

But Jesus didn't wonder. He knew, now!

❈   ❈   ❈

When the *seder* was over, Jesus and his disciples left to spend the night on the Mount of Olives, opposite the Temple Mount. It was well occupied by other pilgrims who were already encamped there. Jesus led his group to the garden of Gethsemane, by the brook of Cedron in the Valley of Kidron at the foot of the Mount of Olives.

"Pray that you may be spared the hour of testing," he said to his followers. "Sit here while I pray."

Taking Simon, John and James with him, he walked on a way and then stopped. The three saw anguish in his face and waited for him to speak.

"My heart is ready to break with grief," said Jesus. "Stop here and stay awake."

They nodded gravely.

Then Jesus went forward a little, threw himself on the ground and prayed.

"*Abba*, Father," he said fervently, "all things are possible to Thee. If it be Thy will, take this cup away from me. Yet not my will but Thine be done."

Simon, John and James heard the words. They strained to stay awake. But the food and the wine and the strain of events had exhausted them. Their eyelids drooped and they fell asleep.

"*Avinu, malkenu*, Our Father, Our King," prayed Jesus. "Why is it happening this way? I don't understand! I came to You to serve You with clean hands and a pure heart, and I received Your blessing, remember? The heavens opened and Your spirit descended in the form of a dove and I heard You say, 'This is My beloved!' and I felt Your love and I knew then that You were Love and that the whole earth was holy with Your love. O heavenly Father, from that moment on You were more real to me than anything on earth! Do You remember? You spoke to me and I heard, and as I heard, I spoke, and I could not help listening and speaking from that moment on! Was my mind on fire with its own flame, and not Yours, O heavenly Father? Did I hear nothing? Did I see nothing?"

Jesus felt too anguished to go on. Fear seized him. He rose to look around. He found Simon, John and James asleep. He woke them up.

"Asleep, Simon?" he said reproachfully. "Were you not able to stay awake a little while? Stay awake, all of you, and pray that you may be spared the test: the spirit is willing, but the flesh is weak."

Once more he went away and prayed. "Abba, Father," he continued. "All things are possible to Thee. If it be Thy will, take this cup away from me. Yet not my will but Thine be done."

Simon, John and James heard and drowsed off again.

"*Avinu, malkenu*, our Father, our King. Does a father deceive his children? Does a king deceive his servants? No! No! The Father of Truth does not deceive—and I heard Truth! The King of Truth does not deceive—and I spoke

Truth! Love is Truth! Love is the language of the Messiah! You spoke to me of Love, and I spoke of Love in the world. I have talked, I have acted, I have prayed, I have waited—I have not made one move without You, O heavenly Father, knowing that Your thoughts are not our thoughts, knowing that Your ways are not our ways. How long, O God, how long? Where is Your promise? Where is Your Presence? Where is Your Kingdom and Your Power and Your Glory? It is late, it is late! Soon it will be too late!"

He thought he heard footsteps and rose quickly to see who might be coming. He noticed Simon, John and James asleep. The noise he had heard came from a group of pilgrims who had arrived nearby and who were settling down for the night. Jesus sighed with relief and woke the three disciples.

"Stay awake," Jesus said wearily. "Stay awake!"

The disciples looked at him apologetically, with drowsy embarrassment. Jesus went back to pray.

"*Abba*, Father," he pleaded. "All things are possible to Thee. If it be Thy will, take this cup away from me. Yet not my will but Thine be done."

Simon, John and James dozed off.

"It is a good thing we do not know what tomorrow will bring," Jesus continued, addressing God. "We never know from one day to the next what turns our lives will take. You play surprises on us every moment. And yet I would do it again, if You asked me to, even though what You have done with me, through me, to me, remains a mystery that I can only vaguely comprehend. I could still get away now and live, couldn't I? But living would be dying. I could save myself. But I would be lost. Life now is death and death, life. Instead of life, I will choose life everlasting. You are the King, the Judge, the Shepherd and the Father. You are my Shield and my Redeemer. I will not be afraid. But why this way? What should I have done? Why didn't they understand? Why did nothing happen? Didn't You say, 'Not by might, nor by power, but by My spirit'? I sought Your spirit! I brought Your spirit! I taught Your spirit! Why did they revile me and mock me and ignore me and, through me, You? Father, were You to send a thousand messiahs, what more could they do? Or is that it, that one person can never do anything for another person, that each soul must reach out to You, just as You reach out to each soul? Is that it? Everyone must be a messiah? Is that the Kingdom of Heaven, the Day in the End of days when everyone everywhere at one time and with one heart sees the heavens open and Your spirit descend in the form of a dove and Your voice say, 'This is my beloved'? Can the world be saved only by all, each one saving that portion on which he stands? Can love be awakened in one blinding flash of Your holy Creation? To You, to whom all things are possible, this, too, is possible! If not today, then tomorrow! I will do my part for its fulfillment. I know that my moment is at hand. Make me worthy of it, so that I may sanctify Your Holy Name. Amen."

His sweat was like clots of blood falling to the ground. As he prayed, his anguish gave way gradually to acceptance and peace.

Again he heard footsteps and voices. This time he was sure they were coming his way. Sensing approaching danger, he hurried swiftly to the three sleeping disciples and roused them.

"Still sleeping?" he exclaimed. "Enough! The hour has come! The Son of Man is betrayed to sinful men!"

As he talked, the danger he had sensed materialized in the shape of the Temple police and officers of the guard.

"Up! Let us go forward! My betrayer is upon us!" exclaimed Jesus.

The three disciples, and the others who by now had become aware of the commotion, rallied to his side. By now all recognized Judas, who approached Jesus.

"Shalom, Rabbi," said Judas, and kissed him.

"Judas," Jesus said evenly. "Would you betray the Son of Man with a kiss?"

Simon was incensed when he realized what was happening. "Lord, shall we use our swords?" he asked, and, without waiting for an answer, struck the High Priest's servant and cut off his ear.

Jesus stopped Simon from going further. "Let them have their way," he said and, turning to the arresting officers, he exclaimed, "Do you take me for a bandit, that you have come out with swords and cudgels to arrest me? Day after day, when I was in the Temple with you, you kept your hands off me. But this is your moment, the hour when darkness reigns."

The police now seized Jesus without a struggle, while the disciples, afraid of arrest, fled. A zealous guard tried to seize a pilgrim who had wandered over to see what the commotion was about. Considering the man was a follower of Jesus, the guard grabbed the linen cloth which the man had wrapped around him for the night, but the pilgrim slipped out of it in his fear and ran naked into the night.

⁂   ⁂   ⁂

Caiaphas and his advisory council—his court of justice, his *political sanhedrin*—were used to meeting for special occasions such as this one. In fact, it was the only reason they ever met, to consider special affairs of state. They met night or day, weekdays or holidays, whenever the occasion required it. They met only when called into special session. Caiaphas had called them into special session the previous night to outline his plan. They had met with Judas. They were assembled now to conclude the matter.

The court consisted of Sadducees, representing the more prominent, aristocratic leaders of the community whom Caiaphas had appointed to assist him in matters of state, with the approval of Pilate. Caiaphas did not need scholars, just "friends" of the state.

It was nothing new, really. The head of state—king or High Priest—had always relied on a court council. Most recently, Herod I had made us of it to an outrageous extent.

The council could meet anywhere, in some chamber of the Temple or at the home of Caiaphas. With Rome now in charge of the country, the council only "deliberated," and then turned the individual violator over to the Roman procurator for final judgment and punishment.

Caiaphas tried to hide his nervousness from the others while waiting for the Temple police to arrive with their prisoner. One never knew what might go wrong, even with the best of plans. He was sure of only one thing, namely, that nothing had better go wrong.

He was tired. So were the others. They had been with their families for the *seder.* After it was over they had come here. It had been a long and arduous day. It was the middle of the night now.

Caiaphas felt relieved when he heard the police arrive. When they ushered Jesus into the room, Caiaphas relaxed for the first time in days.

Jesus stood silently in the middle of the room, while Caiaphas and the others regarded him with curiosity. Two guards remained near Jesus.

Caiaphas remained seated, facing Jesus.

"So, you are the Galilean," said Caiaphas finally, "the carpenter from Nazareth! Jesus, the Son of Joseph, I believe."

Some of those present smiled at the innuendo. Jesus said nothing.

"I understand you have quite a number of followers, including twelve close disciples," Caiaphas said. "Didn't any of them come with you?"

A couple of the others laughed.

'You don't say very much," said Caiaphas. "I'm surprised. I was told that you talked quite a bit. In fact, I was told that you had a great deal to say to us here in Jerusalem, including these gentlemen and me and a few other rather important individuals who don't happen to be present at the moment. I would think you would take advantage of this rare opportunity!"

Jesus remained silent.

"I'm sorry," said Caiaphas with mock apology. "I keep forgetting that you are from Galilee. I should keep things simple, shouldn't I? Why don't you tell us about your ideas?"

Those present smiled. The annoyance of the meeting was relieved at least by some welcome humor.

"I have spoken openly to all the world," Jesus now said with controlled feeling. "I have always taught in the synagogue and in the Temple area where people congregate. I have said nothing in secret. Why question me? Ask my hearers what I told them. They know what I said."

One of the guards struck him in the face. Jesus winced.

"Is that the way to answer the High Priest?" the guard exclaimed.

"If I spoke amiss, state it in evidence," Jesus exclaimed. "If I spoke well, why strike me?"

Caiaphas turned to those present.

"Did any of you hear him speak in the Temple area?" Caiaphas asked. "Did anyone else tell you about him? Have you all heard what he's been saying?"

The men all started to speak at once. "He said, 'I can pull down the Temple of God and rebuild it in three days...' We heard him say, 'I will throw down this Temple, made with human hands, and in three days I will build another, not made with human hands...' He said..."

Caiaphas broke into the babel of voices.

"Have you no answer to the charge that these witnesses bring against you?" Caiaphas asked.

Jesus did not answer.

Caiaphas rose now and confronted Jesus, pausing until there was absolute silence in the room. Then the High Priest spoke in dead seriousness. "By the living God I charge you to tell us: Are you the Messiah, the Son of God?"

Jesus looked quietly at Caiaphas. "If I tell you," said Jesus, "you will not believe me. And if I ask questions, you will not answer. But from now on, the Son of Man will be seated at the right hand of Almighty God."

"You are the Son of God, then?" demanded Caiaphas.

"It is you who say I am," Jesus said.

Caiaphas now flew into a righteous rage as he paced up and down before those present. "Have you ever heard anything like this?" He stormed rhetorically. "Such nerve! Such outrageous arrogance! It's…it's…nothing short of…blasphemy, that's what it is! Blasphemy!"

With that, he tore his clothes, as if in mourning over death. "Does anyone have to hear more?" Caiaphas demanded.

"We have heard it form his own lips! We've heard all we have to hear!" some said, and the rest nodded vigorously in agreement. "He's definitely trouble, big trouble!"

"All right, then, what's your opinion?" Caiaphas asked.

"Guilty!" they agreed unanimously. "Turn him over to Pilate!"

They nodded gravely to one another. They were convinced that it was the only thing to do. Anyway, they only did what Pilate wanted. Too bad, maybe. But they couldn't risk the life of the country for the life of one man. Besides, what choice did they really have?

❦   ❦   ❦

Meanwhile, Simon was sitting outside in the courtyard near the fire, having followed Jesus to the house of Caiaphas. A serving maid suddenly noticed him. "You were with Jesus the Galilean," she said.

"I don't know what you mean," Simon exclaimed vehemently and went out to the gateway.

Another girl seemed to recognize him. "This fellow was with Jesus of Nazareth," she said to some bystanders, pointing to Simon.

"Damn it, I don't know the man," Simon said contemptuously. He moved away, but, some other bystanders noticed him.

"You're one of them!" said a man excitedly. "I heard you a little while ago and saw you with him. Your accent gives you away!"

"I don't give a damn about him!" Simon exclaimed. "I don't know what the hell you're talking about. I was just passing by and stopped to see what's going on. The man means nothing to me. I hope they…"

"They should kill him!" the man exclaimed.

'Yeah, he's a troublemaker!" someone else said. "The sooner they get rid of him, the better, right?"

'Right!" said Simon.

Simon wanted to get out of there. He started to leave. A cock crowed. Simon remembered Jesus' words.

He said it would happen! Simon thought. Peter, Peter! He named me Peter, the Rock—and I crumbled!

He hurried away, weeping bitterly. Had it not been for his tears, which blinded him, he might have seen Judas waiting anxiously in the shadows.

❀   ❀   ❀

Pontius Pilate, sitting in judgment in the trial area of the Antonia, studied Jesus as he was ushered into his presence. He looked like any ordinary man, neither tall nor short, fat nor thin. Pilate thought to himself that had he met Jesus in the street somewhere, he would not have looked twice. Pilate was unimpressed. The Procurator kept studying Jesus as he came to a halt before him. Perhaps there was something more to the man, on second thought, Pilate admitted. He tried to figure out what it was. It was the look of the eyes and the bearing of the body. They had about them a sense of…dignity. Not for long, thought Pilate, not for long.

Pilate looked at Caiaphas and his associates, satisfied that they had brought the man to him without incident, first thing this Friday morning.

"Shalom," said Caiaphas.

"Hail Caesar!" Pilate replied. "Whom have we here?"

"Behold the man," said Caiaphas, fencing with Pilate, "Jesus of Nazareth!"

'Oh?" said Pilate innocently. "What are the charges?"

Caiaphas smiled wryly. "I know that the Procurator is fully informed of the man's claims and doings."

Pilate bristled. "I want someone to tell me what he's done!" Pilate demanded and, pointing to one of Caiaphas' advisors, he ordered, "You!"

Intimidated by the direct command, the man blurted: "We found this man subverting our nation, opposing the payment of taxes to Caesar and claiming to be the Messiah!"

"The Messiah!" said Pilate, mulling the idea. "Will you explain that to me?"

The man who had been singled out found Pilate's eyes burning into him. "Well," he began, with an edge of terror to his voice, "It's an idea that has really been developed over…"

"He's the King of the Jews, isn't that right?" Pilate demanded.

"Well, the only King we have…" the man tried to explain.

"Is Caesar?" Pilate asked, smiling wryly.

"And…God," the man answered, trembling.

"Until the day of the Messiah!" Pilate exclaimed. "Right?"

The man knew better than to try to explain further.

"You!" said Pilate, tired of toying with the mouse, turning to Jesus now. "Are you the Messiah, the King of the Jews?"

Jesus looked quietly at the Procurator and said, "It is as you say."

Pilate smiled wryly and said, "You will not remain ambiguous about your feelings much longer."

Jesus shuddered imperceptibly.

Pilate now called a guard and whispered some instructions. Suddenly Jesus was marched away for no apparent reason. Caiaphas looked to Pilate for an explanation.

"Stay a while," he said. "He'll be back soon."

Pilate looked pleased at his little game.

When Jesus returned a short time later, he wore the purple robe of royalty.

"I see Herod Antipas bestowed great honor upon his countryman," Pilate said and, turning to the guard, asked, "What did he say?"

"He said that he waives all rights to his subject, inasmuch as the final violations occurred in your territory," said the guard. "Also, since Rome is the threatened party, he recognizes your authority and defers to it, and to your judgment, fully and completely."

"And the robe?" Pilate asked suspiciously.

"He knows Pilate appreciates a good joke."

Pilate laughed. "Herod is no fool," he said. 'And Pilate does not hold a grudge. I wish to hold a banquet for him. Ask when it would be convenient."

A messenger left instantly. Pilate now dismissed Caiaphas and his advisors.

"All right," said Pilate, addressing Jesus when the others were gone. "Have you nothing to say in your defense? You are aware of the charges against you, aren't you?"

Jesus said nothing.

"H'm!" Pilate grunted. "You're either a brave man or a fool. I suspect the latter. Either way, you're a fool. So you can't really win. You know that, of course."

Jesus remained mute.

"Do you want me to lose my temper and get angry?" Pilate asked, slightly uncomfortable. "It's not really necessary when one holds the upper hand. One can afford to be patient under those circumstances. I'm glad in a way that you're not pleading your cause. It's such a foolish thing to do, isn't it? It deprives us of dignity, doesn't it? Begging is so degrading, isn't it? Besides, what could I do except listen and then deny your request? It's a false hope, a hypocrisy! Why go through the motions? I commend your dignity. I must say that for you."

Pilate shook his head in bewilderment. "I have ways of making a man speak, you know that, don't you?" he continued. "But there's nothing worthwhile you could tell me under these circumstances that I don't know already. There's really nothing you and I have to say to each other, is there? You lost, I won. The wonder is that you thought you could pull it off! You waited too long to strike, that was your mistake! Barabbas! If you had no intentions of using him, then you are a bigger fool than I think you are. No one can win without Barabbas! You need Barabbas, but you know what? Barabbas needs you even more! Who do you think represents a greater threat to me—you or Barabbas?"

Jesus did not comment. Pilate laughed. "Let me show you something," said Pilate. He went to the gate and addressed the crowd that had gathered outside. "I will release one of the prisoners to you today," he called. "Whom do you want—Jesus or Barabbas?"

"Barabbas!" yelled the crowd. "Barabbas!"

"You shall have him today!" Pilate ordered.

He returned and confronted Jesus. "I have just made myself very popular," he said and laughed. "It will avoid trouble today. You see, men always choose force. But a general is useless without a king. Force can be fought with force. Barabbas will not give me any trouble until he finds a new messiah! That's why I let him go. He is useful to me. He will direct me to the next messiah! But I will release him too late—for you!"

Pilate wondered why he had talked so much. His eyes darted around in momentary bewilderment, then his face became hard and cruel once more.

"Guilty!" he declared. "Guards!"

The soldiers came to attention.

"Flog and crucify him!" Pilate ordered.

The soldiers seized Jesus and led him away.

Judas wondered when he had last slept. He could not remember. His eyes were heavy but his heart was heavier. He had been waiting with the handful of others outside the gate, wondering what was going on between Jesus and Pilate.

All through the night, ever since Gethsemane, Judas had waited expectantly. He had figured that something might happen at the home of Caiaphas. He didn't quite know what, but he thought maybe Caiaphas would dispatch messengers all over the city and perhaps all over the land. The sound of the *shofar* would be heard, the people would rise, the power of Rome would be crushed, Jesus would be anointed by the High Priest before the holy Temple in view of all the world, and the sons of men would journey to Jerusalem to worship and to go forth to do God's will.

But the night passed without the miracles and when Jesus was delivered to Pilate in the morning, Judas followed him.

Of course, thought Judas, this is where it must happen! He had been upset but now he was relieved. Of course, he thought as he drew hope from the final thought which came to him, when despair almost gave way to terror.

Jesus did not want bloodshed, Judas remembered. Jesus never called for bloodshed. Of course, that's it! Pilate, not Caiaphas, was the key to God's drama. He had to be convinced. He was the unbeliever, the instrument of power, the spear and the sword! Jesus had to confront him. Jesus would slay him with love, he would defeat him with the spirit of God. Not a drop of blood would be spilled. Pilate would die, only to be reborn; Rome would fall, only to kneel in worship! Pilate himself would lead Jesus to the holy Temple, Caiaphas would anoint him, and all the world would come singing to Jerusalem!

Suddenly the gate opened. Judas looked over expectantly. For a minute what he saw did not seem real. Judas wondered if he had fallen asleep and was now dreaming. Perhaps he was having a nightmare. He blinked his eyes and looked at the others around him. They, too, had seen what he had seen.

There was Jesus, his body bruised and battered. Blood mingled with the sweat of pain. The body sagged under the weight of the crossbeam Jesus was forced to drag to his own crucifixion. He puffed hard and harshly, his face contorted. A crown of thorns dug into his flesh.

"BETRAYER!"

Judas's head exploded with the sound of the word. He looked around wildly. Jesus had shouted it! Hadn't he? Judas wanted to hide. They would seize him! Why didn't they seize him?

"BETRAYER!"

There it was again! But this time they all shouted it! So that's it! They knew! They all knew!

"I'm not!" Judas screamed. "I'm not!"

Some of the people looked at him curiously, wondering what had gotten into him.

Judas stared back in terror. I must get out of here, he thought. I must get away from here. Or else, or else they'll…he'll…

Judas turned and started to run. He started to run toward the Temple. He didn't know why. I have to think, he thought, I have to think. He knew he was running. He was even vaguely aware of the direction. Suddenly he became aware of something else. He tried to get his mind to focus on what it was. He had his hand around it. It was hard to think connected thoughts. Yes, he was aware of his hand around a bag. That's it! He had his hand around a bag.

"This is for you."

Who said that? thought Judas, looking around as he ran. It was a voice, a familiar voice, but there were no familiar faces around. Whose voice was it? Why had he said that?

"No! No!" Judas exclaimed. He was startled by the sound of his own voice. Had he said that now, or then, or not at all?

"It is not much, just a token of our appreciation for your service to your country."

"Caiaphas!" screamed Judas. "Caiaphas!"

Now he knew what he had been clutching. The silver! The bag of silver! The thirty pieces of silver! The goddamn bag of silver that he never wanted but which he took to be polite or because of the way it was given him or maybe he didn't want it or who-the-hell-knew, he certainly didn't, why the hell he took it!

Now he knew where he was going! Judas stormed past the Levites and priests and guards who recognized him and let him through, figuring that he had some unfinished business with the High Priest.

Caiaphas and his advisors were assembled in their council chamber going over the critical events once more, waiting for word of their conclusion, when Judas burst in. Caiaphas looked frightened, as did the others, who remained motionless.

"Yes?" Caiaphas asked cautiously.

Judas looked around wild-eyed. 'I have sinned!" he screamed. "I have brought an innocent man to his death!"

'There's nothing that can be done about that!" said Caiaphas resolutely.

Judas let out a cry of anguish and hurled the bag of silver at the feet of Caiaphas and ran out.

Judas kept running. A few people stared, shrugged their shoulders and went about their business. Judas kept running, as if looking for a stream that might quench the fires of his inflamed mind now burning out of control.

He stopped running when he got to the Mount of Olives. He looked around, wondering where he was, wondering why he had come here. Gethsemane. He remembered the place, as from a dream, a dream he had last night or in some other life an eternity ago.

Was it a dream or a nightmare? Was he asleep now or awake? Was he alive or dead?

"Judas," he said reassuringly. "My name is Judas."

Somehow, neither the name nor the sound of his own voice were reassuring. Judas looked around at the ground and the rocks and the trees for reassurance.

"This is where it happened, here, last night," Judas mumbled to himself. "I didn't mean it, I didn't, didn't mean it! Here, last night! Or did it happen somewhere else, long before last night? I didn't betray him! I didn't! Or did I? When? Where? Why?"

Judas wandered about aimlessly, hunting for his soul.

"Did I doubt him, too? Did I lose faith in him? Did I find convenient disguises for my own doubts and fears? Did I sacrifice his life to save mine? Are these the games we play in the darkness of our souls? Why do we hide like that? Why can't we see, until it is too late? Why do we deceive ourselves so cleverly? Betray, betray, betray! Why do we betray?

"God! God! Answer me! Please answer me! Why don't You answer me? Did he talk to You, too, here, last night? I'm talking to You now! Answer me, as You answered him! If You answered him, answer me!

"Faith and doubt! Is that it? Faith and doubt! When is faith right, when is doubt right? If he is the Messiah, it is wrong to doubt. If he is not the Messiah, it is wrong to believe! All our life we can have faith in what is wrong. All our life we can doubt what is right! Then it is good to change faith to doubt and doubt to faith! Faith! Doubt! When are they blessing, when are they curse?"

Judas was tired. He sat down. He listened.

"What is the answer, God? Whether we see, or whether we are blind, right or wrong, good or evil, whatever the inclination of our soul, what is the answer when the deed is done? Are You the answer—You and You alone? Your mercy and Your justice, Your love and Your understanding—is that the only constancy for troubled souls in an inconstant world peopled by troubled souls limited in goodness, in understanding, in love?

"Judas? Judas? O heavenly Father, I am Cain, not Judas! Judas is Cain, Cain, Judas! My God, my God, I wish I were Abel. Better to be Abel! Or Jesus. And yet Cain lived and You set your mark of protection on his forehead, so that he would be safe from the wrath and the vengeance and the meanness of men! No one weeps for Cain, but I weep for him now!"

And Judas wept.

Then he got up and walked around, kicking the small rocks that lay in his path. He picked up a length of rope that some pilgrims had left behind or that had fallen by the wayside. He knotted and unknotted it, without really being aware of it.

"What happens now? The deed once done cannot be undone. All the good deeds that I may cram into my life for the rest of my life cannot undo that one deed. All Your love, all Your mercy, all Your forgiveness cannot make me forget. Perhaps my deed is beyond all understanding, which may be enough for others, but I did it, I must understand! Or is this all we can do, to transform life to Your greater glory—sinner can become saint, Cain can become Abel, Judas can become Jesus? Is this the way of redemption?"

Judas leaned against an olive tree and stood still.

"O God! God! I can't bear the burden of Your love, even with Your love! It is too much! I am not strong enough! I am not Jesus! I cannot wait for Your love in a loveless world. I cannot live with their hate and Your love. You are near, You are far—I cannot stand the distance! I must look into Your eyes, I must tear away the final veil, I must know and feel Your love soul to Soul, spirit to Spirit, stripped of all the limitations of the earth!"

Judas saw the rope lying providentially in his hands and he began to fasten a noose. He looked about. No one was in sight. He found a low, sturdy limb and climbed up. He attached the other end of the rope. His heart pounded fiercely. It felt as if it were bleeding to death.

"He should be at Golgotha now," said Judas. "Maybe the miracle will still happen—now, or on the cross. I cannot wait. I could not bear it if it didn't happen. And if it does happen, I, too, will live. I, too, will be redeemed!"

Judas looked around one last time at the earth and sky. Then he fastened the noose around his neck and cried, trembling, "Into Your hands, O Father, I commit my spirit!"

With that, Judas plunged forward and hanged himself.

Jesus and two other prisoners had arrived at Golgotha. Jesus had collapsed several times along the way under the weight of the crossbeam, so that the centurion had pressed a bystander, Simon of Cyrene, into service. Simon laid the crossbeam on the ground at the place of execution and stepped away.

The soldiers worked efficiently. They stripped the prisoners of their clothes, wound a cloth around their loins and lined them up for crucifixion.

Jesus was first.

Two soldiers seized him by each arm, turned him with his back to the crossbeam and threw him backwards against the ground, with neck against the beam.

They knelt on his arms and, when each forearm was flat against the beam, the executioner drove a five-inch nail through the hollow spot of each wrist. Assured that Jesus was securely fastened, the executioner threw his arms up, at which signal the soldiers raised the beam and fitted it into the upright post. Two soldiers took hold of Jesus' legs and crossed the right foot over the left, pushing the feet up high, to make death come slowly. It was the hardest part of the job, but the executioner knew his business. Soon he had the feet nailed to the cross. It only took one nail. Finally, he nailed a board above the prisoner's head. It read:

JESUS OF NAZARETH,
KING OF THE JEWS

The other two prisoners soon flanked him.

Jesus found breathing hard. When he let his body sag, he could inhale but not exhale. The pressure hurt his arms. Breathing was easier if he pushed upward, but his feet then burned with pain. Roman death was slow and deliberate. Crucifixion was death from exhaustion. It was a heathen dance of death.

A handful of people had come to watch—the curious, the coarse, the morbid, the faithful, the pious, the mourners.

Jesus looked down and at the soldiers casting lots for his clothes. The executioner looked up to inspect his work.

"Father," Jesus mumbled, "forgive them, they do not know what they are doing."

The executioner grinned and then returned to the matter of the clothes, making sure he got a fair shake.

"Are not you the Messiah?" one of the criminals hissed tauntingly. "Save yourself, and us."

But the other answered sharply: "Have you no fear of God? You are under the same sentence as he. For us it is plain justice. We are paying the price for our misdeeds. But this man has done nothing wrong. Jesus, remember me when you come in your royal power."

Jesus answered, "I tell you this: today you shall be with me in Paradise."

The man tried hard to smile.

Some of the bystanders knew the whole story. They had been around when Jesus first entered Jerusalem. They had even been taken in by him at first. They admitted it freely. They had found out soon enough he was a troublemaker and phony. Sure they'd been had, but they weren't dumb. They had dropped him fast. It was the smartest thing they could have done. Look what happened to him! Who knows what will still happen to the others and to anyone who remained overly sympathetic!

"Aha!" one of them exclaimed. "You would pull the Temple down, would you, and build it in three days? Come down from the cross and save yourself!"

"He saved others," said another, "but he cannot save himself. Let the Messiah, the King of Israel, come down now from the cross. If we see that, we shall believe."

The others nodded and laughed.

"He said he was God's son—let God save him, if He wants him!"

They laughed again.

Every breath hurt. Jesus tried not to breathe. There was no way to get comfortable. His head sank to his chest. He tried not to move.

He didn't know how long he had been hanging there like that but something made him look up. He could not tell whether what he saw was real or whether he was dreaming. He thought he saw three women and a man nearby. The man looked like his beloved disciple, John. There was Mary of Magdala and his mother's sister, Mary, wife of Clopas. And there was his mother. He thought they were crying softly. Jesus opened his eyes wide to see better. He tried to smile but he couldn't. He wanted to talk but all he managed to say was, "Mother, there is your son."

His mother nodded to her son and then looked up at John.

"There is your mother," Jesus uttered.

The disciple put his arm around Mary to show Jesus that he understood.

Jesus sighed and slumped form the effort. John and the women remained nearby.

Some of the people left after a while. Some passersby asked what was going on and then passed on. A few had been there from the beginning. They had walked the last mile with him. They would stay with him till the last breath. He had said that he was the Messiah and they had believed him. He had given them faith and hope and love, he had shown them love, he had taught them how to love, he had talked to them of God's love and of God's promise, which they knew would be fulfilled. They had waited and they had prayed and their prayers had been answered. God had sent them the Messiah and though he hung now on the cross, nothing was impossible for God, not even a miracle, for the earth was full of His miracles. They watched and waited, oblivious to time.

"*Eli, Eli!*" Jesus cried. "*Lema sebachthani?* My God, my God, why hast Thou forsaken me?"

'He is calling Elijah!" one of the faithful cried, roused form his stupor, misunderstanding the words.

The others came to life. One of them ran at once and brought a sponge which he soaked in sour wine. He put it on the end of a cane and held it to Jesus' lips.

The mockers looked on and smiled. "Let's see if Elijah will come to save him," said one. The others chuckled.

The faithful continued to wait and hope.

There were those who came to mourn. They did not ask who it was—sinner or saint. They came because this, too, was a way of honoring God. To visit the sick, to attend the dying, to accompany them to their final rest.

When Jesus had been on the cross several hours, it became clear that he did not have much longer to live. He would be the first to die. The mourners moved closer so that he could hear and take courage from the tradition of his fathers.

"The Lord is King," they chanted, "the Lord was King, the Lord shall be King for ever and ever."

A silence fell upon the mockers and the faithful alike as they heard the familiar words.

"The Lord is King, the Lord was King, the Lord shall be King for ever and ever."

One by one the others took up the chant.

"The Lord is King, the Lord was King, the Lord shall be King for ever and ever."

Even the soldiers listened now, uncomfortable in the presence of this defiant people.

Jesus roused himself, trying to catch the words.

"Blessed be His name, whose glorious kingdom is for ever and ever.

"Blessed be His name, whose glorious kingdom is for ever and ever.

"Blessed be His name, whose glorious kingdom is for ever and ever."
Jesus held on to life.
"I thirst," he rasped.
They held the sponge to his lips once more.
"The Lord He is God.
"The Lord He is God.
"The Lord He is God.
"The Lord He is God.
"The Lord He is God.
"The Lord He is God.
"The Lord He is God."
Jesus gasped for air.
"It is accomplished," he whispered. "Father, into Thy hands I commit my spirit."
His eyes closed, his lips stopped moving, but he held on one more moment to the last precious breath within him, listening for the final words of the mourners:
"Hear, O Israel, the Lord is our God, the Lord is One."
Then Jesus gave a loud cry and died.

Pontius Pilate congratulated himself with the news of Jesus' death. He had suppressed a rebellion and kept the Roman Peace. King of the Jews! God's Kingdom! Pontius Pilate knew and served but one King and one Kingdom—Caesar and Rome!

Epilogue

The story, of course, does not end here. For Christians, there is no Crucifixion without the Resurrection, just as for Jews there is no Exodus without Mt. Sinai. The one is linked to the other.

Following his death, the body of Jesus was placed in a tomb. Three days later the body was missing. From this day on, there were reports of a resurrected Jesus appearing to his followers.

Despair was turned into hope, defeat into victory. Here was the key: death could be overcome and turned into life; suffering could lead to salvation.

In time, Judaism and Christianity parted and separated. How and why that happened is another story. It is enough to say, for the time being, that Jews survived their oppressors and triumphed over their persecutors. So did Christians.

They did so then.

They have ever since.

And they will continue to do so in times to come.

Postscript

I began work on this book forty years ago. That was 1963. It is now 2003. I self-published the book in 1977 through the publishing company I had set up for this purpose, The Wordoctor (Word Doctor) Publications. Since I do not plan to continue as a publisher, I want to make sure that this and other of my books remain in print.

Fortunately, the print-on-demand (POD) process and POD publishers make it possible now for independent authors to take control of their works, get them published and sold. Because this form of publishing involves digital storage, with books being printed only when ordered, an author's works can be made available in print for years, even beyond an author's life-span.

I have made no changes to the basic book itself. The story remains as I wrote it, from the first chapter to the last. I have also kept the original introduction and dedication.

However, I have changed the title of this book, added a postscript and a bibliography.

As I state in the introduction to this book, I had great anxieties about undertaking this novel. For years, I did not feel up to the task. Who was I, a layman, to write a book about Jesus! I also wondered how such a book, by a Jew, would be accepted by Jews and Christians. Even when I finally made the commitment to write this novel, I still had these concerns.

My anxiety was relieved greatly when I discovered Joseph Klausner's remarkable scholarly work, *Jesus of Nazareth/His Life, Times and Teaching*. In fact, it was the first book I read about Jesus by a Jewish scholar, as I began my research. What struck me was the sympathetic, respectful understanding with which Klausner approached Jesus. It validated my own approach. I felt encouraged that my book, a novel, might find acceptance as well by Jews and Christians. Klausner's book, which I found in the library, had long been out of print. It was so important to me, literally and figuratively, that I wanted to have my own copy. I contacted a book-search service, which located a copy. It cost $27, an enormous sum for a book, and a used one at that, in 1963, but I was glad to pay it.

The title of my book has been changed from *My Jewish Brother Jesus* to *A Jewish Novel About Jesus* for a rather simple reason. Some people were confused by my original title. Some Jews assumed that this was a book written by a Jewish convert to Christianity, who was trying to get them to accept Jesus, while some Christians assumed that this was a book written by a Jew who had accepted Jesus as his Lord and Savior.

Neither case is true, as readers, of course, discovered. I am a practicing, observant Jew, identifying with the Conservative stream of Judaism. I always have. I explained, even in my first edition, that I wrote the book to give Jews and Christians a better understanding of, and appreciation for, Jesus the Jew and his Jewish roots. Most importantly, I indicated that I did not want to undermine the validity of Christianity or Judaism or to convert Jews to Christianity. I simply wanted to create understanding, so we could live together, side by side, respectful of one another, in dignity and peace. That is still my aim.

To do that, I wanted to show that the love of God and of our fellow human beings is as at the heart of Judaism. Jesus learned this as a Jew and made it the heart of his teaching. It became the heart of Christianity. I also wanted to defuse the age-old deicide charge—that the Jews are "Christ-killers"—and show that the Crucifixion—a Roman form of capital punishment—was instigated and executed by the Roman procurator Pontius Pilate, who considered Jesus a direct danger and threat to his rule and Rome's control of the Holy Land.

I found the basis for these considerations in several sources.

I found the most pivotal, most crucial bit of information in *Man's Religions*, by John B. Ross, who, talking about the Romans, states (p. 574): "Though they allowed the Jews as much civil and religious liberty as political considerations (that is, Roman imperialism) permitted, they insisted on a kind of remote control over the Jewish religion. For example, they kept the robes of the high priest stored in the Tower of Antonia and released them only for the ceremonies in which they were worn. This meant that they could control the appointment of the high priest by signifying to whom they would be pleased to release the robes."

In other words, Caiaphas, the High Priest, was the pawn of Rome, represented by the region's procurator, Pontius Pilate. If Caiaphas played ball with Pilate, the High Priest got his robes and remained in office. If not, the robes were withheld from him and he was replaced by a more accommodating High Priest. The three major festivals when the High Priest needed his robes were Passover (Pesach), Pentecost (Shavuot) and The Feast of Booths (Succot).

Caiaphas was a very accommodating High Priest. He was the 13th High Priest, since the time of Herod, who died around the time that Jesus was born. Other High Priests only lasted on average four years. Caiaphas, however, held office from the years 18 to 36 CE. Significantly, the priesthood, which once was hereditary, had become corrupted during this time. It was for sale.

Caiphas understood how to cooperate with Roman governors. He also knew his limits, if he wanted to stay in power. Pilate saw Jesus as a destabilizing, political threat. Pilate wanted Jesus dead. Since Pilate had leverage over Caiaphas, the High Priest was ready to do his bidding. He delivered Jesus to Pilate for Roman execution by crucifixion. Caiaphas acted with the collaboration of his own, appointed cabinet—a *political* council (Sanhedrin), not a *religious* council (Sanhedrin).

This is discussed extensively in two scholarly works: *Studies in The History of the Sanhedrin* by Hugo Mantel and in *Who Crucified Jesus?* by Solomon Zeitlin. The books make the case that the Sanhedrin referred to in the New Testament was really a political advisory council to the High Priest, appointed by the High Priest, with the approval of the Roman procurator. The religious Sanhedrin, was independent of the political advisory council. The religious Sanhedrin would not have considered a case against Jesus, especially not one involving capital punishment, for which there really was no Jewish religious basis against him. In any case, that process would have required more time than was available. The political advisory council had no such constraints. Furthermore, and significantly, the High Priest, A Sadducee, had no control over the religious Sanhedrin, a Pharisaic institution.

So why is Pontius Pilate placed in such a good light and the Jews in such a bad light, in parts of the New Testament? Why is the blame taken away from Pilate and placed on the Jews?

As so often happens in recorded human affairs, we must learn to read between the lines. Not long after Jesus was crucified, the Jewish Temple was destroyed by Rome. Then, shortly after, the Jews tried a final rebellion, which failed, and they were conquered.

Jews were taken into slavery; Christians were being fed to the lions. The young Christian religion was trying to survive. It would not have been politically wise or physically healthy to blame Pontius Pilate or Rome for the death of Jesus, either in speech or writing. So the story got revised. Those living at the time, understood. They knew how to read between the lines. The biggest hint embedded in the story was that Jesus was crucified. That form of capital punishment pointed to Pontius Pilate and Rome, alone.

We cannot, of course, rewrite the Bible. The text is fixed. It cannot be changed. However, it can be reinterpreted in light of new information or new insights. This is done all the time. We need to do this in connection with these issues, for the sake and integrity of history, humanity, our religious communities and God.

Such efforts have been made independent of my own efforts. The deicide charge, for instance, has poisoned Western society for the last 2000 years, paving the way to the Holocaust. Since then, the Catholic Church and the Lutheran Church have been in the forefront of religious institutions who have modified their position regarding Judaism, recognizing it as a complete, authentic faith, nuancing the difficult passages of the New Testament and asserting the incompatibility of Christianity and anti-Semitism.

I believe that Jesus saw himself in messianic terms. That's how I portray him. Jews and Christians differ on whether he is or not. I leave that question where it belongs, with each faith community. Jews and Christians also differ on other theological questions, including matters of Jesus' birth and special relationship to God. Out of respect for Jewish and Christian traditions, I do not deal with these issues, allowing each reader to follow the dictates of conscience and faith.

It is my hope that this book may play its part in bringing healing to our hearts, light to our minds, peace to our spirits and joy to our souls.

Rolf Gompertz
May 20, 2003

About the Author

"If I had not been born a Jew," said Rolf Gompertz, "I might have become a Nazi. I was born in Germany."

He and his parents, Oscar and Selma Gompertz, lived through *Kristallnacht*, November 9, 1938, the Night of Broken Glass, dress rehearsal for the Holocaust that followed. They fled to America the following year, when Rolf was 11 years old, and settled in Los Angeles, California. Gompertz returned to

Krefeld, his birthplace in the Rhineland, at the invitation of the city in 1987. He was asked back the following year to deliver a 45-minute keynote speech in German on the 50th anniversary of *Kristallnacht*.

Gompertz is the author of eight books, including two biblical novels, *Abraham, The Dreamer/An Erotic and Sacred Love Story*, his most recent, and *My Jewish Brother Jesus*, his first published book, now titled, *A Jewish Novel About Jesus*.

Abraham, the patriarch of three religions—Judaism, Christianity and Islam—is the focal point of *Abraham, the Dreamer: An Erotic and Sacred Love Story*, a fast-paced, provocative, biblical novel, which explores the turbulent love triangle involving Abraham, his emotionally distant wife, Sarah, and her handmaid, Hagar, "the other woman," who is assigned to give Abraham a son and becomes the love of his life.

My Jewish Brother Jesus, a highly acclaimed biblical novel, was published in 1977 (The Word Doctor Publications). It deals with the life of Jesus from a Jewish point of view. It was written to set the record straight about the Trial and Crucifixion and, in the author's words, "to create a better understanding between Jews and Christians, so we can live together, side by side, respectful of one another, in dignity and peace."

Other books followed, including *SPARKS OF SPIRIT: How to Find Love & Meaning in Your Life 24 Hours a Day*, a spiritual self-help book; *The Messiah of Midtown Park* (a contemporary play/comedy-drama); and *A Celebration of Life* (poetry and prose, including the text of his one-man show). His articles and short stories on Jewish themes, including *Kristallnacht* and his return to Germany, have been published in major newspapers and magazines.

Following high school, Gompertz joined the U.S. Army and served as a German translator in Washington, D.C. He then attended the University of California at Los Angeles (UCLA), where he earned a B.A. and M.A. degree in English literature. He was honored with the Best Student of the Year Award and named a Phi Beta Kappa.

After college, Gompertz worked as an editor of a weekly newspaper in Torrance, California, and then joined the Press and Publicity Department of the

National Broadcasting Company (NBC), serving as a publicist and then as a publicity director. He left after 30 years to form his own company, Rolf Gompertz Communications. He has been a UCLA Extension instructor since 1974. His two books in the field are the highly regarded *Publicity Advice & How-To Handbook* and *Publicity Writing for Television and Film.* (An earlier PR book is now out of print.)

Gompertz, and his family, are long-time members of Adat Ari El, a Conservative synagogue in North Hollywood. He created, produced, wrote and hosted a local cable TV series, *ADAT ARI EL PRESENTS: Journeys into Judaism*, which ran for four-and-a-half years. He has taught adult education workshops and spoken on Jewish spirituality, meditation and mysticism.

He and his wife, Carol, were married in 1957 and live in North Hollywood, California. They have two sons, a daughter, and four grandchildren: Ron & Ouided Gompertz, Neil and Ryan; Nancy & Jonathan Booth, Sean and Michael; and Philip Gompertz.

Other Books by Rolf Gompertz

ABRAHAM, THE DREAMER
An Erotic and Sacred Love Story
(A Biblical Novel)

This biblical novel offers an intriguing, unconventional and daring interpretation of the life of Abraham, Sarah and Hagar, the "First Family" of Jews, Christians and Muslims.

The biblical text tells us little about Sarah, but the author suggests boldly, as we meet Abraham's wife, that she is a High Priestess serving Inanna, the Sumerian goddess of Love and War. Sarah, who has become accidentally pregnant by her husband, Abraham, orders the child killed, as required of a High Priestess. Reacting emotionally, Abraham revolts against this practice and, in that moment, hears the call of a new, singular, unseen God who tells him to go forth to a new and different land. Ironically, he is also told that he will become the father of a multitude.

Alienated from each other spiritually, emotionally and physically, the childless Sarah offers Abraham her handmaid, Hagar, with whom to have a child, unaware of the attraction that has already developed between the two, culminating in the birth of Ishmael.

When the jealous Sarah gives birth unexpectedly to Isaac, she breaks up the idyllic relationship between Abraham and Hagar, driving the beloved other woman, and her son, Ishmael, away forever.

Abraham has his difficulties trying to understand the will of his new God. In his despair over losing Hagar, he falls back on pagan sacrificial practices, and proceeds to offer Isaac as a burnt-offering, believing that this is what his new God has asked of him. Ultimately, the book asks the difficult question: How can we ever know the will of God with certainty? In the final showdown between Abraham and Sarah, the author offers a surprising and startling answer to this question. (Note: The novel contains sexually explicit material.)

Fast-paced and written with great clarity like his other spiritually themed books, the novel by this Jewish author makes for fascinating, meaningful and, ultimately, inspiring reading.

What others say about 'Abraham, The Dreamer'

*"A powerful, modern **midrash** (commentary) on the life of Abraham, giving it a contemporary ring...The Biblical characters come alive and become very human. It has been meticulously researched and bears the mark of a master storyteller."*

—Rabbi Moshe J. Rothblum of Adat Ari El, a Conservative synagogue in North Hollywood, CA

"A daring look at the Abraham triangle..., unconventional..., engulfing..., the sexiest, most imaginative account of the lives of Abraham and Sarah that ever has been marketed..."

—Ari L. Noonan, *Heritage/Southwest Jewish Press*

*"Anyone who wishes to become more familiar with our Biblical ancestors, so as to identify with them and to learn from them and the essential messages of their lives, will be well advised to read the dynamic **ABRAHAM, THE DREAMER**, which bridges the gap between ancient times and this contemporary moment in which we find ourselves, and explores the profound relationship that links God and humanity in every generation."*

—Allen I. Freehling, Ph.D., D.D., Senior Rabbi (Emeritus), University Synagogue, Los Angeles, CA

"Simply stunningly brilliant and plausible, in every way...A lovely, powerful and important book."

—Rev. Alla Renée Bozarth, Ph.D., Episcopal priest, Sandy, Oregon, author of *The Book of Bliss* and *At the Foot of the Mountain*

"It should be noted that this Jewish author uses explicit language in his effort to meld the meanings of spiritual and physical love and how those relate to one's life and worship. I appreciated that, though explicit, I never found it offensive."

—Carolyn Howard-Johnson, author of the award-winning *This Is the Place* and *Harkening: A Collection of Stories Remembered*

❈   ❈   ❈

A JEWISH NOVEL ABOUT JESUS

This fast-paced novel sheds new light on the story of Jesus and his times. We get to know Jesus the Jew, and his Jewish world. We meet a much more sympathetic Judas, who believes in Jesus but becomes trapped in a deadly political power-play. Meantime, there is seductive Mary Magdalene, who taunts and tempts Judas, but is transformed through him—and Jesus. Yet Pontius Pilate, the Roman procurator, sees Jesus as a greater threat than Barabbas, the violent Zealot leader. Pilate orders Caiaphas, the Jewish High Priest, whose office he controls, to get rid of Jesus. However, Rabbi Gamaliel, head of the Great Sanhedrin, refuses to collaborate with Caiaphas or Rome—he will not deliver Jesus, or any other innocent Jew, to death.

Rolf Gompertz is an observant, practicing Jew, who fled Nazi Germany with his parents. Says he: "I wrote this book as my answer to Hitler, to set the record straight about the pernicious *Christ-killer* charge, which resulted in Jewish persecution for 2000 years, culminating with the Holocaust. I wanted to create understanding between Jews and Christians, so we may live together, side by side, respectful of one another, in dignity and peace."

What others say:

"It is a pleasure to read a description of the trial and ordeal of Jesus from a Jewish perspective."

—Rabbi Moshe J. Rothblum, Adat Ari El, North Hollywood, CA

"You write with an easy, fascinating, living style...You kept my interest to the end..."

—Rev. Carl W. Segerhammar, D.D., Past President, Pacific Southwest Synod of the Lutheran Church in America

"I found it very readable...The story was so well told that I wanted to keep on reading..."

—Dr. A. George Downing, Executive Minister American Baptist Churches of the Pacific Southwest

"(A) fine Biblical novel. I was especially intrigued with your suggesting that there was a political Sanhedrin operating in Jerusalem."

—Rabbi Allen I. Freehling, PhD University Synagogue, West Los Angeles, CA

"(The author) has given us a reverent, enjoyable work, and he has reminded us once again, as we need to be reminded, that Jesus and his disciples were Jews..."

—William Sanford Lasor, Professor of Old Testament, Fuller Theological Seminary, Pasadena, California, *The Reformed Journal*, May 1978

"This book...helps us understand Jesus and his inner circle as Jews, with a more sympathetic picture of Judaism than we see in the Gospels."

—Review, *The North American Moravian*, March 1978

SPARKS OF SPIRIT (A Handbook for Personal Happiness)
How to Find Love & Meaning in Your Life 24 Hours a Day
(Personal Development Guide)

This book is a spiritual training manual. It shows how to develop and maintain a spiritual point of view in our every-day life. It deals with our personal concerns. It is written in clear, simple, contemporary language that's easy to understand. The end of each chapter also features a list of biblical verses, from the Hebrew Bible/"Old Testament," which support the text. This book has been used for meditation workshops which the author has conducted. It is non-denominational and the ideas can be incorporated into traditional or non-traditional belief-systems. The author offers a simple method of meditation, using the verses and chapter contents.

"Your book is inspirational, interestingly written, and contains many practical tools for developing and maintaining a useful and happy life."

—**Dr. Norman Vincent Peale**
Marble Collegiate Church,
New York City, NY

"Many people are troubled these days, and they are searching for ways to find help. Your volume may reach their needs and prove to be most helpful to them."

—**Rabbi Aaron M. Wise**
Adat Ari El, North Hollywood, CA

"I asked one of our discreet priests to read the manuscript. He advises me that the material is very good and will help many people to relate to the God of Abraham, Isaac and Jacob. He found it good material for meditation and was enthusiastic about your ability to write."

—**Cardinal Timothy Manning**
Archbishop of Los Angeles

*"In **Sparks of Spirit**, your thoughts, The Four Noble Truths and the Eightfold Path meet Torah and the Beatitudes—also a little Black Elk and echoes of the reverent religion of the Great Mother of antiquity (and now). You go deeply into your own specific tradition and through its integrity you encounter the universal experience of holiness and mystery.*

—**The Rev. Alla Renée Bozarth, Ph.D.**
author of ***At the Foot of the Mountain*** and
All Shall Be Well, All Shall Be One

❋   ❋   ❋

THE MESSIAH OF MIDTOWN PARK (Play/Comedy-Drama)

Seventy-seven-year-old Shlomo Hirsch is a harmless, kindly, little old man who quotes Bible verses and sits in a park feeding pigeons. He has known for 50 years that he is the Messiah, but he's never figured out what to do about it. It's worried him lately. After all, he's not getting any younger. Suddenly he thinks of a plan: He will go on a TV talk show and tell his message to the world...

This is a delightful, contemporary comedy-drama about what might happen if the Messiah appeared today. It deals with the complexities and conflicts of our various messianic beliefs, not only within Judaism, but among the major world religions. Whose Messiah can we believe in, all at the same time? The play ends on a surprising note which may very well provide an answer that we can accept, without undermining the various belief systems.

❋   ❋   ❋

A CELEBRATION OF LIFE (Poetry and Prose)

How do I get through life? What's it all about? That's the question the author asks—for all of us. The book takes its title from the author's one-man show, whose full text appears here. In *A Celebration of Life*, the author takes his readers (or listeners) on an entertaining, inspirational journey through life, both humorous and serious, in poetry and prose.

The book also features other works, including "The Search: A Song of Man and the Universe," "The Love Song" and other poems from his early and later years, expressing the universal hopes and fears, joys and sorrows of our human condition.

What Others Say:

(Comments about the author's performance of his one-man show, whose text is included in this book and whose title the book bears.)

"I want to thank you for a never-to-be forgotten evening. You have something to say and say it well. I know that I and all the others who were privileged to hear you and to see your performance came away from the event feeling great—and that is what it is all about after all. Thank you again for giving of your time, talents and warmth to make a memorable evening for the rest of us. I personally will remember it for a long time to come."

**—Edith Schlam, Wise Singles,
Stephen S. Wise Temple**

"Your thoughts in poetry and prose evoked many thoughts and memories in all of us. it was a truly delightful evenig, one that will not soon be forgotten."

**—Kimberly Faber, Program Director,
Women's International Network**

*"I just called to tell you how much I enjoyed last night's performance. I think it's more than a performance. It's a **happening** and it's really inspirational. You do a wonderful job of expressing yourself and your life, and you inspire."*

—Blanche Herring, audience member

*"Rolf Gompertz offers us a **Celebration of Life** which is truly that—a show full of life and joy. Something between lecture and performance. Mr. Gompertz's presentation wins our admiration and our affection. He inspires young and older alike to keep plugging when things get rough…and to develop their capacities for love. I heartily recommend Mr. Gompertz as an educating entertainer and an entertaining educator."*

**—Rabbi Susan Laemmle, Hillel Director/USC
formerly Hillel Director, Los Angeles Valley & Pierce Colleges**

How to Obtain These Books

These books are available as paperbacks from the publisher's online book store at http://www.iUniverse.com or from http://www.amazon.com. The books may be inspected and browsed at either place before ordering. At the web site _select_ the _book store_ and _search_ by _author's name_ (Rolf Gompertz) or the particular _book title_. If a title has not been posted yet, it will be shortly. You may also contact the author for more information and updates. Mailto: rolfgompertz@yahoo.com.

Bibliography

BIBLES

Jewish

The Holy Scriptures, According to the Masoretic Text. Copyright © 1917, 1955
(New Edition, fourth impression, 1965). Philadelphia, Pennsylvania:
approved version of The Jewish Publication Society. Grateful acknowledgment is made that quotes from the Hebrew Bible in *A Jewish
Novel About Jesus (My Jewish Brother Jesus)* are taken from here, with
permission.

Soncino Books of the Bible, Editor: Rev. Dr. A. Cohen, M.A., Ph.D., D.H.L.

The Pentateuch and Haftorahs, Second Edition, Dr. J.H. Hertz. London: Soncino Press, 1937.

The Psalms, Hebrew Text English Translation with an Introduction and Commentary, by The Rev. Dr. A. Cohen, M.A., Ph.D., D.H.L. London: The
Soncino Press, 1950.

Christian

New English Bible © Oxford University Press and Cambridge University Press
1961, 1970. New Testament. (Grateful acknowledgment is made that
quotes from the New Testament in *A Jewish Novel About Jesus (My Jewish
Brother Jesus)* are taken from here, with permission.)

A New Translation of THE BIBLE Containing the Old and New Testaments, York and London, Copyright ©1922, 1924, 1925, 1926, 1935 by Harper & Brothers; copyright © 1950 by James. A.R. Moffatt

The Complete Bible: An American Translation, the Old Testament translated by J.M. Powis Smith and a group of scholars; the New Testament translated by Edgar J. Goodspeed. Chicago: The University of Chicago Press, 1939, thirteenth impression, 1949.

The Holy Bible, Containing the Old and New Testaments, translated out of the original tongues: and with the former translations diligently compared and revised by His Majesty's Special Command, Appointed to be Read in Churches, Authorized King James Version, (The Oxford Self-Pronouncing Bible, S.S. Teacher's Edition), Oxford University Press.

The Holy Bible, Containing the Old and New Testaments, translated out of the original tongues, being the version set forth A.D. 1611, compared with the most ancient authorities and revised A.D. 1881–1885, Newly Edited by the American Revision Committee, A.D. 1901, Standard Edition, Thomas Nelson & Sons, New York, copyright 1929 by International Council of Religious Education.

The Holy Bible, The Scofield Reference Bible, Containing the Old and New Testments, Authorized Version, edited by Rev. C.I. Scofield, D.D., Oxford University Press, New York, Copyright ©1909, 1917 by Oxford University Press, American Branch.

The Holy Bible (Containing the Old and New Testaments), Revised Standard Version, Thomas Nelson & Sons, Old Testament Section, copyright © 1952; New Testament Section, copyright ©1946.

The New Testament, in Modern English, translated by J.B. Phillips, The Macmillan Company, New York, 1962.

ENCYCLOPEDIAS, CONCORDANCES, DICTIONARIES, ILLUSTRATED PUBLICATIONS

Analytical Concordance to the Bible, designed by Robert Young, LL.D, 21st American Edition, revised throughout by William B. Stevenson, B.D. (Edin.), New York: Funk & Wagnalls, 1912.

Dictionary of the Bible, edited by James Hastings, New York: Charles Scribner's Sons, 1937.

Encyclopedia Judaica, Cecil Roth, Editor.

Illustrated World of the Bible Library, 5 volumes, 1958–1961, The International Publishing Company Ltd., Jerusalem—Ramat Dan, Israel; McGraw-Hill Book Company, Inc.

The Jewish Encyclopedia, Prepared by more than 400 scholars and specialists. New York: KTAV Publishing House, Inc., 1901.

The Standard Jewish Encyclopedia, New, Revised Edition, Cecil Roth, Editor-in-Chief, New York: Doubleday & Company, Inc., 1959, 1962.

The World's Great Religions, Editor-in-Chief, Henry R. Luce, Time Incorporated; series and book were produced under the general direction of Edward K. Thompson, Managing Editor, New York: Time Incorporated, 1957.

PASSOVER HAGGADAH

The New Haggadah/For the Pesah Seder, edited by Mordecai M. Kaplan, Eugene Kohn, and Ira Eisenstein, for the Jewish Reconstructionist Foundation, published by Behrman House, New York, 1941; second printing, revised, 1942, sixteenth printing, 1959. Out of print.

BIBLE ATLASES

Rand McNally Bible Atlas, Emil G. Kraeling, New York: Rand McNally, 1962.

The Westminster Historical Atlas to the Bible, Revised Edition, edited by George Ernest Wright and Floyd Vivian Filson, with an introductory article by William Foxwell Albright, © 1956 by W.L. Jenkins, org. edition © 1945 by The Westminster Press

BOOKS

Allegro, John Marco, *Zealots: Treasure of the Copper Scroll*, Garden City, New York: Anchor Books, 1964.

Aron, Robert, *Jesus of Nazareth, The Hidden Years*, translated from the French by Frances Frenaye, New York: William Morrow and Company, 1962.

Arnold, William Thomas, *The Roman System of Provincial Administration*, Oxford: B. H. Blackwell, 1906.

Asch, Sholem, *The Nazarene*, translated by Maurice Samuel, New York: G.P. Putnam's Sons, 1939.

—*Mary*, translated by Leo Steinberg, New York: G.P. Putnam's Sons, 1949.

—*Salvation*, translated by Willa and Edwin Muier, New York: G.P. Putnam's Sons, 1934, 1951.

Baeck, Leo, *The Pharisees and Other Essays*, New York, Schocken Books, 1947.

—*This People Israel, The Meaning of Jewish Existence*, translated by Albert H. Friedlander, Philadelphia: The Jewish Publication Society of America, 1965.

Bailey, Albert E., *Daily Life in Bible Times*, New York: Charles Scribner, 1943.

Baron, Salo Wittmayer, *A Social and Religious History of the Jews*, 2 vol., Philadelphia: The Jewish Publication Society of America, 1952.

Bishop, Jim, *The Day Christ Died*, Harper & Brothers, 1957, Cardinal Giant, 1959.

Borg, Marcus J., *Jesus, a New Vision/Spirit, Culture and the Life of Discipleship*, HarperSanFrancisco, a division of HarperCollins Publishers, 1991; HarperCollins Publishers, New York 1987.

Buber, Martin, *Two Types of Faith*, transl. by Norman P. Goldhawk, New York: Collier Books, 1951.

Browne, Laurence E., *From Babylon to Bethlehem*, Cambridge: Heffer, 1951.

Bruce, Alexander B., *The Miraculous Element in the Gospels*, New York: Hodder, 1886.

Bryan, William Jennings, *Christ and His Companions*, New York, Chicago: Fleming H. Revell Company, 1925.

Busch, Fritz, *The Five Herods*, trans. E.W. Dickes, London: Robert Hale, 1958

Clough, William Overton, *Gesta Pilati*, Indianapolis, Douglass, 1880.

Cohen, A., *Everyman's Talmud*, New York: E. P. Dutton & Co., Inc., New American Edition, 1949.

Conybear, Frederick Cornwallis, *The Origins of Christianity*, Evanston & New York: University Books, 1958.

Crozier, William Percival, *Letters of Pontius Pilate*, New York: J. M. Sears, 1928.

Daniel-Rops, Henri, *Daily Life in Time of Jesus*, translated from the French by Patrick O'Brian, New York: Hawthorn Books, Inc., 1962.

Douglas, Lloyd C., *Those Disturbing Miracles*, New York: Harper, 1927.

Drucker, A. P., *The Trial of Jesus from Jewish Sources*, New York: Bloch, 1907.

DuPont-Sommer, André, *The Essene Writings from Qumran*, transl. by G. Vermes, Oxford: Blackwell, 1961.

Durant, Will, *Caesar and Christ*, New York: Simon, 1944.

Edersheim, Alfred, *The Temple: Its Ministry and Services, At the Time of Jesus Christ*, London: Religious Tract Society, 1874.

Enelow, Hyman Gerson, *A Jewish View of Jesus*, New York: The Macmillan Company, 1920.

Epstein, Isidore, *The Faith of Judaism*, London: The Soncino Press, 1954.

Farrar, F. W., *The Herods*, New York: Herrick Press, n.d.

Finkelstein, Louis, *The Pharisees*, 2 vol., Philadelphia: The Jewish Publication Society, 1962.

—*The Pharisees and the Social Background of Their Faith*, 2 vol., Philadelphia: The Jewish Publication Society, 1938; 2nd edit. 1946.

—*The Jews, Their History, Culture and Religion*, Third Edition, in two volumes, New York: Harper & Brothers Publishers, 1949, 1955, 1960.

—*Akiba: Scholar, Saint and Martyr*, Cleveland and New York: Meridian Books, The World Publishing Company and Philadelphia: The Jewish Publication Society of America, 1962; © 1936 by Louis Finkelstein.

Fletcher, Howard A., *Saint Judas Iscariot*, New York: Vantage Press, 1961.

Gaster, Theodor H., *Myth, Legend, and Custom in the Old Testament*, A comparative study with chapters from Sir James. G. Frazer's *Folklore in the Old Testament*, New York and Evanston: Harper & Row, Publishers, 1969; Frazer's *Folklore in the Old Testament*, 3 vol., Macmillan & Company, London, 1918.

Ganzfried—Goldin, *Code of Jewish Law, A Compilation of Jewish Laws and Customs*, Revised Edition, by Rabbi Solomon Ganzfried, translated by Hyman E. Goldin, LL.B., New York: Hebrew Publishing Company, 1961.

Glover, T. R., *The Conflict of Religions in the Early Roman Empire*, London, Methuen & Co., 1917; Beacon Press, 1960.

Goldstein, Morris, *Jesus in the Jewish Tradition*, New York: Macmillan, 1950.

Goguel, Maurice, *The Life of Jesus*, translated by Olive Wyon, New York: The Macmillan Company, 1946.

Goldin, Hyman E., *The Case of the Nazarene Reopened*, New York: Exposition Press, 1948.

Goodspeed, Edgar J., *A Life of Jesus*, New York: Harper & Brothers, Publishers, 1950.

—*The Twelve*, The Story of Christ's Apostles, Philadelphia: John C. Winston Co., 1957.

Granger, F. S., The *Worship of the Romans*, London: Methuen, 1895.

Grant, Frederick C., *The Life and Times of Jesus*, New York, Cincinnati: The Abingdon Press, 1921.

—*Ancient Judaism and the New Testament*, New York: The Macmillan Company, 1959.

—*Ancient Roman Religion*, New York: Liberal Arts Press, 1957.

Grant, Robert McQueen, *The Sword and the Cross*, New York, The Macmillan Company, 1955.

Grayzel, Solomon, *A History of the Jews*, Philadelphia: The Jewish Publication Society of America, 1952

Greenstone, Julius H., *The Messiah Idea in Jewish History*, Philadelphia: The Jewish Publication Society of America, 1943.

Guignebert, Charles, *Jesus*, translated from the French by S.H> Hooke, New Hyde Park, New York: University Books, Inc., 1956.

Hamilton, Edith, *Spokesmen for God, The Great Teachers of the Old Testament, New York: W.W. Norton & Company, 1936, 1949*

—*Witness to the Truth/Christ and His Interpreters*, New York: W.W. Norton & Company, 1948, 1957.

Herford, Robert T., *The Truth About the Pharisees*, Menorah Press, 1925.

—*The Pharisees*, Boston: Beacon Press, 1962.

Howlett, Duncan, *The Essenes and Christianity, An Interpretation of the Dead Sea Scrolls*, New York: Harper, 1957.

Heschel, Abraham J., *The Prophets*, Philadelphia: The Jewish Publication Society of America, 1962.

Housh, Grant S., *Judas Speaks*, New York: The William-Frederick Press, 1953.

Jones, Arnold Hugh Martin, Oxford: The Clarendon Presds, 1938.

Karp, Abraham J., *The Jewish Way of Life*, New Jersey: Prentice-Hall, 1962.

Kazantzakis, Nikos, *The Last Temptation of Christ*, New York: Simon and Schuster, 1960.

Klausner, Joseph, *Jesus of Nazareth/His Life, Times, and Teaching*, New York: The Macmillan Company, 1925, 1926.

—*The Messianic Idea in Israel*, New York: The Macmillan Company, 1955.

—*From Jesus to Paul*, translated from the Hebrew by William F. Stinespring, Boston: Beacon Press, 1961; The Macmillan Company, 1943.

Kligerman, Aaron Judah, *Messianic Prophecy in the Old Testament*, Grand Rapids, Zondervan Publishing House, 1957.

Komroff, Manuel, *Jesus Through the Centuries*, New York: William Sloane Assoc., 1953.

Learsi, Rufus, *Israel: A History of the Jewish People*, Cleveland and New York: The World Publishing Company, 1949.

Liebman, Joshua Loth, *Peace of Mind*, New York: Simon and Schuster, 1946.

Lockyer, Herbert, *All the Miracles of the Bible*, Grand Rapids, Zondervan Publ. House, 1961.

Ludwig, Emil, *The Son of Man, The Story of Jesus*, New York: Boni & Liveright, 1928.

Mantel, Hugo, *Studies in the History of the Sanhedrin*, Cambridge: Harvard Univ. Press, 1961.

Mattingley, Harold, *Roman Imperial Civilization*, London: Edward Arnold Ltd., 1957.

Micklem, Edward R., *Miracles and the New Psycholgy*, London: H. Milford, Oxford University Press, 1922.

Monsma, John Clover, editor, *The Evidence of God in an Expanding Universe*, Forty American Scientists Declare Their Affirmative Views of Relgion, New York: G.P. Putnam's Sons, 1958.

Montefiore, C.G. (Claude Goldsmid), *The Synoptic Gospels*, 2 vol. London: Macmillan, 1927.

Morton, H.V., *In the Steps of the Master*, New York: Dodd, Mead & Company, 1934, 1935.

Mossingsohn, Igal, *Judas*, New York: St. Martin's Press, 1963.

Newman, Louis I., *The Jewish People, Faith and Life*, New York: Bloch Publishing Company, 1965.

Mueller, Francis John, *Christ's Twelve*, Milwaukee: Bruce Publishing Co., 1940.

Nicoll, Maurice, *The New Man: An Interpretation of Some Parables and Miracles of Christ*, New York, Hermitage House, 1950.

Noel, Conrad, *Jesus the Heretic*, London: Religious Book Club, 1940.

Noss, John B., *Man's Religions*, New York: The Macmillan Company, 1949.

Oursler, Fulton, *The Greatest Story Ever Told*, Garden City, New York: Doubleday & Company, Inc., 1949.

Papini, Giovanni, *Life of Christ*, freely translated from the Italian by Dorothy Canfield Fisher, New York: Harcourt, Brace and Company, 1923; 14th printing, 1924.

Perowne, Stewart, *Life and Times of Herod the Great*, New York: Abingdon Press, 1959.

—*The Later Herods*, New York: Abbingdon Press, 1958.

Phillips, J. B., *Your God Is Too Small,* New York: The Macmillan Company, 1957.

Rayner, William, *The Knifeman,* a Novel of Judas Iscariot, New York: William Morrow and Company, Inc., 1969.

Reich, Max Isaac, *Messianic Hope of Israel,* Chicago, Il.: Moody Press, 1945.

Renan, Ernest, *The Life of Jesus,* New York: Modern Library, 1927.

Riddle, Donald Wayne, *Jesus and the Pharisees,* Chicago: Chicago University Press, 1928.

Robinson, Benjamin Willard, *The Sayings of Jesus, Their Background and Interpretation,* New York: Harper & Brothers, 1930.

Ross, Albert Henry, *And Pilate Said,* New York: Scribner, 1940.

Roth, Cecil, *Historical Background of the Dead Sea Scrolls,* New York: Philosophical library, 1958.

Sandmel, Samuel, *We Jews and Jesus,* New York, Oxford University Press, 1965.

—*A Jewish Understanding of the New Testament,* Cincinnati, Hebrew Union College Press, 1956.

Schonfield, Hugh J. *The Jesus Party,* New York, Macmillan Publishing Co., Inc., 1974.

—*The Passover Plot/New Light on the History of Jesus,* published by Bernard Geis Associates, distributed by Random House, 1965.

—*Those Incredible Christians,* published by Bernard Geis Associates, distributed by Grove Press, Inc., 1968.

Schuré, Edouard, *Jesus, the Last Great Initiate,* New York: Theosophical Publishing Co., n.d.

Silver, Abba Hillel, *A History of Messianic Speculation in Israel*, The Macmillan Company, 1927; First Beacon Paperback Edition, 1959, Beacon Press, Beacon Hill, Boston.

—*Where Judaism Differed*, New York: The Macmillan Company, 1956, 1961.

Smith, Arlis Milton, *The Twelve Apostles*, New York: Revell, 1940.

Smith, Asbury, *Twelve Christ Chose*, New York: Harper, 1958.

Spong, John Shelby, *This Hebrew Lord*, New York: The Seabury Press, 1974.

Thompson, J.M., *The Synoptic Gospels*, London: Oxford University Press, 1910, 1928, 1935, 1947, 1950, 1956, 1962, 1969.

Trattner, Ernest R., *As a Jew Sees Jesus*, New York and London, Charles Scribner's Sons, 1931

—*The Autobiography of God, An Interpretation*, New York, London: Charles Scribner's Sons, 1930.

—*Unravelling the Book of Books*, New York: Charles Scribner's Sons, 1929.

—*Understanding the Talmud*, Toronto, New York, Edinburgh: Thomas Nelson & Sons, 1955.

Van Paassen, Pierre, *Why Jesus Died*, New York: Dial Press Inc., 1949.

Walker, Thomas, *Jewish Views on Jesus*, London: G. Allen & Unwin, 1931

Wallis, Wilson D., *Messiahs, Their Role in Civilization*, Washington, D.C., The American Council on Public Affairs, 1943.

—*Messiahs, Christian and Pagan*, World Worship Series, Boston: R. G. Badger, 1918.

Weinstock, Harris, *Jesus the Jew*, New York & London: Funk & Wagnalls, 1902.

Wendland, Johannes, *Miracles and Christianity*, English transl. H.R. Mackintosh, London & New York, Hodder & Stoughton, 1911.

Whitman, Howard, *A Reporter in Search of God*, New York: Doubleday & Company, 1953.

Williams, John Hargraves Harley, *A Doctor Looks at Miracles*, New York: Roy Publishers, 1959.

Wright, Charles James, *Miracle in History and in Modern Thought*, New York: Holt, 1930.

Zeitlin, Solomon, *Josephus on Jesus*, Philadelphia: The Dropsie Colllege for Hebrew and Cognate Learning, 1931, printed by The Jewish Publication Society Press, Philadelphia

—*Who Crucified Jesus?*, New York: Harper Brothers, 1942.

0-595-28437-X